RIOT

RIOT

SARAH MUSSI

*Hodder
Children's
Books*

A division of Hachette Children's Books

ISBN: 978 1 444 91010 0

Typeset in Berkeley by Avon DataSet Ltd, Bidford-on-Avon, Warwickshire

Printed and bound in Great Britain by Clays Ltd, St Ives plc

The paper and board used in this paperback by
Hodder Children's Books are natural recyclable products
made from wood grown in sustainable forests. The manufacturing
processes conform to the environmental regulations of
the country of origin.

Hodder Children's Books
a division of Hachette Children's Books
338 Euston Road, London NW1 3BH
An Hachette UK company

www.hachette.co.uk

Troubled Families 'Have Too Many Children'
Sky News, 2012

Mothers from problem families should feel 'ashamed'. They are damaging society and should stop getting pregnant, according to a senior government adviser. Louise Casey, the Prime Minister's troubled families' tsar, has said it is time for the state to intervene.

They cost the taxpayer an estimated £9bn in benefits, crime, anti-social behaviour and health care, and one fifth of them have more than five children.

Miss Casey warns that the state must start telling families to take 'responsibility'.

In her initial report on the challenge the Government faces, compiled after interviewing a dozen families, she painted a grim picture of generational dysfunction.

See full article at: news.sky.com/story/963120/families-tsar-blames-mums-for-broken-Britain

The Beginning of the End

'The time comes in the life of any nation when there remains only two choices – submit or fight.'

From Nelson Mandela's Statement from the Dock in the Rivonia Trial Pretoria Supreme Court, South Africa, 20th April, 1964

'Revolution Starts with Disillusion.'
Anonymous

They held Patient 5074 down. Two restraint cuffs strapped over the wrists. Two more above the knee. Another two at the ankles.

'Scalpel, please,' said the surgeon.

The orderly passed the scalpel.

'Local anaesthetic.'

The orderly passed the syringe.

The surgeon swabbed a small square on Patient 5074's groin.

'I'd stop resisting if it were me,' he remarked. 'If I don't make a clean incision, it'll be the worse for you.'

Patient 5074 fought back all the harder.

'Call Jenkins,' ordered the surgeon.

The orderly leant out of the door and yelled, 'JEN-KINS!' down the corridor.

A man entered, huge, built like a boxer, and Patient 5074 felt the weight of hands press on both shoulders.

The scalpel hovered.

The surgeon adjusted his sterile gloves. Jenkins pushed down.

The scalpel descended.

A thin line of blood pencilled its way across Patient 5074's flesh. The sheath of skin split.

'Swab etc.,' said the surgeon.

The orderly passed a kidney dish with small dissecting scissors, stitch scissors, sutures, chromic catgut, ties with cutting needles, small curved artery forceps, skin hooks, corrugated drain, adhesive tape, antiseptic solution.

Gauze swabs.

'Hold now,' ordered the surgeon. Patient 5074 tried to scream. Jenkins grunted with the effort of immobilisation.

The taut flesh parted, exposing the tube. There it lay, slim as a flower stalk, bedded in pink-soft tissue.

The surgeon addressed Patient 5074: 'I'm removing two centimetres. I shall cauterise the tubes and stitch the whole back over it. I am required to say for your information: reversal surgery is illegal. Plus it may endanger your health.'

Patient 5074 thrashed on the table.

He snipped the tube twice. He removed the bud of flesh. He swabbed down the bleeding. He stitched up the incision.

'One less for the gene pool, then,' remarked Jenkins.

'The left side?' said the orderly.

The surgeon nodded. 'Fresh scalpel, please.'

The Beginning

'We are not in the least afraid of ruins. We are going to inherit the earth. There is not the slightest doubt about that.

The bourgeoisie might blast and ruin its own world before it leaves the stage of history. We carry a new world, here in our hearts. That world is growing this minute.'

Durruti – Anarchist Leader of the Spanish Civil War, 1896–1936

1

'Masses Against Mass.'
Anonymous

There's a sound like a wave crashing on shingle. A shout goes up. I crane my neck forward, trying to see what's going on. Could be some new security measure for enforcing public order. Like tear gas. They could do that. I wouldn't put it past them. Something's flipping happening, anyway. Booing echoes from the front of the march. People jeer. I shoot a look at Lacey. She's holding up OK. 'Remember,' I grin at her, 'act your rage!'

She looks back at me, slightly puzzled.

Another bout of hooting. This time it's a bit louder. Maybe the Prime Minister's come? Maybe my father's up there too. Bound to be. *Fascist*.

'Let's get with the action,' I say. Waving our placards, Lacey and I step out faster, pushing through the crowd. We're doing it! We're actually flouting the ban on demonstrating! They won't shut us up. Ever. They

3

can't. *We are the future. We are the dawning of the new age.* I get a lovely fizzy feeling. Then I hear that drag on shingle again.

'Maybe they've come with some kind of backup?' says Lacey.

'Probably,' I shoot back. 'Like the SS.'

She shakes her head slightly.

'C'mon,' I say, giving Lacey a confident smile. We push forward. *Dear Prime Minister, we'll stop when you do.* (*Dear Father, I will never stop.*) Oh yes, I don't wanna miss this.

Up ahead a sea of people boils over: some older, but mostly students, teenagers, thousands of us. The ones the new Snip Bill's designed for.

The new Snip Bill. Ha! The forced sterilisation of all school leavers without secure further education plans, guaranteed employment or a wealthy sponsor. Ha ha! What a good idea. Youngsters like me, from moneyed backgrounds, escape. Others, like Lacey, with a single mum on benefits, don't. What a *totally fabulous* idea. Why not give discrimination a chance?

'HANDS OFF OUR BODIES!' someone shouts.

A chant reverberates from the front, back down through the march: 'HANDS OFF OUR BODIES!' I chant along too, loud and proud. *Stop taking orders, start taking over!* Someone adds 'SEXY'. That's quite funny. The chant changes. I join in: 'HANDS OFF OUR SEXY BODIES!'

Overhead the air starts vibrating. Underfoot the pavement shudders. *They steal our dreams, we'll steal their thunder.* The tramping from the march almost drowns out that dragging sound again – but not quite.

Suddenly I know what it is.

It's the sound of armoured vehicles rolling across tarmac.

Instinctively I glance behind me. More than twenty thousand people. All of them crammed tight. All of them pouring into the square. The square that's cordoned off on three sides. A sudden shiver runs through me. It'll be OK. There were armoured vehicles rolling after our last demo. Nothing happened. The army won't actually do anything, will they?

The road shakes again. The juddering underfoot is unmistakable now. The crowd hears it.

They lift their heads, all at once like a flock of startled sheep. Someone cries out above the chant, 'TANKS!' The new cry's taken up. Suddenly everyone's yelling 'TANKS! TANKS! SEXY TANKS!'

Lacey grabs my arm. 'Tia, let's go,' she says. 'I'm scared.'

'Don't be,' I say. 'We've seen tanks roll in before.'

5

'Not at the *start* of a rally,' says Lacey.

We can't give up now. *We are the Barbarians at the gate!* But something drains away inside me. I wouldn't put anything past this government. I pull out my phone. 'I'm gonna Direct Message them all,' I tell her. 'Only a few more minutes. Then we'll go.'

I pass my placard to Lacey. I check the time. The speakers are due to arrive at noon, and it's one minute to. 'All the press'll be here,' I say. 'They won't do anything.'

I watch the seconds as they count down: forty-seven, forty-six, forty-five . . . I feel for my zipper. Then I message forty thousand followers on Darknet7: *Tops Off.*

I did it!

I punch the air. *Hasta la victoria siempre!*

'*For ever until victory!*'

Guevara's revolutionary cry.

And I can almost hear the buzz as forty thousand Darknet7 message balloons ping up on forty thousand mobiles all round the country. And I can't help but smile. Armoured vehicles or no flipping armoured vehicles, I will never let you defeat me, O my father who art not in heaven. Darknet7. My invention. My baby!

Now for tops off. Me too. I struggle with my sweater. There's a roll of noise from the front and a loudspeaker says something I don't catch. Bloody zip. My hair twists down one sleeve. My head flipping jams.

'GO HOME. DISPERSE.' I make it out this time.

I yank at my sweater hard. It gives way. Clear of my top, I whip my head round. Lacey already has her shirt open. 'HANDS OFF' dips and swells across her chest. I scan the crowd. A thousand white T-shirts display: HANDS OFF. MY BODY, MY CHOICE.

Message delivered then.

I smile briefly, tie my hoody around my waist.

'STOP,' hails the voice through the loudspeaker. 'STOP THE MARCH. YOU ARE BREAKING THE LAW. GO HOME. WE WILL USE FORCE.'

Water cannons roll into view. Huge trucks, massive tankers. They line up on a rise that borders part of the square. A cloud rolls across the sun. The cannon on every tank swings round and points directly at us.

In slow motion the march tries to stop. Like a juggernaut turning, it ploughs forward. We're carried further into the square. Buildings tower on either side. Glass fronted. Cold stone. The bank still with scaffolding half covering its front, where the latest EAT THE RICH graffiti is being removed. Such a shame. It was total art: fat bankers being served up with chips. Brilliant.

There's nothing brilliant about what's happening now

though. The protesters at the front are yelling. And we can't stop. Like cattle we crush into each other, unable to do anything else.

At the front, a cordon of police sway. *Pigs*. A sea of yellow and black uniforms: riot helmets, body armour, neck protectors, knee pads, gas masks, crowd-control batons, high-visibility bulletproof vests. *Pigs in vests*. The sun sparkles off their visors. *Even cops hate cops*. Last week they declared a state of emergency, banned demonstrations, brought in daylight curfew. *Of course they were gonna bring water cannons*.

Someone screams, 'DEATH TO THE OPPRESSORS!'

'Tia, I. Really. Am. Scared,' says Lacey.

The riot police link arms, stare straight ahead like zombies. The water cannons point menacingly at us. Mounted police materialise behind the front line, as if by magic. Last week they told us: 'There will be zero tolerance of further disruption on our streets.' But they wouldn't dare turn on us, would they?

A helicopter overhead suddenly illuminates the crowd, spotlights over us, pauses, searches. Its blades flicker through sunlight.

'Maybe they're looking for you,' hisses Lacey.

They could be too. They know I'm here. EVE, of Darknet7, hacktivist, flash mobster. Disturber of the streets. Mother of the Future. I twist my mouth into a wry smile. Not that they know who I really am, of course. I'm not that dumb. I could be anyone. *Hacktivist Rule No. 1: Stay Anonymous.*

I shade my face and look up, tracking the helicopter. That's funny: they're circling back. *Shit, maybe they do know who I am! They might've set up some kind of trackerbot on the words 'tops off' and satellite-mapped it to every square centimetre of the march.*

I act fast. They'll be trying to lock on to my signal, if they haven't already. They'll find out who I am quick enough then.

I pull out my mobile, erase the last connection. A sudden surge in the crowd makes me stagger and I drop the phone. *Shit. I need to turn it off.* I duck down to retrieve it.

It's wedged beside a plastic device screwed to the road. Relieved, I pick it up, turn it off and half straighten up. *A plastic device screwed to the road?* That's weird. What kind of flipping device gets screwed to a road? I look again. It's neat and it's only just been put there. Corkscrews of plastic are still scattered near it. I kick the thing hard. Its cover pops off, revealing a canister. *A gas canister.*

I squat down and look through legs along the kerb. There're more. What a dirty trick.

They've rigged the entire square with flipping gas canisters!

Quickly I pull my T-shirt up over my nose. Tear gas? Pepper gas? Smart gas? Shit. *They've outsmarted us.* They mean business. Last week they outlawed gatherings of more than a hundred people. This week they've screwed gas canisters to the pavement.

They've targeted this rally! Of course they have. *They knew we'd break the law.* They're going to teach us a lesson. *A lesson we'll never forget . . .*

The Prime Minister must be long gone. Out the back, into an army tank; off the roof, into one of the helicopters. If he ever came at all.

He never came, did he?

That's it. He didn't come. And my father, Dr A. J. Thomson, Minister of State, didn't come either.

None of them came.

It's all been set up.

And if anyone does anything stupid, starts a ruckus, starts smashing and grabbing, we're screwed.

We've been flipping set up.

With horror I realise they want us to do something stupid. They want to release the gas. They want to teach us a lesson.

And of course someone *will* do something stupid.

'Let's go.' I grab hold of Lacey. 'We need to go. *Right now.*'

They'll *make* someone do something stupid.

She nods. She buttons up her top. 'At least they never got to promote their campaign,' she says.

'Great,' I say. One up to us, hundreds down to them.

Together we try to edge to the side of the mass. I pull out my mobile. It's risky but I turn it on and quickly DM the protesters: *GAS – GET OUT!* Then I turn it off again.

Instantly the helicopter's back. Lacey was right. It's looking for me. It spot searches, seeks out girls, settles on faces, one by one. They've honed on to my signal. They're trying to pinpoint EVE.

I try to compose my face, wipe off any reaction. I continue edging towards the side of the square. I pull on sunglasses to fix any retina-recog system they might run. The helicopter hovers – it must be running something. Face ident? Movement patterning? But at that distance, with that shake? Can't be very accurate. Not that they can measure it against anything. They can't possibly know who I really am. My Darknet7 identity is encoded. All links scrambled. All posts unspecified. I'm just the mysterious EVE, Mother of the Future. Taster of the forbidden fruit. Database coordinator for the equally elusive ADAM, Commander X of the HANDS OFF

Campaign #OpStopHandsOffActa. But I puff out my cheeks with air nonetheless. I have other reasons for staying anonymous. I don't duck my head though. That'd be like running before hounds.

The spot settles on a girl where I was a minute ago. Long hair, like my webnet avatar. The blades whirr. The spot locks on.

Her.

'YOU.' The loudspeaker hails her directly. The crowd around her shifts.

'DON'T MOVE.'

The demonstrators continue pressing. The spotlit girl can't help herself, she tips forward.

'Stop pushing!' I yell.

The girl sways, tries not to move. The damp morning air condenses on her. Out the corner of my eye, I catch glinting on a rooftop. *Jesus Christ*. They've got sharpshooters too. She staggers, topples. Her top isn't off either. She's wearing a bulky jacket. A bit *too* bulky.

'RAISE YOUR HANDS.'

Ominously bulky.

Suddenly everyone's focusing on the confrontation. Nearby kids try to step away. There's something weird about the way she's holding on to the front of her top as well. She isn't even trying to raise her hands.

12

'WE WILL SHOOT.'

She can't step back, that's for sure. Behind her the crowd wants to see, so they're all shoving forward. She's yelling. Suddenly I'm as scared as Lacey. There really is something suspicious about her. Why doesn't she put her hands up?

'Try to back off,' I hiss at Lacey. 'Make for that corner. Get into that street.' I point to an alley behind us, leading off the square.

We're far too near the girl. If she's got something explosive under that jacket we're gonners. 'Move it!' I shriek at Lacey. I shove out with my arms. I back up. I elbow, poke my way out. I don't care. I'm not going to get blown up by some fanatic. This is supposed to be a peaceful demo. Non-violent, non-cooperation. *Make Sense not War*.

Not gas and marksmen and water cannons and set-ups.

And bombs.

The girl in the jacket moves her hand down its front. She pats as she goes, as if she's locating something. She's fumbling with the zip.

Why the hell hasn't she got her jacket off? That's the whole point: jacket off, slogan screened on T-shirt, every link in the country getting the message.

13

'Hurry!' I scream at Lacey. 'She may be wired!'

Glints of light flicker from the far roof.

'RAISE YOUR HANDS.'

She doesn't move. But we do. Towards the alley. The helicopter hovers closer. The spot steadies on her face. 'She looks like you,' yells Lacey.

A rattle of gunfire.

She staggers.

No blast.

Like ketchup from a squeezy bottle, a jet of scarlet squirts out from her front, sprays the faces around her. A sea of red blooms across her chest. For a moment, the press of crowd holds her upright. Then she just crumples, sags and is down on the tarmac. The crimson pool spreads. Her front soaks red. The crowd freezes. The screaming starts.

No blast. No bomb. No boom. No flash.

Without warning, the police form a needlepoint. They charge into the crowd, swinging batons, cracking bones, thrusting all aside. I'm pressed tight in the mass. A phalanx of soldiers reaches the girl, surrounds her body. The crowd stumbles aside. I stagger, nearly fall. A bomb-disposal agent in thick gear lumbers through the crush. He's slow. He's yelling. People squeeze back.

He bends over the body of the girl. Cautiously he

opens her soaked jacket.

A head blocks my view. I duck and peer. I can't see anything. A tremor goes through the crowd. The bomb-disposal guy holds something up. Something red and tiny with little primrose-yellow booties.

Definitely not a bomb.

A cry goes up from the crowd.

The first brick flies. The first window breaks.

I see someone pull on a hoody, whip a bandana over a face. I look around and suddenly, as if by some signal, there's a load of hooded faces. My heart races. Blood pounds in my ears. This is it. They'll start on us now.

'Run,' I scream at Lacey. Get into that alley.

This is what they wanted. An excuse to mow us down.

'Run!'

There's a roar behind me. Screaming and screaming and screaming.

A rush of people skid past on a column of water, all arms, all legs. I'm knocked back. Knocked over. All water. They're choking and screaming.

I grab Lacey, coughing.

Gas.

I stagger upright and run. I sprint, arms flapping, legs tripping, tugging Lacey. People everywhere. Dodge them. Shove them. Tread on them.

'RUN!'

I run. Lacey runs. We run. Screams and sirens and the wail of water cannons and the rush of helicopter.

And I can't breathe.

I'm falling.

I feel it then. Searing pain. White fire. My legs don't respond. My arms fling out in front of me. I tumble forward. I hit the ground.

Cold tarmac.

Hot blood.

2

'People Against the People.'
Anonymous

I've been hit.

Lacey's here. She pulls my arm.

The pain's unbearable.

She jolts me. 'Tia!' she shrieks. 'Get up, they're shooting.' She jolts me again.

I recoil. I try to get up. I put my good hand to my shoulder. It comes away red. Lacey sees it and screams. Rushing air blasts overhead. The helicopter's still there.

'They're trying to kill us,' sobs Lacey.

I force myself up.

'*Tia*,' screeches Lacey again. '*Hurry*.' Her eyes are wide with horror. She's staring at something behind me.

I look. A huge grey horse is slashing down towards me, iron-shod hooves, massive legs. Its eye rolls white. I spin away. Its muzzle sprays out foam. A row of mounted police are charging straight at us, arms raised. Batons thwack down. People fall.

I struggle up. I limp down the pavement, my arm hanging. 'Wait, Lacey,' I whisper.

There's so much noise. Someone shoves me aside and barges past. I overbalance. There's screaming and gunfire. The world spins. Lacey is here again. '*Hide*,' she sobs. '*We gotta hide.*'

There's nowhere to hide, just people shouting and shoving and everywhere the pain in my shoulder. The street ends. Water shoots across the tarmac. I've been shot. I'm running. I shouldn't be. Running will pump blood to my shoulder. I try to remember what I should do: apply pressure, elevate the injury, remain calm, summon an ambulance.

'*If left uncontrolled, bleeding may lead to shock or even death.*' I hear my mum's voice. '*Blood needs to clot . . . ice won't form on the rapids of a river . . .*'

'Down here,' Lacey hisses.

I follow her. Walls and roads and shops and tarmac swirl. The huge poster of the hand points at me, shouts out its slogan: YOUR COUNTRY IS IN TROUBLE – ARE YOU PART OF THE PROBLEM?

Lacey dips down some steps, round a corner. I just follow, then I don't think I can follow any more. I sink down. The ground feels soft. Lacey drags at me. I think she's saying 'Fire', but I can't hold on to what

18

she means. Overhead, shots rattle.

'Lacey,' I say. 'I don't think I can.'

She looks at me. 'You must.' And somehow we're edging along the paving, creeping into a car park. The world is still red. I think Lacey's holding me.

'That poor girl,' she wheezes out.

I don't say anything. I don't know what to say. The air's thick with smoke. I don't know what to think. I need to get hold of ADAM. He's the boss. He runs the campaign. He'll know what to do.

In some distant past I hear Mum saying: *'In every struggle there are sacrifices.'* Mum would know; she's a front-line aid worker. She saves lives in India. So far away.

'That poor baby,' whispers Lacey.

It's not a car park. It's a delivery area at the back of a huge shopping precinct. It isn't until I try to focus that I realise how badly I'm bleeding. Blood runs down my arm. My front is soaked.

'Lacey,' I whisper. 'I can't go any further.'

'Please try,' she says. 'If they spot us . . .' Her voice breaks. 'They're everywhere. They're firing at people. We can't stay here.'

Up ahead are some recycling pods and one huge dumpster husk. 'Just get me over there,' I say.

We crouch together behind the pods. Lacey helps me take off my backpack. I press down on my shoulder. Stop the bleeding. The pain sends silver edges around everything. I think a bullet's in there. I can't apply pressure. I grind my teeth tight. I try to press harder. *That girl's face. The way the blood sprayed out. Thick like ketchup, but somehow oily too.* I can't stop seeing it. I can't stop the bleeding. I think I cry out.

'Ssh,' hisses Lacey. '*People!*'

'Who?' I catch on to the last word. I've missed something. 'What?' I say.

'Ssh.' She lays a hand over my lips and gesticulates like crazy. '*Looters*,' she mouths.

I look at the corner of the dumpster. Then, suddenly, beyond it, across the delivery area, I see them: young men, hooded up, faces covered. They swim in and out of view.

'Just stay very quiet,' whispers Lacey. 'They'll go.'

I hope to hell they'll go.

I nod and grit my teeth. Don't let them see us. Above, the helicopter whirls back; it spotlights the corner of the superstore. Maybe they'll go, maybe they'll think the helicopter's on to them.

'That first one,' whispers Lacey.

She's peering round the side of the bin. I try to

20

increase the pressure on my shoulder.

'He's got those eyes,' she says. 'I think it's that Cobain.'

'Who?' I whisper.

'That one,' she says. I try to follow her direction. But I can't see anything. They're under a government billboard now, which reads OVERPOPULATION KILLS, and they're much nearer. Hoods up. Faces concealed. They're carrying stuff. There's so much smoke. Can't see how she can make out any of them.

'I'm sure it's Cobain,' hisses Lacey.

I don't understand. 'Cobain who?'

'That guy – the one who's all over the news.'

I search my memory.

'The one with the eyes. Who led those riots.'

Oh, him.

I remember the riots. Our last demonstration, hijacked by stupid louts.

The one they called *'The epitome of what this country has become.'* Some kind of self-styled ghetto guerrilla.

All that hard-won sympathy. All those ruined businesses. Those poor people, they lost everything.

I remember. Me in the prefects' common room watching the television. My father being interviewed. My mates laughing. His monologue.

'We must ask the question. The question that is on everyone's lips: Why do these young adults riot? Is it the lack of education?

'Is it the lack of jobs?

'Is it the lack of community?

'No, it's not the lack of these things. It's family. Wasteful, irresponsible parenting. Mothers who have child after child so they can sponge off the state; work-shy fathers who'd rather breed than get a job. This is the canker in our nation. And it's their children who are rioting.

'And it must stop.'

Then they showed that famous footage. And I remember him, the boy with the cat-green eyes, the Che Guevara boy, the one caught on camera smashing a shop front, the one giving us all a bad name.

The boy with the message on his T-shirt: IF IT AIN'T BROKE, BREAK IT.

I press on my shoulder again. Overhead, the helicopter circles back. My head swims. 'You need to get away,' I whisper. 'I could drag myself to the back of that superstore.'

She glances at the shopping centre behind us. 'I'm not leaving you,' she says.

I look up. The helicopter has swooped in quite low. It's hovering.

22

'*Go while you can*,' I say.

'Uh-uh.' She shakes her head. Her blonde curls bounce. I look at her, small, petite, pretty. She won't stand a chance against those boys. They'll take her mobile off her and maybe worse. Take both our mobiles. All our Darknet7 data. Then we'll be really screwed.

And what if they turn my mobile on? That helicopter will be straight back. She sees what I'm thinking.

'Maybe it's not Cobain,' she whispers.

'Check,' I whisper.

Lacey scoots to the corner of the pod. 'He's tall,' she says, 'and broad shouldered, kinda good looking – you know: dark jeans, dark hightops?'

I grit my teeth; sounds like him. 'Walks like he has swagga?' I whisper.

'Yep,' she says. 'It is him. He's got those eyes.'

'Then you got to go,' I say. 'They're not nice. You know that.' I clasp my shoulder tighter. Blood seeps between my fingers.

'But what about you?' she hisses.

I'm too weak to argue. I want to put my head down and rest. I want Lacey to go.

'Go on.' Something breaks in my voice.

'I'll get help,' she whispers.

'Yeah.'

'Keep out of sight,' she says.

'Let ADAM know.' I rest my forehead on the ground. 'Don't tell anyone anything. Just message ADAM.'

'OK . . .' She sounds unsure. She turns to look at me, her face white with fear. 'You gonna be OK?'

'Yeah,' I say.

She turns away. Shots rattle across the delivery lot, echo off the buildings. Lacey darts forward behind the dumpster, makes it to the trailer bases lined up by the chute outlets, hesitates, looks back, ducks down behind a side wall. She'll make it. *Please God let her make it.* The last I see of her is a flitting shadow on the street as she turns a corner. At least, I think it's her. I sink down.

Above me the smoke swirls.

Above me the helicopter is back.

3

'A Mask is a Face You Can Trust.'
Anonymous

They're coming, all hoods, all durags, snapbacks, jeans busting low. I drag myself in tighter behind the pod. They're carrying swag: bags, screens, boxes. They've finished with the superstore, then.

They stroll from the direction of the loading bay, whooping. That means they left the store at the back, through the stock entrance.

A way in at the back? If only I could get there. I might be able to get help.

Lie low. Stay out of range. They're very near now.

I flatten myself behind the bins, press down on my shoulder. I hear the scuff of their steps.

'Stupid bitch,' says one of them. 'If she'd organised a mob in the high street as well, we'd've got into MaxMart too.'

'And the Plaza,' says another.

'Flash mobs, flash robs,' jokes a third.

'Now the po's cordoned it off.' One of them kicks a can across the tarmac. It rattles. It slams into the pod with a hollow clang.

My breathing goes weird. Footsteps crunch nearer.

'Don't worry, it's burning now,' says a fourth. His tone clears my head. I try to control my breathing. *If they find me*. I cringe. *Please God don't let them find me*. I push my rucksack with my backup Darknet7 gear into a space by the pod. *Don't let them get my rucksack*. I ease my mobile out of my pocket and hide that too. *They'll take everything if they find me*. I peer through the smoke, praying they won't see me.

The lead guy straightens his bandana. For a moment his face is unmasked. Lacey was right. It is Cobain Reilly. I recognise him now. A bolt of disgust shoots through me. *Cobain Reilly*. He must be loving this.

'Think,' says a boy beside him. 'If we could get hold of that Darknet7 EVE, we could organise our own riots.'

In the distance, I hear fresh alarms ringing.

'If I got hold of her she wouldn't be organising nothing,' says one, six foot and nasty.

Cobain snorts, lifts his cat-green eyes and rolls them upwards. 'That girl's nothing special,' he says. He says it all kind of angry, like he knows me and is personally disappointed at my lack of specialness.

26

'Too right,' laughs his friend. 'I don't know why she's so fussed about having her tubes snipped – it's not like anyone'd want to do her, anyway.'

They laugh. Laugh and laugh. I press harder on my arm. *Dear God, let them go.*

'You know why she hides her identity?' says another. 'Why she calls herself EVE? Mother of the Future?'

'No?'

'Because she's so ugly even Frankenstein ran away.'

Cobain opens his mouth and laughs. 'That's good. That's really good. I heard she *really is* ugly.'

'All that lot are ugly,' says his friend. 'That's why they're so angry, because they're panting for it and no guy'd ever look at them.'

'Not this guy anyway,' says Cobain. 'Like would I be bothered about some random bit of pussy that's got to whip up support to get itself noticed?'

Suddenly sirens start, deafening – even the pod shakes. The fire alarms are drowned out. Immediately I know what it is. Daylight curfew. *Christ*, it was only introduced last week! They're not wasting time about using it then. I remember the warnings. '*Gatherings of more than a hundred will be dispersed.*'

'*By force if necessary.*'

Cold sweat breaks on my forehead. Then right on cue

the word: 'DISPERSE' is abruptly thundered out over the urban address system. It echoes across the loading bay. I start to shiver. Can't stop shivering. Maybe I'm going into shock.

'Quick,' says one of the yobs, 'or we'll be trapped in the open.'

'Like hell,' says another. 'This'll stop them.' He throws something. There's a crackling, whooshing sound.

They pound forward. Their footsteps fade as the words: 'DISPERSE . . . PERSE . . . PERSE,' crackle on.

Very carefully I roll over. If I can get to that back entrance, I won't be caught in any curfew sweep. I drag myself up. I think the bleeding's slowed a bit. If I can hide. If I can rest. If Lacey gets ADAM. He'll find a way to save me. ADAM's clever. He's the boss. He helped me set up Darknet7. He'll work something out. He won't leave me here. Though I've never met him in the flesh, he's ADAM. And I'm his EVE.

We didn't think it was gonna be like this, though, did we, ADAM? When we planned our new Eden, our own rebellion against authority. I hacked into the databases, did all the techie stuff. Got our message to go viral. You did everything else — organised the rallies, kept tabs on the government. We didn't think they'd strike back so fast, so savagely.

So venomously.

Not like this.

I'll need my mobile! ADAM can't find me without that! But if I get caught and the army finds it on me, they'll work out who I am. Oh hell.

Hacktivist Rule No. 2: Leave No Trail.

I pull my mobile back out from under the rubbish, snap off the back, take out the chip with all the Darknet7 data on it. I get my personal chip out of my jeans pocket and slide it in instead. That's the best I can do. I wrap the first chip in a bit of paper and screw it up so it just looks like used tissue. Then I tuck it into the side pocket of the backpack. Zip it shut. They'll never find it. It's encoded too. It should be OK.

The effort of doing all that drains me. I lie still and rest for a minute, then I heave myself up. Just let me get into that store. Hide. When I'm there, I'll figure out what next.

I stumble to the back of the shopping centre. It's more of a crawl, a shuffle really, but I make it. I was right, there is a way in. I yank aside a broken bit of timber with my good hand. Somebody's tried to board up the back, make it yob-proof. Ha ha.

Hastily I check around. *Don't be seen.* Tacked on a panel over one window is a picture of the huge hand. It's pointing at me. *ARE YOU PART OF THE PROBLEM?* it demands. You know, if you look at that hand long enough, you start thinking you are.

I crawl through broken glass into the store. My shoulder pounds like some explosion has detonated inside the bone. As I move I try to hold it steady.

Inside, is some kind of Homebase. There's electrical stuff and furniture: polished mahogany tables, chipboard shelves, chairs with wicker seats, light fittings, pads, screens.

Cobain and his crew have definitely been here. Everything's trashed. I hate that. I mean, when someone burgles a place and then they trash it. Why do they do that? Even if they have to take the stuff; they don't have to trash it. I don't get it.

I slump against the wall. Thank God I made it. Thank God they've gone, and it's calm. Except for the fire alarms. They're ringing so loud, it's hard to even think. I try to shut out their wailing. *Thank God the place's empty. I'm safe from daylight curfew here.* I stumble to a sofa and collapse, my head swimming, my throat dry. I need to rest.

I try lying down. The wall races, the ceiling sways. The air still splits with the ringing. I sit back up. It's no good; the room tips sideways. I steady myself against an armrest. Tentatively I touch my shoulder. The T-shirt's

30

ripped. I daren't pull the cloth back. It's stuck over the wound. What should I do?

Mum, I could do with you now. I really could. I know you had to go. I don't blame you. I just wish you'd taken me too. OK, I do blame you a bit. I could have helped. I wouldn't have minded going to school in Ahmedabad. Anywhere's gotta be better than Grandmama's and boarding school in Cheltenham.

Boarding school in Cheltenham! I'm so screwed! How am I going to go back there now – covered in blood? I imagine Miss Dyson's face, she's such a clean-freak housemistress. She'd probably faint. She'd definitely call my father.

I pull at my T-shirt a little. It's still bleeding. *How bad is it?* I hope it didn't hit the bone. *Apply pressure, stop the bleeding.* I really hope it didn't hit the bone. I unwind my scarf and press it on to my shoulder. I'm leaning on a white lace cushion, and I've messed it up. Vaguely I wonder where everyone is. I wonder if they can get the bloodstains out of the cushion. *Just rest a bit.* That's it. I press the scarf tighter until I can feel the pressure. Like a deflating tyre something airy sighs through me. I try to relax, try to stop my heart pounding so fast.

I hope to hell Lacey made it.

I should have known after last time. They did tell us: '*We will use necessary force.*' They told us all right. And now they have. I grit my teeth, try to take my mind off the pain. The protests will have to stop. ADAM will have to drop the campaign. My heart sinks. I close my eyes. I let myself sink. Everything goes dark.

The store fades.

I blink out.

I wake with a start, groggy, coughing. And I'm wet. The flipping sprinkler system's started. I feel so thirsty.

I reach for my rucksack and my water, and it's not there. The flipping bag's still stashed by the pod. Fabulous. No water. And no rucksack. My flipping backup phone's gone too. And all the spare SIMs. What was I thinking? The air's so thick. I'm soaked. I haven't got the energy to crawl out again and get any of it.

I cough. I should go and get that bag. My 5XG backup phone is in it, with all the rest of the HANDS OFF info, plus my money. *My bank card?* I search for my regular mobile, check my card's with it. *Phew*. That would've been a dead giveaway!

I shouldn't have changed that chip. All that data's just out there now: identities, URLs, codenames, IP addresses. Everything to close down Darknet7. Anyone could find it.

I lift myself up. The scarf tears on my shoulder. I wince.

And I cough.

And I look over the back of the sofa.

And I realise why the store's empty, why the ringing's so loud, why the sprinklers are on.

The entire rear end of the store is seething in smoke.

I blink. My eyes water.

Not just smoke.

The store's on fire.

4

'If You Want a Brighter World, Try Setting This One Alight.'
Anonymous

I scream. Smoke catches my throat. I stumble up. Which way? Towards the fire, through the flames? Out into the open? How long have I got? How long have I been out of it? I daren't call someone. They'll have downloaded a hound app on to my phone by now. They'll hunt me down. Finish me off.

They shot that baby.

Go deeper into the mall then? Get on to one of the walkways. The place's huge. It can't all be on fire. But what if I'm trapped? I'm only using the phone if there's no other way. Get up. Go.

The skin on my face stings with the heat. There must be another way. I stumble past the side tables, down an aisle and out of the store. The smoke thins a little. Glass ceilings high above me. On to a pedestrian path between shops. The space rises up to roof level.

No sprinklers. No exits.

I stagger into another store. Look for a way out. Fire escape? Delivery door? There won't be a window that'll open, they'll all be boarded up. There won't even be any windows on this level. Where's everyone gone? *The whole flipping centre's been evacuated.* Get to an exit then. Go along the walkways? Go up to a higher level?

I cough. My shoulder hurts.

Think of something.

A figure appears through the smoke. I think it's a figure. It hovers and blurs just out of focus. Maybe I'm seeing things. Loss of blood, no air. My eyes sting so much. I flipping well hope it's someone. It sways nearer, through the smoke. It's only as it comes close enough to touch, that I see him – tall, broad shouldered. He bends and peers at me. Cat-green eyes.

'*Shit*,' I whisper.

'What?' he says.

I try to turn, get away. Fabulous. Imagine my luck, meeting a flipping yob in here.

'Hey!' he says. 'I'm not going to hurt you.'

Not much. He grabs my wrist. *Shit. He'll take my phone, take my bank card.*

I trip. Stupid low step. I shoot, sprawling, on to the floor. *My shoulder.* I'm on the floor. I can't get my breath. I lie there, expecting the worst. I'm going to pass out again.

Cobain Reilly stands there. Then he bends down, feels for my throat. This is it, I think. This is flipping it.

I try to yell, but nothing comes out except a kind of strangled yelp.

'Great, you're alive,' he says. He removes his hand. I lie spread-eagled, waiting for something to happen.

But nothing does. And I think, where's his gang? They must be around somewhere. Why's he here? How come he *is* here?

And then I feel him catch my arm, my good arm, thank God. I hear him grunt something. My head spins. I can't seem to sit up. I can't focus on him. Fifty cat-green eyes look down at me, all sizing me up for the kill.

'Come on,' he says. 'We gotta get out.'

I'm surprised. I don't know why. Isn't he going to rob me? Or is this some kind of truce until we do get out? Just get me out then, pal. I don't want to die in here.

If I died in here, that'd be the end of Darknet7. My father'd like that. That'd be the end of all his worries. His bill'd get through and the whole flipping nation would be saved. Over my dead body, I think. And that kind of narks me. *Over my dead body*.

No flipping way. I want to see my father lose, hear the

36

news presenters on every channel telling the nation that the No More Children in Need Bill is history. So I sit up. *Destroy what destroys you.*

I can't seem to focus on anything, though. And I'd like to shake Cobain's yobbish hand off me, but instead I let him help me up and guide me towards a huge double bed.

A huge double bed. I must be in some stupid bedroom store. Don't even go there, I tell myself. That's very not funny. I manage to take a tiny sip of air.

'You OK?' he says. 'Cos we need to move fast.'

'I'm fine,' I croak.

'OK,' he says. 'This way then.'

We leave the bed store. Hit the shopping-centre interconnect and stumble into a vast electrical and home leisure outlet. The smoke hasn't reached here yet. Although the staff must've left in a hurry, because all the TV screens are still on. The march, the placards, the T-shirts, all playing over and over, the flying bricks, the burning cars, the hooded-up gangsters.

I stagger past a home-cinema display. Someone is saying: '. . . *It's the additional poverty taxes* . . .'

I hold on to a set of shelves. Stuff crashes to the floor.

There's no shot of the girl. No tiny red bundle with yellow booties. The pictures just carry on playing, the reporter just carries on reporting. '*Something has to be done . . . It's overpopulation . . . There's simply not enough people in work . . . Too few are paying for too many . . .*'

I stumble past rows of the same face, reporting the same story, following Cobain as fast as I can. '*Breaking news,*' announce the TVs. '*Rioting has broken out in seven boroughs across London.*' A dancing light plays across the screens. *SENSELESS VIOLENCE DURING ILLEGAL FLASH MOB DEMONSTRATION.* A collage of images: burning buildings, kids kicking in shop fronts, kids attacking police.

We're almost through the TV section when my father appears. They must be doing a live interview with him. 'Such sickening scenes,' he says, on twenty different screens. '*But beware, you hooligans, the full force of the law will be unleashed upon you. When the Devil is loose you will not curb him again.*'

I know that quote.

When the Devil is loose you will not curb him again.

The words of his hero: *Joseph Goebbels.*

Rioting youngsters flash back on to the screens. Most are hooded up. One face isn't though. Cat-green eyes are picked out, zoomed in on. Then the camera widescreens out. And there he is – Cobain Reilly, smashing a shop front. '*The epitome of what our nation has become*,' spouts my father. '*Criminality, pure and simple.*'

I look at Cobain. He's gesturing me on.

'I know you're hurt,' Cobain interrupts me staring at the screen, 'but we need to move fast, get to some stairs, get off this floor and find a fire escape. The whole mall's going up.'

The reporter's voice fades as I stagger away from the screens. '*Dr Thomson, Minister of State and tsar of the new so-called "Snip Bill" is righteously angry . . . We have seen enough destruction on our streets . . . law-abiding citizens forced to close down hard-won businesses . . .*'

'Why're you here?' I say, confused.

'I saw you crawl in the back of the mall,' he says.

Of course he did. Did I really think I could escape so easily?

'Where're your friends?'

'Them? Long gone.' Cobain flashes me a strange look from his green eyes.

'Then, why aren't you?'

'The whole place was on fire,' he says.

I still don't get it.

'And I started it,' he says.

'Oh,' I say. How bizarre. I'm not sure I'd rush into a complex of burning buildings to rescue some random stranger who was mad enough to wander in. But then maybe he's got a conscience. Imagine that! A yob with a conscience! I really struck lucky. A *stupid* yob with a conscience too! Why not set fire to a whole shopping centre and then get trapped in it?

'So come on,' he says, 'let's get out.'

We take some stairs at the back of the electrical store and climb upwards. Inside the stairwell the smoke's pretty bad, and there's this stench of burning plastic. We go up as far as we can. And then we stop. Cobain hunts around as if he's unsure what to do next. Wonderful. I can't believe it. He doesn't know what the hell he's looking for! That's great. That really is.

'Must be access somewhere,' he says.

I sink down against a wall. Smoke sweeps up in my face. My skin feels tight. The air's on fire. Every breath burns. The building hums. The heat's a thick weight. The sprinklers start again.

And we're trapped.

The first thin blowing of cinders meets me. Fumes curl up through the floor. I try to think of anything that might help. But my mind isn't working.

And all I can think is, we're going to die. My father's going to flipping win. And why the hell did I follow a stupid yob up here, to the top storey of a burning building?

5

'The System Isn't Broken. It Was Built That Way.'
Anonymous

At last I say, 'There.' I point inanely at a door, back down the stairs, on the turn of the landing. It's got FIRE EXIT written on it. God knows how we missed it.

'Yeah,' Cobain says, flashing me a look from those eyes. 'Yeah. Come on.' He bounds back down the stairs. 'This floor's going to collapse.'

He reaches the fire exit and bangs it open. Smoke pours up the stairwell. I struggle to my feet, and promptly start coughing again.

'Pull your shirt over your nose,' Cobain says.

But I can't. My shirt is stuck to the wound in my shoulder. If I pull on it, the bleeding will start again. I try to cup my hand across my face, but it's my left hand – my bad hand. It sends such a spiral of agony up into my shoulder, I let it drop. And I can't use my flipping right hand, because I need that to press the wound.

Cobain twists on the landing, looks at me, turns back, unwinds his bandana and ties it loosely across my face. 'Come on,' he says. He puts his arm around my waist. 'Lean on me.'

I'd much rather not. But I do, because my legs aren't holding me up. I don't know if it's the fumes or the bleeding or the shock, but I grab on to Cobain like I'm even happy to, and I let him help me back down those stairs.

Cobain doesn't try touching the bar on the door. He kicks on it with his foot, then knees the exit flaps open. And I catch myself thinking that maybe he's not so dumb as I thought. That push bar would've been too hot to touch. Except that you've got to be pretty dumb to set fire to stuff and think there's any kind of future in doing that. Well, that's what I think.

'Thank God,' he says.

He helps me through the doors. There's a crash as they're sucked shut behind us. And we're standing on a metal parapet overlooking part of the roof. Above us huge clouds writhe over London. The sky's dark from a hundred blazing buildings.

We're out. *Hallelujah!* I grip hold of the rail and cough and try not to breathe in smoke. I look over the edge of the roof, over sixty metres of empty air. Below me the street looks small, the pavement just a strip. A car's on fire. There's something weirdly awesome about it. *We are the spark that starts the wildfire. We are the lightning on the horizon.*

Suddenly there's the shriek of splintering wood, a terrible smell, and the scream of air long trapped in some substance whooshing out.

'Shit – the floors are going,' says Cobain. 'There's not much time. If the structure folds, it'll take the fire escape.'

My head swims. It looks an awfully long way down. I'm not sure I can make it. And it's weird. It's like being in a film. *Here I am on top of the world, watching it burn.* I stumble forward. Cobain helps me to the steps. He puts an arm round me again. 'Hey,' he says. 'Hold on to me.'

I move. I try not to fall. The metal's almost too hot to stand on. I shift my feet. I can smell the rubber from the soles of my trainers. They stick slightly to the steps. A pole crashes on to a roof below with a screech.

I sway on the step. I can't get my head round it. Why is he doing all this? Yobs aren't heroes. 'Why are you helping me?' I ask. 'You don't even know who I am.'

Cobain clutches me with one hand and reaches his other arm around me.

'Don't care who the hell you are,' he says. 'Just hold on.'

43

And half carrying me, half breaking my fall, he supports me down the curving stairs. Down we go. One step at a time. Round and down. The stair treads clang. And yob or not I'm just praying the hell we make it.

But the lower we get, the thicker the smoke, and I can't stop coughing. Cobain pulls me in closer. I gasp for breath. He covers my head with his jacket. I think it's his jacket. I cling on to him. My eyes sting. I try to wipe them; they sting more.

And inside his jacket it all smells of him, his sweat, his cologne and I'm thinking how I'm breathing in Cobain Reilly, Super Yob, along with smoke and burning air.

But he's all I've got. The metal rail's too hot to touch. Scorching particles sear through my jeans. Sparks burn my arms. And suddenly I'm afraid flames will reach out and snatch us off the fire escape; the stairs will crumble and we'll fall. I let go of my shoulder and grab hold of him tight. I try not to scream. I balance against him and stumble.

'The girders they put in to support these buildings are huge,' he gasps. 'They'll melt and buckle a bit – they won't break. Don't be scared. No need.'

But there is need. And he knows it, so I don't answer. And I *am* scared. I'm so flipping scared, I can't even think about it. My heart bangs high up in my throat, and my lips are so tight against my teeth: I think they're glued to them. When I try to take a breath, the world sways. But I must breathe. I have to breathe.

Suddenly I feel Cobain tense up. A jolt of electricity goes through him. 'This is gonna hurt,' he says.

I don't know what he means.

'Grit your teeth,' he says.

I'm gritting them as flipping tight as I can. Then the world spins. I feel a yank. The air doesn't make it to my chest. I hyperventilate. I scream, but no sound comes out. Then my head's flopping, and I've clamped my jaw down so hard, I've bitten straight into my bottom lip.

Cobain is kicking down on the metal steps. I taste blood. There's a rush of smoke, then thick deadly choking air. And I'm dangling over his shoulder being raced through fire.

I bang and bump and choke and kick. But his grip's like iron.

'Just bleeding relax!' he screams.

I squeeze my eyes shut and try not to moan.

At last it stops.

He puts me down. I slump in a heap before I realise where we are. There, above me, the sky churns with vast mushrooms of smoke. And we're down. We're actually down. Not on the balcony, not on the fire escape, but on tarmac – fifteen metres from the mall.

'My God,' I whisper.

'Sorry,' he says. 'You were too difficult on your feet
. . . If the levels had gone . . . you know the stairs . . .
it wasn't safe.' He's doubled up panting.

I just stare at where we've come from.

And right in front of my eyes the mall seems to leap
up at the sky, as if it's suddenly reached combustion
point and everything in it must explode. The heat surges
out in a great tsunami. The fire escape is engulfed in red-
raw flame.

'We can't just sit here,' he wheezes.

He's right. Carbon debris is swirling in air, fire engines
are wailing nearer. But I can't seem to move. I just stare
at the building and I think, *My God, we were in there.*
Oh My God. Oh My Flipping God.

'Let's go,' he says. 'Look over there.'

Overhead one piece of burning trash seems to be
moving differently from the rest. It spins straight at us.
Above the rush of fire, the blades of a helicopter swirl
into view, banking and swooping, channelling through
the grey fumes.

I let him help me up. For a moment he supports my
weight, but once on my feet I struggle to stand. 'Quick,'
he hisses, 'move.'

As fast as we can, we sprint to the side of the loading bay. I say 'sprint', but I can't sprint. I stagger and weave around. I'm so flipping dizzy. I have to let him help me again. Finally we make it and crouch down behind burnt-out cars.

'Thanks,' I croak out.

'You OK?' he says.

I nod. But I'm not OK. I've just been flipping shot, and flipping roasted in a burning building and now I'm crouching down behind a row of flipping trashed cars with a flipping yob. But I don't say anything. That's one thing about me, I'm a coward.

I try not to be, but I am. For instance, if you told me you just adored cupcakes and didn't I too? I'd say yes I really adored them, even if I hated them. And then if you offered me a cupcake and said you'd baked it all by yourself, I'd eat it. Even if it made me throw up. Wonderful. I just hate that about myself.

Cobain wipes some of my blood off his jacket with the palm of his hand to show me that I'm not OK. I whisper, 'Sorry,' like it's my fault. Which is exactly what I mean.

'Don't worry,' he grins, 'it's only a jacket.'

And then I feel I really ought not to be so cowardly, so I say, 'I saw you earlier.' I pause, then I go for it. 'You'd got stuff.' I want him to somehow know that even though

47

he just saved my life, I don't think it's OK. I don't like looters. And I hate yobs. I really do. Although I haven't got the nerve to say *that*, of course. Plus, if he hadn't set fire to the building my life wouldn't have needed saving.

'So you think I can steal myself another one.' He laughs.

That's not what I meant.

'Whatever,' he says, 'but I'm not a thief.'

Before I can explain, before I can remember that he's right, that he wasn't the one carrying the stuff earlier, the helicopter whirls into view. It hovers and seems to be searching the loading bay.

It stays right there, whirring away above us. Somehow it must still be locked on to me. That's what I think. I press up closer to the car. If it comes any nearer, its heat-imaging sensor will find us.

Then all of a sudden, a fire engine careens round a corner into the loading area. And someone runs out from behind the dumpster husk. For a minute, my eyes bulge. It's a girl, blonde hair, petite.

Lacey?

But it's not Lacey. This girl's short but quite different. She's got longish hair and baggy jeans. And she's carrying *my* rucksack.

I know it's mine. I stuck neon strips on the back of

it, so when I'm out on my bike, cars can see me. And that rucksack has neon strips on it. She must've hidden behind the pods and found it.

I watch as she pauses, opens up the rucksack and searches through. My heart sinks as she pulls out the phone.

My 5XG phone.

My only backup cell, that I've downloaded shedloads of apps on to, plus all my expensive smartware.

She's nicking my phone and my rucksack.

Plus the HANDS OFF chip is stashed in that bag and if anyone gets hold of that, they'll have total access to Darknet7.

Without thinking, I hiss at Cobain, 'That stuff's mine.' I make to get up and go over and take it off her. I may be a coward about hurting people's feelings, but I'm not a victim. I need that bag back. Plus it *is* mine. Cobain lays his hand on my shoulder. 'Leave it,' he whispers. I look at the fifteen metres of open tarmac. He rolls his eyes up at the helicopter. I sink back down, unsure.

'Wait,' he says. 'Use my phone. Video her. Get it back later.' He pulls out his phone.

Cobain certainly isn't as stupid as I thought.

My 5XG Supertouch, that she's holding right now, has about a zillion *FindMe* apps on it, so unless she goes off the worldwide grid into outer space, I can track her down anywhere. But videoing her is a good idea. In case she thinks I'm dumb, and tries to claim she doesn't know anything about it.

But I don't want to use his yobby phone. Yuk. So I get my other one out. He rolls his eyes like So You Have Two Phones and puts his away. And then I'm screwed, because now I'm going to have to use it.

That's what I mean about being a coward.

Still, I reassure myself, it'll only be on for a minute. Plus I won't go online. And I did change the chips.

The girl turns my 5XG phone on.

Instantly the helicopter rises ten metres in a vertical ascent. I shrink back, scared it's picked up my signal. But it's not looking at us. Its searchlight locks on to *her*. And before she can raise her head or duck or scream or race for cover, it just rattles out a round of fire.

BAM.BAM.BAM.

Just like that.

And the girl seems to pop right there in front of us. Just pop into a pattern of holes and a spray of dark paint. Like a balloon deflating, she shrivels up and crumples down on to the tarmac.

I can't believe it. They just shot her. And she just shrivelled up. Right there in front of me. And she's lying

50

there. And they just shot her for nothing. She wasn't looting or anything. I can't believe it.

They just shot her.

And all she was doing was using my phone.

6

'All Freedom is Insurrection in the Eyes of Power.'
Anonymous

'Run,' says Cobain. 'The helicopter's seen us.' And half heaving me up, half carrying me, half leaning together, like we're in a drunken three-legged race, we run, away from the heat, away from the flames, away from the fallen girl, out behind the cars, past the pods, away from the helicopter.

We dodge, make it under the barrier arm. Coughing and heaving, we leave the car park and get into the street. The sirens seem to have a new pitch, like the baying of hounds. And I'm thinking: *Christ, they just shot that girl. She had my bag. They thought she was me.*

I glance back. The store's still standing red against the sky. It's wavering in the heat. Bits are breaking off, swirling around like leaves in a storm.

'C'mon,' says Cobain.

The helicopter whirrs into view. It swoops down, does

an abrupt turn our way. Its bloated body, like a bluebottle's, pitches and rolls as it tries to get us in view.

'What the hell did you do?' Cobain says.

I'm trying so hard to stay on my feet and get them to move, I haven't got breath to answer. I don't know what to say either. Like, I was fine when I woke up this morning. I got up as normal. I got my slot in the bathroom. Got down to the dining hall, got my breakfast. The teachers on duty sat and chatted with each other. One even said, 'Hi, angelcakes' to me. Nobody tried to flipping kill me. I got my exeat pass stamped, got on the coach.

I don't know.

'They really don't like you.'

Remembering this morning helps. At least it means they don't know I'm Tia Thomson. They don't hate her. If they did, they'd have got me then, wouldn't they? When I was on the coach. They could've stopped it anywhere up the M4.

But what *did* I do?

I try to work it out.

1. Belong to the HANDS OFF Campaign?

2. Build databases to message supportive people about where to rally?

But none of that's flipping illegal. The campaign's a

huge thing. There's loads of people working on it. And I'm not the only one. I just set up Darknet7, that's all. I don't hack into personal data (even though I could) and I don't reveal anything or leak sensitive stuff. I'm a sixteen-year-old schoolgirl, for Christ's sake.

Though – if I totally tell the truth – I have been known to hack into 'other' stuff. Maybe that's it? But I haven't done anything like that for ages. And all I did was plant our message everywhere: *We are Anonymous. We do not forgive. We do not forget.* And anyway that's what Hacktivists totally do and Rule No. 1 always applies.

So even if it could be that – it can't, can it?

I feel my mobile buzzing in my pocket. Lacey will've contacted ADAM. It'll be them. I flipping hope it's them. I hope Lacey's OK. She'll be trying to get me. I know she will. But I'm not at the pods any more. Nobody'll know where to find me.

Suddenly it dawns on me: *My mobile shouldn't be buzzing.* I glance up. The helicopter's circling right over us. *Shit. Shit. Shit.*

'And you need to get that shoulder looked at,' says Cobain.

I yank out my phone. *Holy shit. It's still on!* I rip the back off and flip the battery out. *Stupid.*

'I could take you somewhere?'

I'm so mad at myself, I can't concentrate on what he's saying. *They just shot that girl. And my phone's still on.*

Cobain seems to be waiting for an answer. 'It'd be safe,' he adds.

I glance up again. The helicopter's still there. *Where the flipping hell can he take me, with half of London burning?*

I can't believe I did that. I just can't believe it.

'You need help,' he continues.

'No,' I say, 'not a hospital.' I should go to a hospital. But if I do, they'll want to know who I am. They'll call my school or, worse, my father.

Cobain laughs. 'Hospital? You'll be lucky. There's no A and Es left alive this side of the river.'

Of course. An emergency a day keeps revolution away.

'It's someone I know,' says Cobain over his shoulder, as if I'd asked.

'Just let's get out of here,' I say.

Suddenly a familiar howling starts. It's so loud even the windows on the buildings rattle.

'Curf-ew a-gain,' calls Cobain.

I cup my good hand over an ear. I can't hear him properly.

'*Hourly day-light cur-few alert,*' he yells.

I'd figured *that* out.

'C'mon.' Cobain drags on me. 'They're gonna sweep the streets again.'

Inside the howling, police sirens start.

'Can we hide?' I say, although I've no idea where we are, where we could hide. With a funny little gasp I realise Cobain's all I've flipping got. If he turns round now and blows me off, what'll I do?

And as if he's thinking the same, he says, 'I don't know how you became my problem.'

I don't want to be. I don't want to be his flipping problem. But now I'm trusting him to take care of me. That's got to be funny, though, hasn't it? Trusting a stupid flipping yob.

'What's your name anyway?' he says.

'Tia,' I say. I shouldn't tell him, at least not my real name, but somehow running like this for our lives, it'd be weird not to.

'Tia,' he says, as if he knows something I don't. Then he turns his head away. 'Tia,' he says again. He holds out his hand, as if I should take it.

And we come out of a side street. Straight into the sights of the waiting helicopter.

Cobain shoves me sideways, so hard it hurts. He drags me into a passageway between the houses. The helicopter dips out of view. We race the length of the passageway, veer out down a dark alley, jump piles of old trash, slip on rotten cardboard, gasp and run.

'Keep going,' he orders.

In the alley, he pulls me to a stop. I'm too out of breath to say anything. He drops us back, into an entrance, against a bricked-up doorway. He's panting and sweating. His face is half lit, half in shadow. He lays a finger over his lips. I try to stop wheezing. My shoulder throbs. My chest is on fire.

Cobain motions with his hand as if he's waiting for someone or something to happen. I freeze. Terrified.

Down the alley passes a beam of pinkish light. It moves slowly and methodically, like a car headlight surging down a narrow lane.

As it draws nearer, Cobain presses me up against the brickwork. 'Close your eyes and hold your breath,' he whispers.

The pink band of light passes in front of us.

Cobain keeps me pressed against him. His body's warm. I feel the beat of his heart. I smell his sweat.

After long seconds filled with nothing, except his face on my face, he releases me. A cold front fills the places where we touched.

'What was that?' I gasp.

'Recog-imaging sweep, from a drone,' he says.

'A drone?'

'They released it as soon as we lost them.'

This must be a new all-time low, even for this government. 'They're using military drones on civilians?' I can hardly believe it.

'Unmanned aerial vehicles.' He grins. 'Remote electromagnetic-spectrum sensors, gamma-ray sensors, biological and chemical sensors, cameras, radar systems, electromagnetic-wave detectors . . .'

I look up in awe at Cobain. He's not such a stupid yob then! He really knows this stuff. I'm surprised. Shocked even. I never thought yobs knew anything, except how to collect benefits.

'Technologically capable of identifying the airborne presence of various micro-organisms and other biological factors, like DNA. Your DNA. Can be used to analyse the concentrations of each element in the air and set on target like a tracker dog . . .'

Christ. Remote, electronic, DNA tracker dogs. Great. If we weren't screwed already, we flipping are now.

'. . . can be programmed to activate on finding target.'

'Activate?'

'Detonate.'

'You mean shoot us all by itself?' I say.

'You've got it.' He grins again.

58

And I have. More than he thinks. He's not the 'epitome' of anything! Except maybe of geeky-right-on-spec-up-to-date-techno-lowdown! The media's got it all wrong. He's not stupid at all!

Immediately he shoots up in my estimation. Like a zillion notches. He knows way more than ADAM ever warned me about.

And he's just saved my flipping life again!

'Did it see us?' I gasp.

'Did it *tag* us,' he corrects. 'Can't tell, but I don't think so.' He laughs. 'Otherwise we'd probably be dead.'

I breathe a sigh of relief.

'Has to get eyeball ID and/or DNA and/or a chemical profile. But if it did tag us, it'll know who we are by now. It probably got incomplete data and is awaiting orders.'

'Then it'll follow us?'

He just laughs again.

Now *I'm* being stupid.

'Let's move it,' he says. 'If it's tagged us, drones are virtually impossible to shake off. But if we move now – before it gets orders, with all this carbon in the air – we may lose it.'

We creep down the rest of the alley, dart into a side street, and out into scruffier areas of town.

I wheeze out, 'Where d'you learn all that?'

'College of Hard Knocks,' he says. 'Plus I used to dream of flying remote piloted aircraft.'

Somehow the idea of Cobain wanting to fly model aeroplanes is bizarre.

'When I was a kid, I mean. You know the kind of things: radio-controlled, multi-engined, rotary-winged airborne vessels. Kinda like toy drones.' There's this gleam in his eye like he's going to break out into a long series of instructions on how to build one too.

I know exactly what he means. My little cousin had loads of that stuff. He wasn't really into it. It was his dad, my Uncle Phillip, who was. My little cousin, Auden, pretty much trashed all of the planes Uncle Phillip bought. He used to try to fly them over the wall of the walled garden at Grandmama's. Those walls are pretty flipping massive, and he was totally dyspraxic, so mostly the planes came to a spectacular end two thirds of the way up.

'Not that I ever did,' Cobain adds. And I don't know why, but suddenly that makes me feel sort of bad.

We keep on moving, even though I'm majorly knackered. My shoulder is bleeding again. But Cobain doesn't let the pace drop. I wait for that drone to come looping over some flipping wall and splat us. But it doesn't. Nothing happens. We just get down some alleys, past some locked doors, into a part of the city I've never been to. The houses look pretty shabby, and the streets are very narrow. There's kind of broken furniture and sodden mattresses piled up on the pavement. The government posters are smaller too.

One flaps in the breeze. It's totally ripped up, but you can still read it. It says: SO GLAD I'M NOT A DAD with a pukey picture of a young guy out on the town with girls and booze while his mate is stuck at home babysitting a screaming brat. A little further on another says: STAY YOUNG. DON'T BE A MUM.

Why are all the posters from the SAVE OUR NATION FROM OVERPOPULATION campaign like that? Like getting off your head and sleeping about with randoms is better than being a caring parent? I wish my father were more caring. I even wish he'd get off with a flipping random, at least it would show he was human.

Cobain sees I've slowed. He pulls me on. 'Keep moving,' he hisses. 'They'll still be scanning for us.'

I remember how they used to show really horrible clips on TV of thin, cold children all huddled up together with a teenage girl, barely old enough to be their mum, all trying to share one bag of chips. I hate all that kind of stuff. And I know it's not like they're a bunch of real kids. They're all actors, for God's sake, and they get paid for doing it, but I still hate it. It's so horrible. There really *are* poor kids out there and they don't get paid anything.

Then I see that Cobain has turned round and is looking at me. 'Not much further,' he says in a kind of worried tone.

Suddenly I start to feel really hazy. The street looks like it's rippling. I sway a little and reach up at my shoulder. I should have kept the pressure up. All this running and jolting is probably the worst thing for it. I feel the sticky trickle of blood down my arm. I try to sort it out, but a rush of vertigo catches me and I almost fall.

'There's this lady,' says Cobain. 'She can patch you up.'

I nod. *If only Mum were here, she'd patch me up.* But she's not. She's not been here for a long time. She's patching up other girls in India. I remember her letter from the sanatorium, that horrible place my father shut her up in after he packed me off to boarding school. She wrote: *The doctor at the clinic here thinks I can practise again.*

And all of a sudden I'm not feeling so good. The street around me goes fuzzy.

He has a surgery in India, she wrote.

It starts to go dark.

Cobain stops, peers at me. 'You OK?' he says. 'She'll sort out your shoulder and the burns.'

The burns? What burns? I wasn't aware of any burns. I look down at my hands. They're trembling. They're grimy with ash, soot, caked blood.

Gently he takes them in his. I turn to him, bewildered. 'I can't go back to school like this,' I say.

'I don't think you'll be going anywhere for a while,' he says.

'But I've got to,' I gasp. 'I've only got exeat for the weekend.'

It's true. If I don't get back before high tea on Sunday the school will inform my father. They'll find out I didn't go to Grandmama's. He'll hit the roof. Sweat prickles the back of my neck. And my housemistress will be so disappointed. I don't want my father to find out. And I don't want Miss Dyson to know I lied to her.

Cobain's touch is warm. 'We'll think of something,' he says, 'after you're fixed up.'

I need to get fixed up. 'OK,' I say. 'Take me there.'

'Great.'

'And thanks,' I whisper.

We creep down side streets through housing estates. I hold on to Cobain and slow him down. I know I do and

I know he's jumpy. But he doesn't say anything. He doesn't get snappy or rough. At least, not with me.

But I'm sure I hear him muttering under his breath. And he starts kicking out at trash like he wishes it was somebody's property or something.

At last, behind a railway siding, he knocks on a door. It opens immediately.

'Get in quick,' says a woman.

We get in.

'Did anyone follow you?' She looks as shaken as hell.

Cobain shrugs.

'The shit's hit the fan,' she says, and then, accusingly: 'You were part of it again?'

'She needs help,' Cobain says.

The woman leads us down a narrow hall. We go along by the stairs and down two steps into a kitchen. The TV's on.

'She's hurt,' says Cobain.

'*The armed services have been drafted into central London,*' says the TV.

The woman is tall and thin. She pulls up a chair, sweeps a pile of junk mail off it and dumps it on the table, pushes me down and says, 'This is the bloody limit.'

'*The police are currently looking for two suspects believed to be behind the recent rioting,'* says the TV.

'She took a bullet,' says Cobain.

'Is she Eve?' asks the woman. 'She bloody well is, isn't she? Put the kettle on.'

Cobain's picture flashes up on the TV screen. Behind him you can just make out the figure of a girl. *'Cobain Reilly is known to have terrorist associations,'* says the TV, *'and his cooperative is presumed to be the Darknet7 agitator, known only as* EVE, *Mother of the Future . . .'*

'This is my aunt, Pat,' says Cobain.

'I'll try not to hurt you,' says Pat.

'She's going to be OK, isn't she?' asks Cobain.

The picture of us is very indistinct, as if it was taken from far away and zoomed in on. I'm standing behind Cobain. You can't see much of me, thank God. But I'm pretty shocked. How did I go from being a schoolgirl, bunking off exeat to join in a totally politically correct rally to *terrorist cooperative* in one afternoon?

The reporter continues, *'. . . They are responsible for the coordination and mobilisation of thousands of violent demonstrators . . .'*

No wonder they're targeting me, then. But it's not fair if Pat's blaming Cobain. And for some stupid reason I want to stick up for him. 'It wasn't Cobain,' I say, 'it was ADAM.'

'Adam?' says the woman.

'He's the one who's responsible for the coordination of the demonstrations,' I explain.

The TV screen flicks back to the picture of us. My face is obscured, but the camera focuses in on my jacket, then concentrates on my hand. In one corner of the screen it shows a clip of my avatar on Darknet7, a cartoon girl pointing back at the hand poster saying HANDS OFF. Same turn of the wrist, same ring on the index finger.

'Hold still if you can, while I clean it,' says Pat.

I can't believe it. They must have had thousands of teams of experts working on that image, isolating every little flipping detail, digging around and being total detectives until they found that ring. The ring my mum sent me from India. They probably cracked open a bottle of champagne when they found it. Amazing. I just don't believe it!

Both are dangerous . . . says the TV.

I look down at my hand. It's really trembling. I take the ring off and shove it under some of the junk mail on the table. I'll have to leave it. I'm kind of sad about that. I liked it, plus my mum gave it me. I don't have much from my mum. Vaguely, I wonder if my father will recognise it? I try to remember if he's even seen it before. I can't imagine he has. I don't let him know much about the things my mum sends me.

Cobain's looking at me in a strange new way, like a cat waiting at a mouse hole, or something. Like he's surprised I tried to bail him out. The woman's intent on my wound. Very gently she drips water on to the caked T-shirt.

'. . . *and should not be approached* . . .' says the TV.

The water soaks into the cloth. It's warm. The blood and the tightness soften. It flipping hurts. I grit my teeth.

'. . . *anyone who has seen either EVE or Reilly should report to the police – on the number below, where an incident room has been set up.*'

'So you're not Tia,' Cobain says.

I don't know what to say. Like: Yes I am. I'm Tia (Letitia, but I hate that. It sounds so nobby and old and stuffy). Tia Thomson, daughter of Dr Tony Thomson, Minister of State, granddaughter of Lady Thomson and the late Lord Thomson of Moreton-under-Marsh, boarder at Cheltenham Ladies' College, with a mum in India who's a doctor and an aid worker and activist for the rights of women (Go, Mum!), and who I'm really proud of and want to be like. And, yes, I'm EVE too – technical wizard, political campaigner, dispatcher of Smart Mobs, member of Anonymous. Whatever. Oh and by the way I've also got a few other identities tucked up my sleeve – just in case. Happy?

So I don't say anything.

Cobain turns to his aunt. 'A helicopter followed us,' he explains. 'They sent in a drone. I lost that. But looks like they already got a picture.' He sounds like he's used to disappointing her.

'But now they'll figure out where you both are,' says the woman. 'They'll check every address, however long it takes. You know they will.' You can hear the exasperation in her voice.

'She's gonna be OK though?' repeats Cobain.

'You won't be able to stay here long,' says Pat. 'Two days at most. You'd be better going in the morning.'

I wince. The water seems very hot.

'They've been running your pictures for twenty minutes.'

I flinch as she tries to tease the T-shirt away from the wound.

'. . . *the Minister of State, Dr Thomson, Government Tsar in charge of the No More Children in Need Bill, has asked for parliament to grant an emergency, special-measure licence to the army for immediate shoot-on-sight powers. "EVE and Reilly are known terrorists," he says. "We must not underestimate them."'*

Shoot on sight?

So now I'm a flipping *known terrorist*!

68

At least it proves he can't have guessed. He wouldn't shoot his own daughter, would he? Plus parliament will never grant it. This is Britain, isn't it? We don't shoot people because they demonstrate. That's ridiculous.

Cobain leaves the room. The woman reaches for the scissors, cuts the T-shirt away. 'We'll need to check that bullet's out,' she says.

I don't know why, but suddenly I want to laugh. Though it's not funny. That tiny red bundle with its sad little primrose-yellow booties. That girl with the baggy jeans. But it's not ridiculous either, is it?

Shoot on sight.

Check that bullet.

This is Britain and of course we shoot demonstrators.

And how typical of my father!

Shoot first, legalise later.

7

'News Cameras Are Police Cameras.'
Anonymous

I'm barely aware of anything except that the room is dark. I'm strapped into a bed by a very tight sheet. It feels like a tight sheet anyway, but when I pull on it – to loosen it a bit, so that I can sit up – I find it's more like a band fastened across the upper part of my torso. There's a terrible pain in my arm. I feel so flipping ill that even when I figure out how to loosen it, I can't sit up. Somebody comes into the room, not quite sure who. Their face fuzzes up and I shut my eyes. I'm vaguely aware of them going. Someone peers in round the door and then walks off down the corridor.

I lie there and remember:

My mother soothes my brow. I'm small. I lie curled up on her lap. My throat is sore. I have a headache. My small body feels feverish. Her touch so cool.

'You'll be fine,' she says. 'I'm a doctor and I can tell.'

I know she can tell. She can do anything. I'll be fine. She's beautiful and I love her.

She wraps her arms around me. She sings quietly. I can almost remember the song. I will be fine. The pain will go. I feel better already. My temperature will cease.

The door opens. A hurricane bangs in.

'What are you doing?' shouts my father.

My mother freezes. A bolt of alarm runs through her. It runs through me.

'You stupid, stupid woman,' he shouts. 'Get her to a doctor.'

'I am a doctor,' my mother whispers. 'She only has a cold.'

'A proper doctor,' he yells. 'Not an imbecile.'

The pain in my throat is back. I can't swallow. I hold on to my mother.

'This is why I can't trust you. Why I can't leave her in your care.'

'She'll be fine.' My mother tightens her arms around me.

'Do you dare to contradict me?' His voice rises. His words tower over us.

In one swift movement, he drags me from her.

I scream.

'See what you've done,' he bellows. 'Now she's crying.'

'Please,' says my mother.

I can't hold on to her.

He's too strong.

71

'She won't be fine,' he thunders.

And suddenly I know I won't.

The memory fades.

My shoulder throbs. My throat hurts. My head aches. Pat comes in. She's older than I first thought. Maybe sixty. She takes my temperature and forces me to eat a little soup. She says sorry, but she had to clean it and stitch it and that meant something like chloroform. She doesn't explain what. She wishes it had been less basic. She knows I must be feeling very sick. She tells me I've been lying here for thirty-six hours and she's been worried. She reassures me she's a nurse. The bullet just left a clean gash. She thinks I'll recover, and if only I'd eat a little more I might feel less like vomiting.

Thirty-six hours! That means we're halfway through Monday! I should be back at school by now! I should be in Biology!

They'll have raised an unauthorised absence. They'll have phoned my father. They'll have phoned my grandmother. They'll have flipping phoned everyone!

'Don't think I'm happy about all this,' she says. She gently peels a dressing off the wound and swabs down my shoulder.

She's not happy about it!

'I'm not happy about you hiding here. Cobain's put

himself at considerable risk to make sure they don't look for him at this address. It'd be much better if you could get to a regular hospital and get the wound treated,' she continues. 'You've lost a lot of blood and you need proper medication, if we're to avoid septicaemia.'

What the hell am I going to do now?

'Why exactly are they after you?' she says.

Good question! I wish I knew! 'I think they want to stop the protesting,' I say. *Thirty-six hours!* 'I think we've grown too big. We defied them, that's probably it. We still rallied after the ban.'

I really don't know why they're after me. If they needed to go after someone, they should go after ADAM. And suddenly it occurs to me that maybe they are going after ADAM too.

I should warn him.

'Don't believe it,' she says. 'It's in their interests to have a bit of opposition.' She rips off the last bit of gauze. I flinch. 'Mostly so they can discredit it.'

That flipping hurt.

'Put yourself in their shoes,' says Pat. 'What better than a protest march descending into a riot – then they can point fingers and condemn the whole lot.'

She's probably right. But they've already done that and we're still rallying and still getting support. So if that was the plan, it hasn't worked, has it?

I've got to do something.

It's too late to call Miss Dyson and feed her another lie. I'm kind of relieved. She's nice. I hate lying to her. I could call up Jessica; I've covered her back enough times. Maybe I *should* call her, and see what's happening.

'Is it healing?' I ask. I wonder if I'm OK, and if I dress up now and get back to school – like really quickly – and talk some crap about missing a train and being too scared to travel with all the rioting and everything – whether they'll buy it?

'That doesn't explain why they want you dead,' she continues. 'Much better to catch you, try you, condemn you and snip you, then they can hold you up as an example. They've been snipping all convicts, you know, for a while now.'

She obviously has no idea who I am. I totally don't think my father would want me snipped. And he definitely *wouldn't* want me held up as a public example. I mean, it would hardly reflect well on him, would it?

For a minute I'm tempted to tell her who I really am. She seems kind of sensible. Maybe I could, maybe I could beg her to help me, get her to phone the school for me?

I decide not to. I don't really know her. Cobain trusts her, but I don't really know Cobain either.

Suddenly, I wonder where he is, where he's gone, why he hasn't been in to see me. But then why would he? He'll be off looking out for himself now. And then I wonder what Pat exactly meant by: '*Cobain's put himself at considerable risk to make sure they don't look for him at this address.*' Has he been staying away, been seen at other locations, to protect me?

Pat straps my shoulder back down and tightens the cloth belt back across me. She apologises. 'Your shoulder needs to be as immobile as possible,' she says. 'At least for a day or two.'

A day or two? I haven't got a day or two!

Chill out, I tell myself. *Maybe the school's not looking for you yet.* Christ, it's only Monday. You've known boarders get back on Wednesdays after exeat and nobody's batted an eyelid. There's curfews and riots – they can't expect you to be back on time, can they? They'll just think you're stuck.

'What's happening?' I say. 'Are they still rioting?'

'They've cleared the streets,' she says. 'But they can't stop the riots. There's a new saying.' She laughs.

'What?'

'*Night time is the riot time.* Kind of funny, isn't it?'

There. That's it. They'll just think I'm delayed.

'So after dark, even though there's a curfew, they come

75

out,' she goes on.

'It's pretty serious then?'

'There's been total loss of control in Bristol and Birmingham, thousands rampaging up north too.' Suddenly she sounds worried. 'All the boroughs south of the river are burning and most of the East End.' She adjusts the cover over me. 'During the daytime the army patrol, fire fighters get the blazes under control. Don't worry, they aren't near here.'

'But?' I say. I can hear the 'but' trailing in the air behind her.

'They've been out rioting every night since they killed the baby. It's very scary. The army have been shooting. They don't tell us how many. You can see for yourself. Now you're awake, I'll bring the telly in from the kitchen. The rioters are trying to close in on Zone One.'

'Zone One?'

'Parliament Square.'

She disappears. I gaze at the ceiling. I wonder what I've done with my phone. I hope to hell it's off. I need to make a plan. In a minute I'll try getting up, see if I can get back to school. Maybe that's the best idea: just turn up there with a long story.

But if the rioting's out of control will I even be able to get anywhere? And what about my father? His precious

No More Children in Need Bill goes before the House for its Third Reading tomorrow morning. Surely he'll be far too preoccupied with that and the riots to care if I've gone AWOL?

I've got to do something. Make a list. Get up and see.

Warn ADAM, he's in charge of the campaign. Let him know what's happened.

I'm definitely not using my phone. I need a computer. And I need money. Everything I had was in my rucksack. *Shit, they have the flipping rucksack – with my other phone, and that SIM card!*

1. I really need to move.
2. Get some money.
3. Get myself to a computer.
4. Get hold of ADAM.
5. And stay alive to do it.

8

'Help All Fugitives, Even the Innocent Ones.'
Anonymous

Pat reappears with the TV. It's an old-fashioned widescreen. My heart sinks. If only it'd been a Smart TV. 'I'll put it on for you,' she says.

'Have you got Internet here?' I ask.

She shakes her head. No Internet. She sets up the TV at the side of the room and clicks it on. She passes me the remote. I mumble thanks and lie there thinking.

I need to find out where I am first. Get myself to the nearest cashpoint. Then an Internet café. I try to sit up. Instantly my head pounds.

Everything I had was in that rucksack. If I hadn't kept my bank card in my phone cover they'd have that too. Thank God I've got my bank card.

How safe is it going to be out there? Quickly, I flick through the channels to find the news. A voice drones out. *'New census data shows a record thirty-four per cent increase in population in England and Wales, up by 56.1 million to 75.147 million. Population figures have nearly tripled since the turn of the century . . .'*

I click that off and search again.

I see a familiar scene. It's the square. The crowd and the demonstration are being replayed from an angle that's new to me. The camera pans across the faces at the front of the march. You can't see or hear any police anywhere.

A cool, rather plummy news voice is saying, *'Since the latest rally against the No More Children in Need Bill, where a child and his mother were shot by angry protesters, factions of jobless young people have taken to rampaging in the streets.'*

I shift in bed. *Shot by angry protesters.* Surely that's not right? They were shot by some kind of sniper, weren't they?

'Whether they have any real political point to make, or are attempting to bully politicians out of a long overdue and necessary measure by ruining hard-won businesses . . .'

I flick channels. That shuts her up. Everybody's going to think the demonstrators were armed and violent. They didn't shoot anyone. Somebody will have filmed it on their mobile. It'll be all over the Internet by now. The reports are rubbish. How can they say that?

The picture switches to a hall of some kind. I think it's a community hall. The cameras are trained on a woman, plump and high heeled, the stop-at-nothing reporter type. She has very straight hair and looks like she'll get her story across whatever the cost. She's interviewing a couple of teenagers. Nice, middle-class girls. Well chosen. But still in the shadow of the snip. Maybe she'll give a news update soon. I really need to figure out what's happening.

'Hel-lo?' her deep voice rings out. 'Media South,' she says, 'the TV channel that records the throb of the nation.'

The throb of the nation? The throb! My eyes!

'We're here to find out from teenagers themselves how they feel about EVE of Darknet7. Has she got it right? What does the normal girl-next-door think of EVE's HANDS OFF mob action? Does she think EVE discredits the Anti-Snip Bill Campaign? Or does she believe that despite violence erupting in the aftermath of EVE's rallies that EVE should still be allowed to carry on?'

I don't like her. She's not on our side.

Plus, what does she mean? How can I *discredit the Anti-Snip Bill Campaign*? Like I'm not part of it, like I don't liaise with ADAM on every flipping flash mob.

'So, here we are with Emma Parks and Krystal Selhurst, girls that will soon have to think about meeting the Snip Bill *requirements. Now, girls, what do you think of the HANDS OFF Campaign?'* she says.

I pay attention, hoping Emma and Krystal aren't stupid.

The girls look at each other as if they've never heard of any campaign. One of them giggles nervously.

'Are you members of Darknet7?' tries the interviewer.

I don't like the way she says 'you', as if decent teenagers, like them, wouldn't be. I carry on watching. I'm interested now.

'Yes,' says one of them, bringing her chin up.

Good. She's not going to be bullied.

'Did you know the website is linked into the Underground Internet, the online communication choice of government enemies, common crooks and paedophiles?' the interviewer continues.

I was so right. She's definitely not on our side.

The girl snorts.

'And would you say this elusive EVE of Darknet7 has got it right? Or that the government have got it right when they say that a limit has to be placed on public gatherings and she deserves to be stopped?'

I mentally correct her. *Shot on sight, more like.*

'EVE's a hero. She—' says the girl.

The woman quickly swaps the microphone to the

other one. 'What about you, *Krystal?*'

I hate that. She's got this rushy way of talking, like she's going to get all *her* points in and nobody's going to stop her, but when it's somebody else's turn, she cuts them off. That sort of thing makes me so mad.

Luckily the second girl, Krystal, makes it worse for her. '*EVE is AWESOME,*' she says. '*She started hacking when she was like eleven; she's part of Anonymous, you know . . .*'

I smile. *We are Anonymous. We are legion. We do not forgive. We do not forget. Expect us.* Yep, I'm part of Anonymous all right. Anonymous, the anarchic digitalised global brain of the Hacktivists. The Robin Hood and his Merry Men of the cyber sphere. And as soon as I've got a fast computer under my touch I'll prove it.

Krystal nods her head vigorously. '*EVE's a totally White Hat, Elite Hacker. She's so fighting for us. I think she's totally amazing.*'

I love that girl. If they put this bill through, I'll get on a computer, I'll hack into all the government records, I'll name and shame all the doctors, I'll scramble the databases. Make sure that girl never gets her call-up number. Krystal Selhurst. Got it. I'll make sure you're absolutely safe, Krystal. I won't let anyone snip into your body and remove any part of your fallopian tubes. I promise. I really do.

Suddenly I feel violently nauseous. Christ, the horror of what they're planning to do to kids like Krystal hits me.

Predictably the camera is whipped away from the girls and on to the woman. She starts speaking immediately. All rushy again, of course.

'Media South faces the difficult questions of today, here in St Matthew's church hall, and asks: Have these rioters fully grasped the crisis that faces us all? Do they really understand what overpopulation means? Do they realise that while thirty per cent of our national budget is spent on welfare, a huge fifty-five per cent of that goes on hidden costs relating to the least productive members of our society? Do they understand the enormous price of housing single parents, providing their unplanned children with free education, free health care, free school meals, free bus passes and free dental care? To say nothing of tax credits, social workers' salaries and prison places – yes, the statistics show that eighty per cent of young offenders come from broken homes. Do they realise that much-needed funds are being diverted to pay for community policing and anti-social behaviour control? Do they know that population figures are soaring out of control? That energy is in crisis? Do they know that even

with the new rationing programme, food resources are under
escalating pressure?

'*Are they aware starvation is a very real threat?*'

I change channels. I can't stand to listen to her any
more. Nothing she can say will convince me. Nothing
gives anyone the right to operate on sixteen-year-olds, for
Christ's sake. She's detestable. She's vile.

The screen flickers and suddenly there he is.

My father.

His face is huge and shiny, filling up most of the
TV screen. '*My daughter,*' he's saying, '*is very precious
to me.*'

Oh shit. The school's already called him.

My heart sinks.

'*If you are out there helping her, if she's wounded or
frightened – please don't hurt her.*'

Does he think I'm kidnapped?

'*Please don't hurt her.*'

My God, he sounds like he cares! He really does! I
even have to swallow a lump that rises in my throat.
I almost want to find my flipping phone and call him,
straight away, and say: 'It's OK, *Daddy*, I'm alive, and I'm
so sorry and I'll get straight back to school.' But I stop
myself. This emotional hijacking of millions is his
speciality. Vaguely, I wonder why he's bothering. You'd

think he'd got more to worry about with his flipping bill and half of England rioting.

But the angst in his voice sounds so genuine, I almost gulp. He reaches up to his face, touches the corner of one eye, presses it, pauses, struggles to master his emotions. Boy, he's good.

One thing's for sure, none of this is about me. Either he wants public sympathy or, more likely, he wants to demonstrate how tough he can be. I know I'm right when I hear his next words.

'*But if you are holding her hostage*,' a note of menace laces through his words. It actually sends a shiver down my spine, '*know that I will not stoop to being bullied and when I find you . . . if you have hurt my daughter . . . the Devil will truly be loose.*'

The message comes across loud and clear. He isn't going to pay. If kidnappers out there hoped otherwise, or thought he might drop the bill to get me back, they can cut me up into little pieces for all he cares – *in fact, they should* – it would provide him with an excellent reason for going after everyone who opposes him.

I roll my head to one side on the narrow mattress and press my face into the pillow. My throat closes up. But I don't cry. I don't cry over much any more.

And then I see the TV again.

85

And on the screen is me.

There I am in every shade of Technicolor right alongside him. It's an old video clip of us walking through the grounds at Grandmama's house. We're right by the old gamekeeper's cottage. He's dropped the menace now and is appealing for information.

Where am I?

Who's housed me?

Will they make contact?

I sigh. He knows exactly what he's doing. If I'm with friends, out of his clutches, I'm not going to be there for long. If I'm with enemies, they better kill me right now while they still stand a chance.

I lie still and close my eyes.

Flipping marvellous.

My picture being broadcast nationwide. Cobain will see it. Of course. What will he think? *Great, I risked my neck to save Tony Thomson's daughter?* Excellent. That'll go down like a bomb, won't it?

I struggle to sit up. I'm flipping going before Cobain gets in. I flipping am. I'm so gone.

Plus, I don't want to bring my father's 'Devil' down on him.

I gulp and press my lips together. *It's just his eyes. There was something so cool about them.*

But nobody deserves to be on the receiving end of my father.

Nobody.

Not even a yob.

And especially not a clever lovely yob with nice eyes.

9

'Better Sorry Than Safe.'
Anonymous

I get off the bed. If I don't move, I'll lose my nerve. I'll walk out of here and get to a cashpoint and go and find a computer. I'll be careful. I'll have to change my appearance, cut my hair, because these days they have CCTV at every ATM. When I use my card, I'll keep my hoody up and my head down. Make it look like I'm the kidnapper and I forced the card off poor little Tia Thomson. Then scarper.

Well, I've got to do something. And I need money. We outsmarted the drone – didn't we?

Then I'll report to ADAM. I probably need to meet him face to face. Explain, tell him the access code to all the other sensitive stuff stored in the StormCloud. Everything else may be hacked by now. He needs to stop using Darknet7 anyway. And we need to decide how we warn the mobbers – the police will have their names and everything.

After that, I don't know. I'll ring Mum. From a public hub. Let her know I'm OK. The thought of ringing Mum fills me with trembling excitement. I'll ring Mum.

And I won't go back to school. I'll keep moving. I'll disappear. I'll survive.

A rush of something very wonderful surges through me. I could go to India. I could go anywhere I like, and ring who I like.

Suddenly I'm longing to ring her. And I'm up. I can stand. I balance myself against the wall, and move slowly towards the door.

Voices are coming from somewhere down the corridor. *Maybe Cobain's back already?* I pause and take a deep breath. Oh well, least I can say thanks and bye. Beads of sweat break out on my forehead. I'm not sure why my heart's beating so fast. I inch down the corridor.

Anyway, my shoulder feels better. That's good, and I can flex my hand. I splay my fingers and then form a fist. It's sore, but it works. I can bend my elbow too. It's my legs that feel trembly, but they're not aching, just weak.

I reach an open door and pause. The voices are louder. I hear someone say my name. Cobain. So he *is* back. I press my lips tight. Have to face him, I suppose. Then leave.

I catch my name again. They're talking about me. So I listen.

'She'll have to go.'

It's the woman: Pat.

'Why?' It's Cobain. He sounds annoyed.

'She's all over the news, that's why! In two different places! Shoot-on-sight EVE, Mother of the Future, and the lost little Tia Thomson, for Christ's sake! If her father finds out she's here . . .' There's an exasperated sigh. Her voice trails away leaving a scud of worry behind.

'Yeah?' says Cobain. Even the way he says 'yeah' sounds angry.

'And she's been shot. She could die.'

'Thing is,' he says, 'it's not up to us, is it? She's a person. And she'll decide what she wants to do next.'

For some silly reason that comment makes my heart skip a beat.

'You're playing with fire,' says the woman's tired voice.

'Whatever,' says Cobain. 'Look, Pat, I'm just helping the girl. Thomson doesn't scare me.'

I can't imagine anything scaring Cobain.

'That's not what I meant,' says the woman. 'She's a very pretty girl.'

There's a laugh from Cobain, as if he's in pain, as if all

the prettiest girls in the world were somehow out of his reach. 'No fear of *that*,' he spits out. 'She's not pretty enough for me.'

My heart suddenly trembles against my chest. I lean up against the wall, strangely deflated. I try to swallow. A thick dry feeling coats my mouth.

Who cares? Mum would say: *'We're not Beautiful, We're not Ugly, We're Angry.'*

'Exactly,' I mutter to myself.

'And it's not safe,' says Pat. 'While you've been out trying to throw the police off the scent, your friend Tariq called. He said both Moss and Shakka were picked up this morning.'

'Moss and Shakka?' says Cobain. 'But they weren't even out at the weekend?'

'Well, they've been picked up, and Tariq wanted you to know.'

'But Moss and Shakka only just got out of prison, like me,' says Cobain. 'They're on licence.' There's a genuine note of surprise in his voice.

'Tariq seemed to think the police will figure out you're here pretty soon. They've already been to all the places you've led them to. If they come here, they'll find her. You need to get going and start looking out for yourself. She can go back to her father.'

I don't need to hear any more. I step out into the doorway.

I step too soon and too boldly. And my stupid leg crumples at the knee. I stagger, slamming my bad shoulder into the door frame.

Cobain and Pat spin round. They look like little kids caught raiding the cookie jar. Their faces all wide and surprised.

I try to straighten up, stand up for myself. 'Don't worry yourselves,' I say and attempt a smile. 'I was going anyway.'

For some reason I think Pat will be happy I'm going. Then I realise she's not. She just looks worried.

'You don't have to go,' says Cobain.

'It's OK,' I say. I don't even look at him.

'You're not really well enough,' says the woman. I can hear that 'but' trailing again.

I give a little shrug. I sit down on the arm of an old sofa, mostly to stop myself toppling over.

'Thanks,' I say. 'Thanks for everything. I'll be fine.'

Out of the corner of my eye, I watch Cobain. He's got this look on his face. He frowns. I follow the furrow of his brow, the tense line of his jaw. He looks furious. I try to work out what it is, if he's disappointed in me? If it's because I overheard him, because I'm Tia Thomson?

92

Anything, just a clue. He catches me watching. I turn away, confused.

And as I do that there's an almighty knocking on the front door.

10

'Charming Ruins: Coming Soon to This Location.'
Anonymous

The sound of the knocking is so loud I almost jump off the arm of the sofa. My pulse rockets as if I'm on the starting line of some kind of race. I look at Pat. She's gone completely white.

'Who is it?' I hiss. And suddenly I'm scared. I remember the drone and the helicopter and the girl with the baggy jeans. I'm scared. I really am.

'Get going, you two,' hisses Pat. 'I know that kind of knock. I told you they'd be here. Just go. I'll hold them off.'

I turn into the corridor, stumble back to my room, struggle to pull on my clothes. I try to race, my heart pounds. My arm goes numb and a tingling pain shoots into my shoulder. *Shit. Shit. Shit.* I notice someone's washed the clothes, the blood stains are gone. There's a fresh T-shirt. Painfully I yank it on. I grab my jacket, check my phone's inside.

I hear Pat in the front hall. 'Who's there?'

'POLICE. OPEN UP.'

'Just a minute,' she calls. 'I'll get a key.'

She hastily signals to me to hurry and to get out the back door. I *am* hurrying. I'm hurrying so fast, I'm nearly hyperventilating. The police hammer again on the front.

'Hang on!' she calls. 'Just looking for it.'

'Quick, this way,' hisses Cobain.

He's waiting for me by the entrance to the kitchen. He ushers me through to the back door. I hear Pat fumbling with the keys, like she's eighty years old and very stupid, saying over and over 'Com-ing! Com-ing!'

'Go-ing,' says Cobain, and draws back the bolts on the door, yanks me through and we're out into the yard.

'And keep going, and don't look round.'

I don't need telling twice. If the police have worked out where we are, it won't take them long to work out the house has a back door, will it? Hastily I glance up. Thank God there're no helicopters.

Cobain sees me. 'Don't worry,' he says, 'they'll get here soon. Lucky for us they sent the police first.'

I don't know whether it's lucky, but I see his point. When we're clear of the alley that serves the back of the terrace and hurrying through a neighbouring estate,

I say, 'Just put me on the right road. I need a bank or a cashpoint and then I'm good.'

'Oh yeah?' he says. There's this mocking tone in his voice.

I don't want to sound selfish – like I'm just looking out for myself, so I add, 'You all right? Got somewhere?'

'Why the hell didn't you tell me who you were?' he says.

If he thinks he's going to embarrass me, he's wrong. 'I should have thought that was pretty obvious,' I say as snottily as I can.

'So that jerk really is your father?' he says.

I don't bother to answer. He can despise the hell out of me, if he wants. I'm not going to apologise to him for being me.

'Does he know you're good old EVE too?' he questions.

We dart round a corner before I say: 'Nobody knows that, except my friend, Lacey, you, and now Pat.' Then I add, 'And I thought I could trust you.'

'You didn't exactly tell me, though,' he points out.

'I didn't lie either,' I say.

'So what else don't I know?' he demands. 'Your mum works for the National Front maybe?'

'My mum works in *India*.' I say sarcastically. 'Her clinic is funded by Save the World. They don't employ people

96

who belong to the National Front.'

'Your dad scared her off, did he?'

His guess is so near the mark I don't know whether to laugh or cry.

He laughs anyway. 'And he wants you dead. That's kind of funny.'

It's not funny actually. Not flipping funny at all.

'It's not like you're Mr Didn't-Do-Anything,' I counter.

Cobain looks up angrily.

'Why are the police so keen to get *you*?' I go on.

'Look, keep up,' he says. 'They'll be looking for us by now.' He pulls me on and not very gently either. I get the message. He's quite happy to question me, but he doesn't want to answer stuff about himself.

'What did you do? Nick somebody's mobile?'

He shoots me a withering look.

'Sorry,' I say sarcastically. 'Too small fry. You looted an entire mobile-phone shop.'

He quickens his pace, doesn't answer.

'Still too pathetic? So what the hell *did* you do? Rob a bank?'

'You're just pissed because I found you out,' he says.

'You don't have to tell me anything, if you don't want to,' I say, still kind of snotty. I can be quite snotty when I want.

He doesn't. He just carries on walking.

For some reason, though, I want to know. There's heaps of yobs out there, looting, out of control. So why're the police so keen to get him? Something Pat said, or hinted at, niggles at me. So I query, 'You've got something to do with fuelling all this rioting, haven't you?'

That must be it. Right from the start the media singled him out, gave him that stupid title: *The epitome of what this country has become.*

But Cobain shakes his head. 'I wish I knew,' he says. And my chest suddenly tightens. *I wish I knew why they were after me too.*

I try to figure it out. There must be a reason.

'Well, someone's behind the riots,' I say at last. 'Those yobs in the crowd were all ready for action.' I remember: the hoods going up, the bandanas over the faces. 'And they had bricks. You don't just find bricks lying around, do you?'

'Well,' says Cobain, 'I didn't hand any out.'

But now I've thought of it I can't get it out of my mind. *Those guys weren't protesters at all. Everything was set up: the gas canisters, the helicopters, the yobs in the crowd.* I watch the path ahead of me and step over a snail. *And I was the one who sent out the call.*

'You really sure you wanna go to a bank?' he says.

I nod. Like obviously.

'They're going to have totally upped the security around any kind of money outlet,' he continues.

'I know,' I say. It's true. 'I was hoping I could change my appearance, but we left in such a hurry.'

'You're gonna have to,' he says.

At least I don't have to convince him why I need money.

'I thought I could cut my hair,' I say, 'and change my jacket.'

'You can borrow mine,' he says.

As we hurry along one of the walkways in the estate, he strips off his hoody and passes it to me.

'I'll give it back,' I say, 'if you come with me.'

He nods. And on the spur of the moment I say, 'Will you cut my hair too?'

He doesn't answer, but a few metres further on, he pulls me into an empty stairwell. 'Put on the hoody,' he orders. I stand there and struggle to get the hoody on over everything else.

He pulls out a knife, flicks it open. Why did I know he'd carry a blade?

'It's a shame to cut it,' he says.

'Better than being snipped elsewhere,' I say, trying to

make light.

And I stand very still, as he gets hold of chunks of my hair and saws through them. And when he's satisfied he's cut it all off, he picks up an old plastic bag, wraps the locks up in it and stuffs everything under a pile of old car tyres by the stairwell. *Hacktivist Rule No. 2: Leave No Trail*. Must be a yob thing as well.

'Thanks,' I say. 'And I'm sorry I didn't tell you about my father.'

'You still shouldn't go into a bank,' he says. 'Use an ATM. Although you look a lot better now.'

'Only if I have to,' I promise.

We leave the stairwell and hurry out of the estate on to a road. I wonder what I look like. I try to catch glimpses of myself in car windows. I feel kind of shocked that I've just had all my hair cut off. It's kind of like going past some point of no return. It makes everything so much more serious. And that's weird, because having a haircut is nowhere near as serious as being shot at.

But it was my decision to cut it, that's the difference. It's like I've accepted all this madness. I know it's stupid to care about your appearance when you're running for your life, but suddenly I really do. It's as if I've got to find myself again. I can't be EVE any more and Tia is lost and gone. Now how I look has changed too. So who am I? I

100

need to know.

Just at that moment, as I think *Who am I?* a helicopter whirrs overhead.

Cobain instantly stops. All of a sudden he pushes me flat against a wall, stands over me. 'Pretend we're making out,' he hisses.

I catch his eyes, wide, clever, alert. The helicopter whirrs nearer. He presses his body against me. 'Just pretend,' he says.

And I do. I pretend. I raise my face to his. Our lips meet. A strange bolt of electricity shoots through me. I almost close my eyes, but I'm pretending, right? I keep them wide open. I look straight into his green ones, as our lips press together. He looks straight into mine.

And without me being even aware of it, I'm moving my lips against his, and curling my arm around his waist, and hooking my thumbs through his jeans belt.

The helicopter dips, closes, whirrs a circle. Cobain presses his knee between my knees, my legs splay open a little. He nuzzles my cheek, gently bites at my lip, parts them and drives his tongue deep into my mouth.

And all the time we look into each other's eyes, unflinching.

His hands inch up under my T-shirt. They're warm. He's moving them up my back – around to my front.

My heart's racing. I can feel it banging in my chest. His heart's banging too. My shoulder's on fire. I don't close my eyes.

The helicopter hovers, seems to decide we must be genuine, passes away. Abruptly Cobain steps back from me.

I lean against the wall for real now. Blood pounding.

'That was close.' He laughs.

I look at him.

Then he turns his back on me and simply starts walking again.

I follow. My knees are shaking. I'm shivering all over.

And it's not just because of the helicopter.

11

'Without Money We'd All Be Rich.'
Anonymous

We get to some kind of local high street. The riots have been right through it. Everybody's off the streets. Except a few, out with brooms, trying to clear up or maybe salvage stuff. Everything's boarded up. Three shops are burnt out. Two grey, skeleton cars are sunk on blackened rims.

All the cashpoints and ATMs are down. The first one flashes out in blue strobe: OUT OF ORDER. The second is more honest. It displays the message in yellow typeface across a green screen: ALL CASH DISPENSERS FOR THIS BANK ARE SUSPENDED.

'I'll have to go in then,' I say. 'They'll probably have working ATMs inside . . .'

'You certain you wanna do that?' asks Cobain.

I don't know. I glance behind. The helicopter's gone. I need money. Internet cafés aren't free, are they?

'Have to,' I say.

He shrugs. I find myself watching him, fascinated by the curve of his cheek, feeling slightly light-headed and wondering what he'd be like if he stopped being so angry.

But maybe he's right. Maybe going into a bank is too risky. But what else can I do? Keep on walking until I find a cashpoint that hasn't had its service suspended? And how long is that gonna take? Being out on the street is risky too. Everything's risky. Plus I need to contact ADAM as soon as possible. It's already Monday. The police have had that data for over twenty-four hours. They'll have decoded it by now. They'll have made a list of suspects, they'll be making house arrests. People need to know that their names and addresses are on that list. They also need to know that's all the evidence the police may have on them. They need to cover themselves. Your name on a list is not enough to arrest you, if you've got an alibi. I need to warn them.

'You don't have to come in,' I say.

He doesn't reply, just tugs his snapback lower and keeps his eyes cast down.

All the bank branches we pass are closed. But at last we get to one that's open. It looks like it's the only one that is. We walk right past, while I try and size it up. The bank's guarded by two policemen in high-visibility, yellow riot jackets, all bulky over their bulletproof vests. They're on steps, just off street level, by glass doors. Truncheons held tight in gripped fists.

But at least the bank's open.

'Wait for me?' I say. I don't know why he should. But I kind of want him to.

'I'll wait.'

I feel a bit better. A lot better actually.

'Keep your chin tucked in. Pull the hoody halfway down your face. Jiggle around. CCTV has very poor quality, even worse on moving images. Don't leave fingerprints and get out immediately.'

Automatically I register the advice. The voice of experience? I pull my hoody down. It's only as we stop outside an Underground station and hover, that I think: *What experience?*

What *was* he inside for?

Maybe he *did* try to rob a flipping bank!

I tuck my chin in anyway. If he was done for robbing a bank, he wasn't very good at it. I pull my hood closer. It means he got caught?

I hope to hell I don't get caught.

I hope to hell the police by the bank don't recognise me, either.

I grit my teeth and wait for a chance to go

back, and get past them.

Outside the bank a car pulls up. The driver, an old guy, wants to stop right there, right by the police, to let his wife out. The policemen move off the steps, down to the kerb, and tell him he can't. He's gesticulating and saying he's way too scared to let her out further off. But the police are too scared to let him park in front of the bank as well.

I'm scared for totally different reasons.

But I keep my calm. I chew my lip and wait. I wait until they're all arguing, then I stroll back to the bank and nip past the guards and up the steps. I turn briefly by the automatic glass doors to catch sight of Cobain. There he is, on the far side of the Underground station, almost hidden.

No sooner have I got through the doors than I feel it. Hostility. Everyone's so jumpy. There's this long queue of people, and they're all staring at me. I look around for the ATMs. And I can't see any! Fabulous. Just my luck, they've been flipping boarded off!

Shit.

And now everyone's staring even harder, and I don't know what to do. OK. *Keep your hoody down. Jiggle around. CCTV has very poor quality.* Stay Anonymous.

I find reasons to hide my face. I make out I've got

something in my eye, I can't think of any other way of covering up. I wriggle a bit. *Cobain was right. I shouldn't have come. I'm bound to be recognised. My face's been broadcast so many times, I'm probably etched into the national memory.*

I should walk out right now.

But then what am I going to do?

I try to think of other ways I could get money. Would Grandmama send me some? She probably would, but it wouldn't solve anything; she'd still have to transfer it through a bank. Maybe Lacey would? Maybe she'd meet up with me some place and bring cash. But I'd have to use my phone to call her, and that wouldn't be a good idea. Hold your nerve, I tell myself, at least join the queue and try. Use your card at the counter. Key in your pin. Keep your head down. It's too risky using your phone and it'll take too long if you have to wait for Lacey.

I watch to see if anyone pulls out a mobile, snaps me or tries anything funny. I slide to the back of the long queue, my heart racing.

This is stupid. I can't do this.

And then I start thinking, even if I get the money, how am I going to get out? I'll have to time the guards again, and I'm not going to get lucky with another old couple, am I?

I turn and watch others leaving. How're they managing it? They just step right up and through the doors. All confident and relaxed. I can do that then. The thought of it makes me feel faint.

Nervously I jiggle from one foot to the other. The queue in front of me hardly moves. How long's it gonna take? Everyone is twitchy. The woman nearest me is obviously paranoid. She doesn't like me standing so close. She inches away and looks at me down the side of her nose. The big guy in front of her turns round and says to me, 'Sure you're in the right place, love?'

I look at him. 'Yeah,' I say.

'Only this is a bank.'

Like obviously, I think.

And then I get it.

I don't look like the kind of person who should be in a bank! Dressed in Pat's spare T-shirt, ripped jeans, faded hoody, I look like a train crash. That's why they're staring. That's why the woman's so paranoid. They probably think I'm in with rioters. Probably think I'm in here scoping the joint out for a raid!

I look at my beat-up, half-melted trainers. I angle my body until I catch sight of my reflection in the polished stone of a counter. For a second I don't recognise me. I'm so thin, and scruffy. My eyes look huge. My hair all cropped. I blink. Of course no one's recognised me. I look like a yob. I look like Cobain. No, much worse. Cobain looks nice, in a cool guy kind of way.

I definitely don't look like the kind of person you'd want in a bank. *I look poor*. Then I read the notice over the counter. And I realise why there's one long queue.

DUE TO THE RECENT RIOTS ONLY CUSTOMERS WHO PASS RETINA RECOGNITION WILL BE SERVED.

They've changed the system. No more chip and pin at the counter. I've got to walk up and do an eyeball ID. My heart sinks. A vein in my temple starts to throb. I can't do that. What a stupid waste of time. All that risk for nothing. Cobain was right. *Why the hell did I come in here?*

I start to sweat. And how *am* I going to get out? If the guards stop and search me, they'll find the wound. And I can't lie and say I got hit in the rioting and I lost my phone and lost my memory and ended up in a bank, can I?

It'll be a nightmare: they'll find out everything; who treated me, who stitched up my wound, who cut my hair, who I really am. Even if I refuse to talk, my father'll find out. He'll get every security check in the capital on

109

it, every CCTV camera, every satellite scan. I know him. There're no mysteries he won't break. He'll break the mystery of me quicker than you can break dry spaghetti.

And then he'll find out I'm EVE too.

And then what?

I won't have warned ADAM. And everybody will be totally totally screwed.

I step out of the queue. I slip my phone into my hand, ready to dump it if they stop me. I cross my fingers. Confidence, right? I reach the glass doors. I keep my head up. Be bold, I tell myself. Step out. The doors slide open. I pass.

I'm through.

I turn to take the two steps to street level when a voice calls out.

'Just a minute, young lady. Not so fast.'

12

'Everything for Everyone and Everyone for Themselves.'
Anonymous

*S*hit. *Shit. Shit.*

Holy flipping shit.

I don't know what to do. What the hell am I going to do?

'Step to one side if you don't mind, miss. Routine stop and search.'

'Why?' I say. I probably shouldn't say that. Police don't like being spoken back to. But why? Why me?

A tall, bearded policeman runs his eye from the top of my short haircut to the faded hoody, torn jeans and beat-up trainers. His look says it all.

It's so unfair. I want to say something. But I don't.

'Just turn around. Raise your hands. Spread your legs,' he says.

Now I *am* screwed. We're all screwed. I can't raise my arm. It's hard enough to even bend my elbow. Why the

111

flip did I stop? I shouldn't have. If I'd raced when he called, I'd have been down those steps and gone. *Dump the phone.* I look for a place, but there isn't one. No bins. Just my luck. No flipping containers at all.

I look down the street, hoping Cobain's seeing what's going on. Hoping like mad he can do something. But what can he do?

And that's when I see them, down the street, streaming out of the Underground. A scary bunch of people.

Hoods up, black balaclavas stretched across faces, carrying things wrapped in long, dark socks. One of them holds up a sledgehammer. And they're shouting their heads off.

When they see the bank an excited cry goes up. Someone – one of the leaders, a really huge guy – throws a brick straight at the front of the bank. It whizzes by, really close. It smacks into the glass with a crunch. Another great cry goes up.

I look at the policeman. But he's not looking at me any more. And I'm thinking: *Wait. Time him. This is your chance. Get away. Disappear into the crowd. He's got bigger things to worry about now.*

So I tense up. Poised for action. I scan the group. Expecting to see Cobain there with them, lobbing the next brick. And I'm right; there he is. I'll head for him.

That's what I'll do. I'll head for Cobain. Right next to the big guy in the black hoody.

The policeman half turns back to me, half watches the street, unsure what to do. I wait. Wait for his grip on my arm to loosen.

Police sirens start. As if by magic, an army of rioted-up, stun-gun-bearing police appear. Blue lights start to flash. Another brick comes shooting towards the front of the bank and smacks into the glass doors. This is it. The doors crack, but they don't shatter. *This is my chance.*

The policeman flinches. His hold on my arm loosens. I raise my foot, focus and kick him one, right on the shin. The crowd sends up a cheer. I twist my arm free. The crowd cheer and cheer like I scored a goal. And I'm down the steps. And I'm jumping sideways into the mob.

I think the policeman raised his baton. I think he leapt after me. I'm not sure. I wasn't watching, but someone in the crowd yells, 'GET HIM.' Another yells; 'DEATH TO THE OPPRESSOR!' Someone raises their phone up, starts filming. Other phones go up. There's an enormous push and they surge forward and engulf me and start lashing out at the policeman.

And suddenly I'm surrounded by the mob and pressed up against them – big, square male shoulders, stubbly chins, angry fists, sweaty armpits – and they're protecting me and they're passing me back through the crowd and they're yelling, 'Fuck the pigs!'

They charge the bank. And turn on the policeman. They drag him down. Hands pass him into the belly of the mob. He goes under. Flashes of his neon jacket bright against the tarmac. And there's arms with clubs being raised, and boots being brought down. The sledgehammer thumps into something yielding and a grunt of satisfaction ripples through the crowd.

I hide my face. The mob strains forward. And stamps down.

And when they've finished stamping, they straighten up and head towards the shattered doors of the bank. And one of them is passing over our heads a ripped-up riot barrier, steel and mesh, and they're battering it at the line of yellow-jacketed police.

I see a lump of neon tarmac slippy with blood. I turn away. My stomach heaves. Huge, empty convulsions.

This isn't what I'm fighting for.

I try to push my way back, get away, get out. I can't think. This isn't what we campaigned for.

I turn and shove against the tide. Stubbly chins, angry fists, sweaty armpits. Surely these aren't the people I was DMing on Darknet7. These are grown men. They aren't kids protesting about their futures. They're all carrying weapons: baseball bats, hammers. They're not in danger from any bill. They planned this. They aren't protesting about anything. Maybe I'm wrong. Maybe they are. I'm not sure. I say, 'HANDS OFF,' to the guy next to me. He turns briefly, doesn't get it.

'What?' he says.

He just looks back, puzzled. Then the penny drops. 'Too late for that,' he says.

I was right, he's not one of us. He's just rioting for the hell of it, just trying to get into the bank, like this is his idea of fun.

It's not mine. I don't want to be in a mob rushing a bank, a mob who stamps down policemen.

'Look at this,' says the man. His face is shining. He shows me his phone. He's filmed the brick on the glass doors. He's filmed me on the steps. Me kicking the policeman. Me escaping. The policeman following. The mob pounding him to the ground. The blood splatter. He's taped the grunt of satisfaction, the mob championing me, raising their fists, shouting, *'Pick on someone else!'* He's finished his little film with a death's head and the title *SHANK A BANK* followed by the slogan: *Before I attack banks, I ask myself: What would Jesus do?*

'We rescued you,' he says. 'It's gone live.'

'It's gone live?' I whisper.

He grins at me. 'You're a hero now. All a the nation gonna be watchin' it. All a them gonna be lovin' it.'

13

'Make Trouble and Influence People.'
Anonymous

Broadcast to the entire nation: Tia Thomson Joins in Angry Mob on Bank Raid. Tia Thomson Incites Mob to Murder. In Cheltenham, the school will see it. In her drawing room, Grandmama will see it. In Westminster, my father will see it. In India, Mum will too.

'Thanks,' I mouth at the man with his phone shoved in my face and his silver-toothed grin. Brilliant. He just helped stamp a policeman into the tarmac. He just filmed himself doing it. And he's laughing. He's loving it. Totally flipping awesome.

I shove the palm of my hand against my mouth. This mob can do anything. They can turn on anyone. I think I'm going to be sick.

Suddenly Cobain's at my side. 'I told you not to go in there,' he says. 'Now look what's happened.'

He yanks me through the crowd, pushes me hard,

like it's my fault. I stop feeling sick. I'm glad he's shoving me. It stops me thinking. My legs are trembling. They just stamped on that guy's head. My legs actually aren't working properly.

'The police are bloody everywhere, so bloody keep up.'

'Sorry,' I say. But my voice is faint. 'It wasn't my fault.'

'Shut the hell up,' he says.

He looks as scary as the others. He's grey with fury. I can see a vein down the side of his face, pulsing.

'Where did all those guys come from?' I ask.

'Don't ask,' he says, shoving me again. His arms are angled, like at any moment he's going to smack someone in the face. His jaw is clenched.

But who are they? And where did they come from? They had clubs and masks. They must've known the bank was open.

'They planned it,' I say.

'Of course they planned it,' he says, like I'm a stupid moron. 'All of it.' He puts on the plummy voice of a news presenter: 'Today's headlines: *Peaceful Protest. Hooded Hooligans. Rampage and Riot. Army Aggression and Countrywide Clampdown.* Of course they bloody planned it.'

He means the government?

Of course they planned it.

And he's right. I am a moron.

I can almost hear the TV Breakfast debate: *'Today we are considering a new angle to the introduction of the No More Children in Need Bill.*

'Recent riots have shown us that an element is loose in society. It's volatile, dangerous and out of control, and it's growing in momentum. We are asking, do we want it spawning? Do we want it replicating itself? Shouldn't we be saying enough is enough?

'Do we want another generation of youngsters like the ones we're seeing destroying our streets?

'We're asking: What kind of parents will these rioters make?'

I pull my hood up over my yobby haircut. My heart's hammering. It's all wrong. Cobain is kicking out at the kerb. We're back on the high street, walking past the boarded-up shops, past the burnt-out cars. All the destruction.

And I can't get used to it.

Is it my fault? What if I'd never started Darknet7?

I go back in my mind, back to how it all started.

It's the Christmas holidays. I'm at my grandmother's. Since Mum left, since she started working in India, I come here during school holidays. Grandmama is nice, a little stiff. You can't cuddle her, not like Mum. She's my father's mother, but she's not like him. She's kind. She has her traditions though. One tradition is that on Boxing Day I must handwrite thank-you cards to all the family. She supplies me with embossed New Year's greeting cards, a list of addresses, the details of each family member, an inventory of the presents they sent.

My father has left, gone back to the flat in Westminster. This afternoon Grandmama will show me where the hunt used to meet on her estate. We will walk part of the way towards the copse and talk about other traditions, ones long gone.

She will tell me news of my mother, hand me a present from her – a new tradition we hide from my father – tell me that she has arranged things. My heart will skip a beat. She will have arranged a visit from my mother, maybe in the spring when Father is very busy. She will tell me she is a mother too. She will ask my school for exeat.

It will be our secret.

My father is far too busy to be disturbed over all this. We will nod our heads. Far too busy.

But until then I must write thank-you notes. I'm bored. I switch on my laptop. I want to download music from an illegal site. I decide to venture into the Darknet, the anonymous Internet underground that can't be accessed by normal web browsers like Chrome, can't be mined by regular search engines. First, I access an anonymising network service called Tor, secret and secure for servers and users. Tor is an Onion Router and I've already downloaded its browser bundle. Like an onion, it has layer after layer of encryption. It bounces me around a global network of relays, hosted by sympathisers, well-wishers, those who lend their services to protect identity, location, today's date.

Suddenly I am anonymous.

Now I can browse the regular Internet securely; but I can also access the Deepnet, the Darknet, the hidden services, the servers delivering web pages that can't be accessed by regular browsers like IE.

An Internet only for other Tor users.

A thrill tingles down my spine. Forget downloading music. Now I can say what I like, be who I want. It never fails to thrill me. I message out over an underground net forum: Disarm authority. Arm your desires.

I'm only playing at first. At least, I think I am.

But I get a message back: How did you find us?

I smile. This is fun. Better than writing thank-you notes. I reply: Through the subterranean pathways, through the rubble of empires. For those who know the paths to liberty, freedom isn't given, it's taken. I smile. This is a good game.

The message says: I'm ADAM, Do you want to take this further?

And I'm sad and lonely and I think: Why not? Why not be a rebel? No one has to know. Why not see where ADAM wants to take this?

And a heady feeling sweeps over me.

I can be reborn, live a free life, a different life. Online I can be anyone. Online I can be Anonymous.

I can do all the forbidden things I want.

I can save the world like Mum.

So I message back:

I'm EVE. Are you interested in apples?

No. I wasn't wrong.

I was bored and sad. And I wanted to do something. It wasn't my fault. I was just dreaming of being free and being different. Are we supposed to just accept everything? Never try to change things?

I stub my foot on a broken paving slab.

But how stupid. Did I really think I could start a little Internet site and post a few messages and organise a few flash protests and everyone in the government was going to roll over and go: 'OK, fair enough, we can quite see the bill is unfair and unpopular and it won't work, so we'll think of something else then, OK?'

Did I really think that?

And now look where we are. All this.

And now what? I can't go back to school. I can't go anywhere. Maybe I could go to Lacey's? If she made it, she'd help me. I hope to hell she made it.

And suddenly I decide. After I've contacted ADAM, I'm going to upload the film of them shooting that girl – the one who took my backpack. Demand justice for her. There's got to be justice for someone. They can't get away with it. They can't just go around shooting people. I'd like justice for that policeman too. But I don't know how to start with that.

I'd like to tell everyone on Darknet7 to stop.

STOP.

No more shooting. No more riots.

And I need to tell them the police have their details. They can find them, arrest them, incriminate them. They need to be prepared. I think of that policeman. The charges may involve murder. They need to have alibis. It's serious. And everyone will say we deserve snipping. And there'll be no justice for anyone. Everything we've worked for will backfire.

We get past a burnt-out petrol station, when all of a sudden Cobain says, 'They arrested Pat.' There's a new tone in his voice, like he's struggling to breathe. 'They found your ring.'

I take that in. I carry on walking. They found my ring.

The ring my mum gave me. The ring I was wearing when the helicopter got us. The ring I left at Pat's. I feel numb.

'What've they arrested her for?' I say. They've got to have a reason. They can't arrest you for owning a ring, can they?

'Don't know,' he says.

'What do we do?' My voice is suddenly very small.

'I don't know,' he repeats like an alien.

My mouth dries up. 'My fault?' I whisper.

'No,' he says. He chooses his words. '*They* arrested her; you didn't.'

I wish he'd blame me. I want to say, *They traced us to her, didn't they? They found out I'd been there*. I want to say that this is what my dad does; this is what he means when he threatens. *I should have somehow made you both understand properly*. And I want to say: *Sorry*. But I don't say anything.

Cobain's arm tightens on me. 'Just keep walking,' he says. So I do. We walk and walk.

We walk away from the police and the blue flashing lights and the mob and the ambulance sirens. We walk into the centre of the city. And we keep on walking. It's only when we get near Trafalgar Square, and the buses and the cars and the people and the police, that we sit down on a low wall. Cobain just sits there, tapping his fingers against stone, scanning the streets, scanning the skies.

At last he says, 'You've got to make a decision.'

I look at him.

'I'm going to propose something.'

I'm confused.

Propose what?

14

'Let's Break the Law So Hard it Can't Be Fixed.'
Anonymous

'Look,' he says, 'I can use you.'

His grip on my arm tightens. A double-decker plunges past. All the people on board peer out.

'You can use me?' I repeat. The minute I say it, I regret it. Like, how's he gonna use me? And do I really want to know?

'But first,' he says, 'you gotta grow up. No more games. No more defeat the Snip Bill. Get back at Daddy. Play at saving the world like Mummy. This time we play for real.'

'My mum isn't playing,' I say. 'She's saving lives. She's a doctor.'

But he isn't listening. I don't bother with the rest. He should leave my mum out of this.

'So I propose you join forces with me,' he says.

One of the buses pulls up really near us. A girl stares

126

out from the top deck at Cobain like he's fit. She shoots me a look, as if to say: *What the heck's he doing with her?*

'You're a hacker,' he continues. 'I need someone like you who can hack into some specific files.'

'Like?' I say.

'I'd like you to hack into the websites of the Department of Justice, and get hold of some prison files.'

'Why?' I say.

'Look around,' he says. 'This is why.' He takes in the square with a sweep of his arm. 'We've brought London to a standstill. We've got crowds out on the streets, guys ready to smash into anything. But we can't bring it down by rioting alone. Now we need help. We need to hack into the banks, government files, organisations, where the money is, and close the UK down for ever. But we need to cover our tracks first; erase our records, all our identities from current files, police-data banks, get rid of all those fingerprints.'

The sun sinks over Trafalgar Square. It catches the rooftops and shimmers in crimson pools on the tarmac.

His shoulders slacken a tiny bit. 'We need to be very sure that whoever, whatever comes, after all this, never gets their hands on any of us.' He looks down. 'I'm tired of being targeted, I guess.' He scuffs at something on the pavement. 'We could do it,' he says, 'we really could. The

Arab Spring in London,' he says. 'Imagine.'

And I do imagine. And I don't like it. More mobs? More riots? More heads stamped into a slippy mess? Put men like them in power?

'Hacking is illegal,' I say. 'It carries a long custodial sentence. If you want me to hack something for you, you really need to tell me why. Everything. What will it achieve? And exactly why you want me to do it?'

'You know very well,' he says. 'The system's unfair. Firstly, the rich get richer and the poor get poorer – or they have babies, or get drunk, or anything, except getting richer.

'And secondly, the government controls everything. They make the laws and they make sure those laws benefit them.

'Thirdly, we're living in a police state. Our taxes fund the people in charge. Our money keeps them powerful, so that they can carry on making more unfair laws. And our money pays the police to enforce those laws too. It's one big cycle, do what I say and shut up – or else. It's a kind of slavery, you know.'

And I kind of see what he means, but I also don't. If we break everything down, what happens then?

'Did you know,' he says, 'that one in five youth between the ages of sixteen and twenty-four is out of a job? That the gap between the rich and poor just keeps on growing? That no one listens to you if you're a nobody?

'That they can bring in the Snip Bill or any bill they like and you're screwed?

'And,' he concludes, 'they're using us.' He pauses. 'Those mates of mine who were arrested weren't anywhere near the riots. But does that matter? They want their names and faces, so they can flash up offenders on the TV to show the nation these riots are all the work of criminals. And nobody'll speak up for my mates neither. Nobody'll believe them.'

I take that in. I know he's right.

'Nobody gives a damn. You can die in police custody in this country and only your mum'll make a fuss.' He pauses again and looks troubled. 'Plus, I saw something just now outside that bank. Something that makes me think these riots are being masterminded by the government itself. And I need to prove it.'

'What?'

'Are you with me?'

'Well,' I say as evenly as I can, 'I might have been, but the way you've asked actually put me off.'

He raises his chin up, looks puzzled.

'You don't like the way I asked?' he says.

'The way you said "I can use you".'

'What I'm trying to say,' he slows down to make his point, as if I'm five, 'is much more important than the way I say it.'

Now I'm beginning to feel insulted. Plus it's getting dark. Very dark. There's a power outage, and no lights are blinking on any adverts. I'm hungry and I'm getting cold and I still haven't warned ADAM.

'We want the same things. There's no reason why we can't join forces,' he argues.

'Actually right now I just need a fiver,' I mutter.

'When the system collapses the Snip Bill goes with it.'

'Is this why you've been helping me?' I ask.

'Kind of,' he says.

'Well, you've been wasting your time,' I say.

He tilts his head.

'And you could've saved yourself a lot of trouble.'

'Why?' he says.

Where do I start? I don't know. I'm not the same girl who got on a coach from Cheltenham two days ago. I don't think I believe in things any more. I'd never have believed the police would shoot into a peaceful protest. I wouldn't have believed the government would use drones on civilians. That a helicopter could open fire on an unarmed teenager. That a mob could lynch someone and film themselves doing it.

I don't know what to think any more. There aren't any simple answers. And I don't believe bringing down the government will change anything. Not if the plan is to put the mob in charge, anyway.

So all I manage is: 'I don't know.'

15

'The Economy is Stumbling.
Let's Kick it Down.'
Anonymous

'Is this about your mother?' he asks.

My mother? I blink. How can it be about my mother?

'Because I said she plays at saving the world?'

'It's not a game,' I say. 'She is saving the world – well, a small part of it. You don't even know what she does.' Suddenly I want to tell him, make him ashamed. 'She's got a clinic with another doctor – he's Indian – they use microsurgery to repair the bladders and internal pelvic organs of girls who've been raped or forced to deliver children too young.'

He looks suitably shocked. But doesn't apologise.

'She's doing more to save the world than you are,' I add.

That nettles him. 'Don't even try to compare us,' he says. 'Your wonderful, save-the-world, give-me-the-Nobel-Peace-Prize mother ran away to India to save other

132

people's daughters and left her own to survive alone.'

That was uncalled for.

'And I had to step in to do her job for her.'

He doesn't understand. My mother had to leave. And I'm glad she did. I remember what it used to be like.

The door slams. The hurricane is back.

'Where's your mother?' He stands there in the door frame to the kitchen. Fire blazing in his eyes.

'She called,' I stammer, trying to cover for her. 'She said they brought in a crash victim, a little boy, his hand was nearly severed off, she said she has to stay to complete microsurgery before the nerves shut down, before the tendons shorten . . . I don't know,' I end lamely. I wish I did know. I wish I could convince him with lifesaving medical details that she's doing something very important, something that will make the difference to a child's life. But my voice is gone now. I shut my mouth.

'And you're here alone?'

I nod. But it's OK. I'm ten and there's Mack, Daddy's trusted-with-everything secretary – he's always here and a driver brought me home and the house-help stayed and gave me something to eat.

My father slams his fist down on the table. The table bounces on the wooden floor. I flinch. I don't dare cover my ears.

'This is the end of it,' he mutters.

Later, when I'm not asleep, I hear them. I hear him. He's shouting. He hits something that resounds with a dull thump. There's a cry cut short. A silence.

I hear him shout. 'No wife of mine is going to be out, while my child is in the house alone.'

I hear a cup break, a plate shatter. I hear him shouting again and again. I can't hear the words. I don't want to hear the words. I cover my ears. Another thick noise. Another series of thumps.

I hear footsteps on the stairs.

I hear weeping from another room.

My mother never goes to work again.

But Cobain isn't finished. He's angry.

'Listen, rich girl, you don't know anything about anything. You're just a starry-eyed little flash mobber who wants to slum it a bit with the have-nots, before you swan off to university, and get a degree and a job and a husband and however many kids you want. You're not in any real danger from the bill, are you?'

He's angry. So I don't say anything.

'After all, your dad's the minister in charge, isn't he? He's not going to snip off his own family tree, is he?'

But I don't have to stay and listen, either. 'I'm really sorry about Pat,' I say, 'but I think it's time I was on my way.' I stand up. 'And I need to message ADAM.' I turn on my heel.

Like lightning he's on his feet. 'STOP.'

I don't stop.

'Don't,' he says. He races after me, lays a hand on my arm.

'I'm sorry if you didn't like the way I asked. I'm sorry that you won't work with me, but you've got no experience of surviving out here on the streets. You're a target. And you don't know what it's like when you're a nobody. You won't survive.'

I just look at him. Did I ask him for his opinion?

'And they got to Pat,' he says. 'It's not all some kind of game. How sure are you about this ADAM?'

'He runs the campaign,' I say.

'But everything's changed,' says Cobain. 'Britain's on the brink of meltdown. People do strange things. ADAM may have changed sides. How much does he know about you?'

I try to remember if I've ever told ADAM I was Tia Thomson.

'And you've met him?'

'I've seen his avatar,' I say.

Cobain rolls his eyes. 'Tia, that's mad. He could be anyone.'

'Like me,' I say.

Cobain looks at me, puzzled.

'Like me being a minister's daughter?'

He sucks in his cheeks. 'Not like you.'

'And who exactly are *you*?' I shoot out.

'OK,' he says. A dark shadow passes over his face. 'Have it your own way.'

I walk on.

Cobain drops his hand.

I carry on.

And he doesn't.

16

'Lead No Followers and Follow No Leaders.'
Anonymous

I walk down the street as fast as I can. Cobain's wrong. You can't destroy things and expect anything better. That's where we're different. I want to fix things, build things, dream big. And I can't see how trashing everything will help.

And really, I didn't like the way he asked.

But I cast a glance back, anyway. He's still standing there, looking after me. I raise my good hand, give a tiny wave. In another time, another world, maybe I could have got to know him better. Found out why he was so angry. We might have hung out a bit. Gone somewhere nice. You know, sat on the grass on a sunny day and talked politics and whether saving the world was better than destroying it. I don't know. I guess he's got his reasons for being angry.

And if he'd asked me for help, as a friend to a friend,

I'd have hacked his records for him. I still might. I could. He did save me. I could do that for him. At least I'd get to know exactly who he is, what he did.

I look back again. He's still standing there.

I glance a third time. But the standing figure's gone. He's gone.

I stuff my hands in my pockets and carry on walking. I don't know why my chest suddenly feels so tight. I hoped he might come after me. Kind of expected him to. I don't know why I expected that.

But maybe it's good he didn't.

Because I know what I've got to do.

And I've got to do it, because I'm not like Cobain. I'm trying to fix things. But it's hard. And that's what he wouldn't understand. He thinks being a 'starry-eyed rich girl' means everything's easy. But it's not. It's harder in some ways. For one thing, it means you've got a lot more to lose. And right now, I'm probably going to lose everything: all the things I could have had, that college place, that degree, that nice young man and that future. Because I've got to decide whether I'm going to open up my phone and log into Darknet7 and warn ADAM or not.

You see, I have a choice: I could basically walk away and fool myself that it's not my responsibility any more. That the users of Darknet7 signed up to the campaign all on their own. I never twisted anyone's arm. It was their choice, and they must accept whatever consequences that choice brings. Just like the rest of us. I can tell myself I don't have money, and there're no cashpoints working. So what the hell can I do? Do they expect me to walk across London for ever, searching for ATMs? And are they gonna buy me a coffin, if the police shoot me down?

The thing is we grew too big. We didn't quietly stop when the government wanted us to. So now I'm in the firing line and the other campaigners are too. So it's every man for himself, isn't it? Plus I've got a future. I've a duty to take care of myself. And that's my excuse.

Or I can simply use my phone.

And I know what I want to do, but I know what I ought to do. And I know what Lacey needs me to do. And I know if I was one of them what I'd want me to do. And I'm trying to decide, but really there's no choice, is there?

Because if the police arrest them and they're convicted, they'll be snipped. And that's what I'm fighting against. What we're all fighting against. And it'll mean we've lost. It's so ironic it's not funny. They're snipping convicts right now – at this very moment – in every prison across the country, and we'll have played right into their hands.

And the bottom line is that data was in my care. So I've got to let them know the danger they're in. I owe that to everyone on the site. There's no other way. Even though opening up my phone is probably going to bring that helicopter straight down on me. And if I'm not lucky I'm going to pop, just like that girl.

It's good Cobain's gone.

No need to put him in danger.

I should have done this hours ago.

Before I can change my mind I pull out my phone. My hands tremble.

Quickly I open up Tor, access Darknet7. There's about a zillion messages and the chat room's buzzing. *'Parliament is calling for emergency sittings to discuss the future of the Snip.' 'Looks like we're winning.' 'Are they about to back down?' 'ARRESTS ARRESTS, be aware – they're swooping in on us.' 'Is it about harsher measures, further violent clampdowns?' 'We shall not be moved.' 'We must rally on parliament itself!'*

I look up, scanning the sunset for a helicopter. Then I get on with it.

They're showing reruns of the baby and his mother being killed. There's a thread focusing on whether or not the shots came from the crowd. I navigate away from that. I can't watch it. Instead I look briefly at the reruns of the guys throwing rocks. There's a hot argument there too on whether or not yobs are of any use to the campaign.

I hit that strand first with one of my pseudo identities.

JaneBond007: – *Yobs are no use to us.*

I look up again, waiting to hear the familiar whirring of blades.

Then I go into ADMIN and quickly post on to the home page:

URGENT. BREAKING NEWS. URGENT. BREAKING NEWS.

WE'VE BEEN HACKED. THE POLICE KNOW ALL OUR NAMES AND ADDRESSES. WE NEED TO STOP. EVERYONE SHOULD STAY AT HOME AND CEMENT THEIR ALIBIS FOR THE WEEKEND. WE MUST IMMEDIATELY STOP ALL CAMPAIGN ACTIVITY, INCLUDING ANY PLANS TO PROTEST FURTHER AGAINST THE NO MORE CHILDREN IN NEED BILL.

FIRSTLY, WE ARE PLAYING INTO THEIR HANDS.

SECONDLY, YOU KNOW WHAT'LL HAPPEN IF YOU'RE CONVICTED OF FLOUTING THE BAN ON DEMONSTRATING, BREAKING THE CURFEW OR RIOTING, AND ARE SENT TO PRISON. REMEMBER THEY ARE LOOKING FOR WAYS TO SNIP US.

THIRDLY, THIS IS WHAT CAN HAPPEN. HIT THIS
LINK.
JaneBond007//filmvid-?com.links-post-a-pic.html

EVE

I upload the film from my phone. The film of the girl in
the baggy jeans. I don't have time to reconfigure it and
post it through ADMIN. The quickest way is through my
JaneBond007 ID. So I do that. It's clumsy, but I link it
through to EVE's board. I can't watch it though. Even if
there was time, I couldn't. So I just type in:

PLEASE SEND THIS FILM OUT. LET THEM KNOW IT
HASN'T GONE UNNOTICED. WE DEMAND JUSTICE
FOR THIS GIRL.

I log out of the chat room. I DM all the followers:

EVE IS ALIVE AND WELL. THE CAMPAIGN GOES
ON, BUT WE NEED TO BE CAREFUL. THIS IS
ABOUT FURTHERING FUTURE LIFE, NOT GETTING
OURSELVES SNIPPED OR KILLED.

EVE

It isn't the coolest message, but I want to get something out. Let those who are monitoring me know the fight's still on.

Then at last I see it. A dark spot on the skyline. They're here. They've found me. I try to hurry. I've only got a few seconds now.

I log out as JaneBond007 and in as EVE.

There're five messages from ADAM:

Where are you, EVE?

You OK?

There's a rumour out you were shot?

Message me?

Please make contact. Worried. A.

I message him back on his board.

EVE here. **THEY HAVE GOT ALL OF THE DATA ON EVERY MEMBER OF DARKNET7. BY NOW THEY WILL HAVE DECODED IT. THE WEBSITE IS NO LONGER SECURE.** Please post out general warning to support mine on Darknet7 on the Anti-Snip Bill Campaign website, and a campaign statement re our position re further flouting of bans. **HAVE THEY TARGETED YOU? IF NOT THEY WILL, IF THEY CAN. KEEP YOUR IDENTITY SECRET. I BELIEVE THEY ARE READY TO KILL ALL OF THE RINGLEADERS OF THE CAMPAIGN. WARN ANY KEY OTHERS COORDINATING WITH YOU.** I'm OK. But need help. Long story. May be my last login. Can we meet? Have key passwords to the Storm Cloud to give you. Plus I've figured something out. Chose public location. Post venue on the pre-planned websites, in central London. In trouble. EVE

Then I stop. I can already tell they're trying to pinpoint me exactly. The speed is slowing down. It takes ages for the post to send. The little whirling thing on the server goes round and round, but the post doesn't send. Impatiently I tap on the screen, but it whirrs on. Just when I can't stand it a moment longer, *at last*, it goes.

And so do I.

The helicopter hovers over the rooftops. I know what they'll be doing. They'll be covering the street, hook up to the CCTV, running it live into their programming banks.

I cut into a side street. But before I log out or have time to shut my phone down, the Darknet7 news bar flashes up. And I read:

BREAKING NEWS: EVE IS DEAD. THE POLICE CAN NOW REVEAL THAT THE NOTORIOUS EVE, SELF-STYLED MOTHER OF THE FUTURE AND INSTIGATOR OF THE RECENT RIOTS, WAS SHOT DEAD IN AN

EXCHANGE OF FIRE IN PARKING AREA J OF SOUTHFIELDS SHOPPING CENTRE ON SATURDAY AFTERNOON. POLICE HAVE BEEN WORKING ON RELIABLE EVIDENCE FOUND AT THE SCENE AND HAVE ESTABLISHED HER IDENTITY AS DAISY COLLINS OF SURBITON . . .

A photo of the baggy jeans girl flashes up on my screen.

My mouth literally drops open. I can't believe it. I feel a sudden mad desire to shout up at the helicopter: 'It's not true, I'm here! I'm not dead!' But that would be totally crazy. They're up there, zooming in on me, for a reason. And if they thought I was dead they wouldn't be, would they? Or would they? I'm confused.

The response from Darknet7 is instantaneous. A 'spokesperson for EVE' writes on the forum wall: *EVE may be dead, but the cause lives on! Hasta la victoria siempre! We call on all supporters of the HANDS OFF Campaign to take to the streets.*

And on every strand runs the message: *THE CAUSE LIVES ON. WE MARCH FOR EVE.*

I jog to the corner of the street. The helicopter sweeps so low even the dust starts to rise up. I wipe my screen on my T-shirt. I flick through the web pages. Everywhere it reads: *WE MARCH FOR EVE. WE MARCH FOR EVE.*

WE MARCH FOR EVE. Except one, where it reads:

THE NEXT MESSIAH AND OUR NEW SAVIOUR,
TIA THOMSON, ATTACKS THE HEART OF OUR
PROBLEMS: THE MONEY LENDERS, THE TRUE
THIEVES, 'THE DEN OF ROBBERS' – OUR BANKS.

I check on other sites.

WE MARCH FOR EVE.

I check on the Clearnet. It's everywhere.

I've got to do something. I post on EVE's page:
NO. STOP.

And they post back:

'Shame on you. You are a government plant.'

'You are trying to stop us from overturning the Snip Bill.'

*'First you kill her. Then you hack her account!! Is there
no limit!!'*

'STUPID! We've seen the video of you killing her!
JaneBond007//filmvid-?com.links-post-a-pic.html
**Shakes head at serious stupidnessiosity of those in
"authority"*'*

'But you will never win. We won't stop.'

'We won't stop for anything.'

17

'Life is Short. Don't Waste it in Submission.'
Anonymous

Desperately I message ADAM again.

IT'S NOT TRUE. I'M ALIVE. CAN PROVE IT WHEN WE MEET. YOU MUST STOP THEM MARCHING. EVE.

Then I switch off my phone. And run.

I make sure my hood's down tight. I come out of the side street. I check for face-recog sweeps. I sprint to the corner and duck into an alley. I look up to check if they've got CCTV. I can't see any. I move fast: there'll be aerial coverage. They'll be heat imaging. They can zoom in on the alley. They're probably trying to do that right now.

Underground, that's the best bet. There'll be cameras in the stations and maybe some on the platforms, but once I'm on a train I can hide myself amongst others, switch lines, platforms, carriages.

Keep going. Lose yourself in the crowd. There's safety

147

in numbers. Sometimes.

ADAM will know what to do. He'll post a place to meet.

Just survive long enough to get there.

I get out on to the main street, dodge between people. *Don't attract attention. Stay calm. Blend in.* But it's not easy. In the distance smoke's funnelling up into the sky. Make it to the Underground, through the barriers, behind a large lady with bags.

School students don't pay on the Underground, but they need a card. I don't have one. Nobody cares though. The guys working here look too tired to argue. Nobody has money, anyway. Not since they froze salary increases and introduced the 'Poverty Taxes'. What a great idea that was. 'This Country is on the Verge of Bankruptcy. We Must All Tighten Our Belts. This Recession is Going to Go on For a Very Long Time. New Tax Payments Will Be Levied to Keep Our Welfare State Going – Just Not on the Super Rich. British People For Great Britain.'

Way to go.

But I worry anyway. I don't want some zealous guy to stop me and demand to see my travel pass. I take off the hoody and keep my head down. Nobody challenges me.

I head for the escalators. It's no use trying the lifts. Even when the power's on they rarely work. Since the austerity measures began, we're all on power sharing. The escalators don't work either, of course, but you can still use them as stairs.

I make it to the platforms. Take the first train. I'm scared. What happens if they figure out I took the Underground?

I jam myself in with all the commuters. *Thank God for commuters. Thank God there are still some jobs for people to go to.* I shrink into myself, become as small as possible. Pressed between backpacks and elbows, I breathe in.

I try not to gulp air. I try to stay calm. Try to guess which station everyone will get off at. Make a plan. *Look like you know where you're going. Any hesitation will show up on cameras.*

I'll have to get off somewhere. I'll have to use my phone again. How long will it take ADAM to set up a venue? I better wait a while. Be sure he's set something up. I can't risk using my phone too often.

I'll wait. I know ADAM. He'll take his time. He'll be very careful to choose somewhere very open, very prominent; under such obvious surveillance that covert systems aren't needed – if there is such a place.

Everywhere's under covert surveillance these days. Every street. And what with the riots, with the HANDS OFF flash mobs, they'll be watching everywhere.

ADAM'll know best, though, however covert. He has his sources. That's why he's run such a successful Anti-Snip campaign.

Well, I hope he'll know best. He's managed to keep the spotlight off himself, anyway.

Unlike me.

Yes, wait.

Suddenly I feel dizzy. If I wasn't held up by the press of bodies, I'd keel over. I'd sit on the floor of the train and never get up again. I wish Cobain was here. Maybe it's my ears, but the noise of the train is deafening. One step after the next, I tell myself. Mum used to say that. *'When it feels like you can't go on, remember, darling, it's just one step more.'*

One step after the next.

I get out at Piccadilly Circus. I follow the rush of people. I check behind me. I don't recognise anyone. I daren't look behind again. Like all the others I keep going.

At Eros I stop. I stand by the statue, as if I'm admiring it, like everyone else. I pull out my phone like I'm taking pictures. Last time I stood here, I actually was taking pictures. They weren't of Eros, though. They were of the best ever piece of EAT THE RICH graffiti. Don't ask me how the artist did it: Leonardo da Vinci's *Last Supper* in street tag right over the flashing Coke ad, with Jesus serving up every head of state from every rich country on a bed of boiled rice! Complete genius.

Boy, that must've annoyed the hell out of them. It appeared overnight, before a huge international economic summit. The government went mental.

It isn't there any more. Obviously. Just people snapping boring old Eros. I join in, or pretend to, while I scan the streets.

Everything looks normal. There's an energy in the air, though. It's dark, and a chill wind has sprung up. Shops are shutting down, boarding up, as if they expect the rioting to reach right into the centre of town. No neon lights sparkle out across the streets.

When I'm sure nobody's looking, I turn my phone on again. I type in my link.

ADAM and I have a code. When we want to pass sensitive information that's too unsecured on Darknet7, we use book blogger sites. We're working our way through the alphabet. It goes like this: you type in book blog and then *A* or *B* or whatever letter we've reached, and then find the first numeral on the page. Using that numeral, you count down the sites. You'd be amazed at the number of book bloggers there are. We find the site; then go to the most recent review and use the *comment back* section and paste in our message there, disguised.

I find the site. I read: *This story should be read in Westminster Abbey. It offers a fascinating bridge to the world of olden-day political debate. I'd double the star ratings and give it nine and a half (only God makes ten out of ten) if I could. Ah, well, I'll have to give it the same old, same old. Five Stars. Read it!*

It tells me what I need to know. Words seven and thirteen, my birthday and his. Westminster Bridge. 9.30 p.m.

Westminster Bridge.

I check the time. It's nearly nine already. I need to get back across London then. I click my phone off and I'm gone. The whole operation took only 3.08 minutes. But I'm not dumb. It'll pinpoint me. And they'll be here soon. I'm just hoping Piccadilly Circus will throw them a bit. Too many people. Too many phones.

I try not to look like I'm panicking. I race down the pavement. *Pace yourself,* I say. Stay calm. Get to the Underground again. You'll make it. It'll take them more than three minutes to get here. A film of sweat coats my forehead. I start to feel hot. I just hope I can make it in time to Westminster. ADAM won't wait. That's the rule. Exact time. Exact place. Dead drop. Move on. If you're there or not. His rules, I remember. Back in the days when it was fun to play at being secret agents, when all we ever did was message each other in codes about dropping off hand stickers for guerrilla-marketing sticker-bomb runs.

If I miss him?

I sprint down the platform. I just make it on to the train. The door practically snaps to behind me. If anyone was trying to follow me, I've lost them for sure. I squeeze through people. Still lots of people. Nobody could have followed me this time. Sweat pours down the side of my face. I wipe it off with the sleeve of my jacket.

On the train I find a seat and sink into it. I stare at the window opposite. The girl sitting beside me has immaculate hair. She's only about six. She's got earphones in as well. She looks so self-contained, so happy. She's not staring around like me. Her mouth is all drawn up tight, biting on her lip as she plays with her HD tablet. I see her reflection in the glass in front, right beside mine. I don't look half as happy as she does.

Westminster Bridge, 9.30.

See, Cobain? You were wrong. ADAM is OK.

Westminster Bridge is very out in the open. I hope to hell he's right about this. I'd never dare go to Westminster Bridge on my own.

I try to imagine what ADAM will be like – how old,

how tall, how skinny? I realise despite hundreds of messages and hours of online chat, and loads of planning and codes and rules and dead drops, I've never met him. I don't know what he looks like, apart from his avatar. I wonder if he looks like his avatar . . .

But why Westminster Bridge? It starts to worry me. I knew he'd choose somewhere obvious, but Westminster Bridge? It's too near my father's flat. What if I strike unlucky and bump into *him*? I imagine the news headlines, probably circulating already:

DR THOMSON APPALLED OVER DAUGHTER SCANDAL.

I close my eyes. ADAM doesn't know who I am, doesn't know I'm Tia Thomson. ADAM wasn't to know that anywhere *except* Westminster would've been OK.

I wish Cobain were here. I almost miss those eyes. I wish he'd helped me just because he liked me.

The girl beside me suddenly taps my arm. I nearly shoot out of my seat in alarm. 'D'you know how to get online?' she says. 'My mum's asleep.'

I notice the lady on the other side of her has nodded off.

I smile at the kid. 'You can't on the Underground,' I say. 'There's no coverage here.'

'Oh,' she says, disappointed. 'It never goes properly,

154

even at home,' she says.

'I can set it up so it does, as soon as you get off,' I say. 'If you'd like me to.'

She passes me her HD Kiddie-Pad tablet. I fix her wireless network connection for her.

On a sudden impulse I say, 'Can I message someone from your tab?'

'Sure,' she says, smiling happily at me.

I message Cobain. I just want to. It seems weird to just disappear without a goodbye. I wish I had his email, although it probably wouldn't be secure. He must be under complete electronic surveillance. I access his social media site, anyway, and post a *friend-me* request with my message. I make sure it goes to *pending*. When we hit a pocket with coverage, or the little girl gets off, it'll send. It won't pinpoint where I am. It's the most obscure I can make it. Nobody will suspect a *friend-me* add from a six-year-old's tab, will they? I write:

Sorry I wasn't what you wanted. Will you still friend me? Meeting A at Westminster Bridge. I'll sort out your stuff – just this once – but that's all. Think of it like a thank-you.

I hope it's cryptic enough. And not too cryptic. I figure he's smart enough to realise it's me and that I mean I'll sort out his records. That I'll hack them, erase them for him.

I pass the tablet back to the girl and whisper, 'Thanks.'

She says, 'You're welcome,' very nicely.

Sweet kid.

The train judders to a halt. The little kid and her mum get off. She waves bye at me. Some people get on. I sit tight. I watch carefully to see if there're any faces I've seen before. Nobody looks at me. They don't look at anybody. They just get on and stare at the floor.

Next stop. Nearly there. How will I recognise ADAM when I'm on the bridge? I don't know what to look for. But there's only one spot that's totally in the middle of Westminster Bridge, and if there's a guy standing on it, that'll be him, won't it? That's why he chose the place. So I wouldn't make a mistake. That's clever, actually.

I start to relax. I made it on to the train. I won't bump into my father. ADAM will be there and I can prove I'm not dead, give him the passwords to the StormCloud and we can stop the marching, make sure we don't play into any more government set-ups.

Parliament Square is still full of people, plus police. They're always there. I stop and look at them. I look up at the Houses of Parliament. The No More Children in Need Bill will be passed here tomorrow. Outside, the podium has already been set up behind the police cordon.

That's where my father will announce the news: '*The bill is now law.*'

And inside that building, between now and then, they'll decide the future, whether some of the next generation will ever play with their children, hold them, admire them. Whether Lacey can have a child, whether she can't. They will decide the future of Cobain.

A shiver goes through me. *Snip Cobain?* They can't do that? Can they? He'd never let them.

Suddenly, the horror of it all hits me again. I think of scrubbed hospital surfaces, of dissecting trays, of scalpels, of blood. Of snipping teenagers. *They can't snip Cobain.* I tilt my chin up so nothing will show on my face. The grey stone of the building towers above me. Shadows stretch out over dark pavements.

This is where they'll decide.

I look around the square, hemmed in on all sides. I look at the huge barriers around the entrance to the Houses of Parliament. If they riot here, they won't stand a chance. The police could cover every exit.

A policeman catches my eye. He smiles a bit. I smile too. So strange that we can smile at each other when tomorrow he'll be the enemy. Perhaps he's smiling for a different reason? Quickly I scan the square. I duck my head down before he can remember me, pull up my hoody. I head off.

The streetlamps are bright. No power outages in Westminster, then. I'm lit up on every side. My shadow stretches out in three directions. The rest of the nation can grope around in darkness, but there'll be no blackouts here. Under each lamppost the tarmac shines in pools of light. I can't resist stepping into the shiny bits and seeing if it lights my shoes.

I hurry past the barricades and the crash barriers, past the scaffold that now protects all the building fronts, out past Big Ben, down towards the river.

No one stops me, but I hurry anyway. And with every step I like the location less and less. *Why did he have to choose here?* My heart thuds. ADAM's clever, though. It's probably like a double bluff. If you meet up right under their noses they won't suspect a thing.

That doesn't calm me at all. What if they do suspect?

I'd much rather have met somewhere else.

Up ahead the river stretches in shimmering darkness. It's a fine night. The water is gleaming a strange, witchy-black. The lamps are lit all the way along the bridge, each one a small shining star. Big Ben towers up, floodlights down, its clockfaces glowing. The river silently slips by, dangerous, deep green.

I tread cautiously, trying not to keep looking over my

shoulder. Sweat breaks out across the back of my neck. What if they've cordoned off the bridge? I'm right in the centre of London. I cross my fingers. Please don't let the bridge be cordoned off.

But what if the rioting has reached the South Bank, and I do get on to the bridge? I won't be able to get off it again. I wish I could message ADAM and change the place.

Keep your nerve, I tell myself. *You asked for this meeting. You've got to prove to ADAM you're alive and give him codes, so he can message every single supporter individually, and get them to stop.*

I hesitate, pretend I've got a pain in my leg, semi-stoop to rub my calf. Frantically I scan around. *Stay calm, Tia. It'll be OK.*

At least there isn't a barrier cordoning off the bridge. There aren't any people on it either. I try to stay as small as possible. I try to slide along by the huge, cast-iron balustrades.

Nobody?

But there should be somebody.

There should be one person, anyway.

There should be ADAM.

Check the time. I can't turn on my mobile. There's Big Ben right beside me. The time is shining out. It's

9.25 p.m. Five more minutes. I relax. Of course ADAM won't hang about on the centre of Westminster Bridge, waiting.

I slow down, let my pace become a stroll, look out over the river, as if I'm admiring the view. I even raise my hand to my eyes to shade them, as if the sun is bright and I'm looking down the reaches of the Thames in some quaint period drama.

Anyone can see that I'm not a tourist, though. They can see it's not the middle of a sunny afternoon or the eighteenth century.

And there's still no ADAM.

I bring my hand down. I go even slower. I glance up at Big Ben again: 9.27 p.m. Maybe he'll come on a bike. That's it. He'll come on a bike. He'll come soon. I must reach the centre of the bridge.

9.28 p.m.

It's getting very dark. For a second I'm confused. Did shading my face somehow make things darker? I glance behind me. All the lights in Westminster have suddenly gone out. Parliament Square is in darkness.

I can't even see the time on Big Ben.

Parliament Square is never in darkness.

The government sits and meets. Their debating and planning goes on past midnight, past dawn. I know. My father's one of them. And tonight they'll be bound to be there. All the hospitals can be on generators, all the traffic lights can blink out. Cars can crash and life-support machines go off. Computers stop dead. But not here.

Not in Westminster.

Big Ben rises like a monolith, its clockfaces gone. Only a pale moon is shining, way off, down behind St Paul's, illuminating the skyline in a ghostly show of silver grey. The dome of the cathedral stands outlined, like an age-old etching. I stare at it, as if I am going back in time.

And that's when I see the red laser dot.

Hovering over my chest.

That's when I hear someone shout, '*TIA!*'

18

'My Dreams Are the Nightmares
of Politicians.'
Anonymous

I duck. I swerve. I weave. I run. The red spot dodges, finds me. I stop. I turn. I curve out into the road. I race forward. I run and run. My heart bangs. Blood pumps through me like a jet.

I hear the voice again. It's far away. Too far away.

'*TIA!*'

I don't know who's shouting. *ADAM? Where is he? They must have intercepted my message. His message. They must know. They've hacked us. They got him.*

I don't know what they must know. I can't think. Only sprint and dodge.

And you can't outsprint a red laser spot.

It follows.

It seeks you out.

I hear a crash. I see the spray. I hear the bullet. It prangs off the edge of the ironwork.

162

Christ, they're shooting at me.

The ironwork.

Get behind the ironwork.

I race to the balustrades. The spot follows.

If I get over the ironwork?

Before I think about it I'm over, dangling above the river, balancing on my tiptoes in the frets of the parapet. Crouching. Hanging on. Beneath me the river floods. My heart explodes in my throat. The red spot is gone.

And no ADAM.

Thank God there's no ADAM. Thank God he didn't come. He must have figured out they knew, must have tried to warn me.

I hear a whirring in the air above me. *Christ, they've sent out a helicopter.*

Think straight, Tia. Think hard. No way back, no way forward. Think.

Maybe I can work my way, crouching behind the ironwork, tiptoeing along the edge of the parapet. Maybe I can make it to the South Bank. *I'm trapped. I knew this was stupid.* My breathing's gone weird. *Breathe.* It was a stupid trap. *They've killed ADAM.* No, he got away. *But he called out?*

I start moving. Another bullet prangs off the iron. *This*

is no joke. My knuckles ache. *Work your way across the river. Keep going. One foot in front of the next.* Everything is aching. *You can do it. One foot in front of the next.* I can't hang on. My shoulder can't take it.

I'm above the last pier when I hear the helicopter again. It's definitely there. It's so dark I can't see it. It sighs through the air. Its whirring drowns out the rush of water.

I'm trembling. This can't be happening. I can't die like this. I won't die like this. I hear the shouting again. It's still coming from a long way off.

'*JUMP!*' it says.

I look down. *I can't jump.* The river's too deep, too dangerous. The current's too fast. My heart stops.

If I can only make it to the last pier, I won't be so far from the shore. The whirring above me is loud. Then I see there is no shore, only a sheer brick quay rising straight up from the riverbed. If I float downstream? *Could I do that?* I try to work out where I'd have to get to? Greenwich? *Could I?* Another shot crashes into the ironwork.

'*Jump!*' comes the voice again, much nearer now. Is it coming from the river below?

I hang off the parapet. I peer through the gloom under the bridge. The smell of water, of city water, raw like

164

rainfall on tarmac.

A boat, a row-dinghy, under the arch. The voice coming from it. *ADAM?*

Thank God. I ease myself down on to the brickwork, the last pier. I don't have to float. I don't have to drown. There's a boat down there. I peer at the water beneath me. If I hang down by my fingers, if my shoulder can take it, even for a second, I can slip into the water only metres from the dinghy. I lower myself down. The fretwork ends in the last sweep of the supporting arch. I feel with my toes for a toehold. I panic. *I can't find a toehold.*

One foot in front of the other.

The river is close. I should let go. Slime-black water.

The whirring above me blasts my hair against my face, whips my face. The red dots appear. So many now. They skitter over the ironwork, scuttle up the brick pier, scurry, search, like cockroaches caught in torchlight. Now on my side of the river. Now overhead. The helicopter hovers. The boat manoeuvres nearer. *I've got to let go.* Let the water carry me under the bridge.

So I do.

I let go.

There's one mad rush of panic. Air whips my face. I feel the water, cold, very cold. It closes over my head.

And I keep on going down and down, and I know I must do something, but I don't know what.

Kick.

I must kick my legs. I must fight. I must.

Kick harder.

Fight back. And I open my mouth, but there's still water. *I can't breathe.* I kick and kick. How much longer? *Open your eyes.* I open my eyes. It's dark. It stings. I close them again. And just when I think it's all over and I'm going to drown, my head breaks surface. I don't even know. I don't even breathe.

I open my mouth and I *can't* breathe. It's like something in my throat has closed down. All I can do is heave and splutter and kick.

And sink under again.

19

'A Cause Not to Die For.'
Anonymous

And as I sink, I remember Mum's letter, the first one I ever got from her, and how it will get soaked and the ink will run.

My Dearest Girl,

I hope so much this letter gets to you.

After you left for boarding school, Tony said I was not to contact you, never to visit you, not to interfere with his arrangements, that he'd send you to his mother's in the holidays and I was to stay indoors and submit to his will entirely.

I couldn't bear it, Tia. It was only you that kept me going. But Tony didn't see it like that. When I resisted he told me I was unwell, needed help. He had me sent to a private mental health clinic, convinced them I was depressed, a danger to myself, a danger to you.

And I was depressed, but not clinically ill. I'd been

stripped of my profession, my self-esteem and finally you, my dearest darling, and I felt my life was not worth having. If it hadn't been for Dr Shah, I think I'd have given up. It was through Dr Shah that I learnt Tony intended to keep me in that clinic on medication for as long as it suited him. Dr Shah was a true friend. He taught me that life is a gift, that I had everything to live for. He saw through Tony. He thought that I could practise again. He gave me hope.

He gave me a fresh start.

So I'm writing this now from my little veranda in India outside the back of the clinic Dr Shah has started. Yes, he has a surgery in India! And I am employed in it! We have funding, and every day I help him treat such sad cases and we are making a difference.

I know it must be so hard for you, my darling, having to face things on your own. But I believe Grandmama Thomson is a decent woman. She promised me that once she'd satisfied herself that I was no threat to you, she'd pass on this letter. She promises she'll deliver more too. Let me know if you get it, so that I can write to you at length, safe in the knowledge that Tony will not punish you for anything I do, and that Grandmama Thomson is as good as her word.

Your loving Mum XXXX

A hand grabs my back, grabs the hoody. Pulls it off me. I feel myself being hauled, dragged, stomach over gunwales, into the boat. And there I lie gasping, heaving, trying to breathe. ADAM throws a cloth over me, says, 'Stay down.'

At least, I think it's ADAM.

And I can't do anything except stay down. I can't even inhale properly. I'm shaking and gulping and so cold. The cloth is thick. Darkness. I'm alive. *Stay alive*. At last I suck in air and heave and push it out again. I twitch back the cloth. I can see brickwork above me. The oars creak. Someone's rowing? We're not moving.

I struggle to sit up. A hand firmly presses me down again. I'm grateful to lie still and stay alive and wait until my breathing returns to normal.

Someone just tried to shoot me. They just tried to flipping kill me. That means . . . I don't know what it means. It could mean anything. It means someone figured out how I contacted ADAM. Figured out his reply. It was just two words in a coded list, a random website. How could anyone figure that out?

Suddenly I feel like I've got a person inside my head. Someone who's reading my thoughts and decoding them. Reading them and telling my father. And it's freaky, it's flipping scary. I start to shiver. Because there isn't anyone else inside your head, except you, is there?

But someone knew it was me. And someone tried to kill me, and that's a fact.

A fact.

A fact that makes me shiver and tremble and lie still, until my mind is clear of red spots. *I jumped into the river!* I just can't believe I did that. *And they're still up there, looking for me.*

'Try to sit up and get your breath,' says ADAM.

Except it isn't ADAM.

I'd know that voice anywhere.

'Yeah, it's me,' says Cobain. 'The bad penny.'

I don't say anything. My mouth just sags open.

It really is him. Cobain Reilly, sitting right beside me.

'Just stay quiet. The heat imaging from the helicopter won't pick us up through the brickwork and as long as they don't suspect we're here, they won't check.'

For some reason I'm insanely happy! I look up. We're moored under Westminster Bridge. *And Cobain is sitting beside me!* How can they not suspect we're here? I open my mouth to ask. Cobain reads my mind.

'Look.' He points upstream. A helicopter is hovering low over the river, its spot searching. 'Luckily you jumped off the right side of the bridge to get swept under it by the incoming tide. I hooked you out and floated your scarf upriver. They've picked that out already. So right now that's where they're looking. Clever eh, otherwise it'd have been a bit more tricky.'

Bit more tricky!

'But in about ten minutes the tide'll turn,' he says. 'In fact, it's started turning already and they haven't noticed. We'll wait for five and then we'll have a very short window to scull this dinghy that way,' He points downstream, 'before the entire place is crowded out with police.'

Already I can hear the familiar sound of sirens. They wail from both banks. Their headlights shine out across the river, shine towards the searching helicopter.

'But how?' I splutter out.

'How did I know to get this boat?'

I nod.

'Well, I got your message for a start, so I figured you'd need rescuing again. And I'd been following you, so I knew you were in trouble.'

'Not possible.' I can't believe it. He's gotta be kidding me.

'Yeah, you were pretty good at dodging trains. But I worked out your pattern. Very neat, follow the thick of the crowd. You're smart. But, I admit it, I lost you eventually.'

I look at him. I can't believe someone could've even followed me on to the tubes, let alone from train to train! A cold thread snakes around my ribs: if Cobain followed me, then anyone could.

'So anyone could've followed me,' I say.

'I'm not *anyone*,' snorts Cobain. 'Not anyone can do what I do.'

'But the boat?' I glance quickly upriver. The helicopter's still searching. The police have reached the bank.

He shrugs in a smug way. He's enjoying this. I'm too surprised to care. 'Well,' he says, 'I lost you, but I knew you were going to meet ADAM, and I knew where, and I could hardly wait on the bridge, could I? So I just thought: if I was ADAM and a dickhead and a government plant, what would be my plan? After that it was pretty simple. If they didn't kill you, you'd have to jump.'

'A government plant?'

'Well, *somebody* snaked you up.'

I shake my head. 'Not ADAM. He set up the Anti-Snip Campaign. Organising flash mobs was just my end of things. If they're trying to take me out, they'll be trying to take him out too.'

It couldn't be ADAM. It was *me* who asked to meet *him*. And it still doesn't explain how come Cobain's here, with a dinghy, under the bridge.

172

Maybe we shouldn't be here under the bridge, either!

'Don't you think we should go?' I say.

'Can't row against the tide,' he says. He puts one hand in the water, checks the flow. 'We'll go soon.'

I glance back upriver. I'm sure I can see the headlights of a police motor launch, out there in midstream.

What if they decide to move back up to the bridge? My heart hammers.

I pull my mind away from the police launch. I turn to him. 'Doesn't add up. That wouldn't have been enough to make you hire a boat.' Though I know for sure he didn't 'hire' it.

'OK,' he says. 'I have other ways of knowing things.'

'What ways?' *Perhaps he did rob a bank. Perhaps he got out of jail early on some kind of plea bargain. Perhaps he's the government plant!*

'Someone snaked you up,' he says. 'I know the frequencies of a load of police radios. I like listening in to that kind of thing. For some reason they were clearing an area around Westminster Bridge, not a normal surveillance op. They spoke about *Code Garden of Eden* needing to be a *one-man op* as *credibility* was still *intact*. After your message, I'd have had to be an idiot.'

'*Code Garden of Eden*?'

'Yeah.'

173

I lie there, trying to let that soak in.

'ADAM and EVE,' he says.

'I know that,' I mutter.

'So I stopped following you halfway round London and came straight here, borrowed this dinghy and waited.'

I stare at him. I don't get it. Why would he do that for me?

I think the question must have scrolled across my face, because he smiles, and says, right on cue: 'No, not because you're pretty.'

The dark arch of the bridge looms overhead. I can make out each brick. My clothes cling to me. They stink. The water slaps at the dingy. I'm so cold. And I'm absolutely sure that launch is getting nearer.

Cobain looks at me and there's this look in his eyes. I don't know what it means. The look stays there, and then it flashes out. It didn't find what it was searching for? I didn't react how he wanted?

My chest deflates. A strange, soft feeling flickers down my throat. I swallow.

'So why?' I ask very quietly. I wish we could just go.

'Because I can still use you,' he says.

I look at him. What's he thinking? Because I said I'd erase his police records? That if he carries on rescuing me, I'll hack the Pentagon for him?

And it's a joke, isn't it? Here we are on a dinghy, under a bridge, on the river, hiding from bullets, waiting for the tide to turn and the police not to arrive. Fabulous. How does he imagine I can help anyone? Even if we do get away from here in one piece? Out there, sharpshooters are still looking for us, and they aren't giving up.

'Well, I thought, now you're Ms Shank a Bank, we could hack them too. Do a little bit of payback, ya know?'

So now he wants to do a Robin Hood? Mr Big-Heart Urban Guerrilla? Redistribute all the wealth. Pocket a load himself? Yo, show the world. *Dear Prime Minister, Redistribution is the Solution?*

He sees my face. 'I'm just joking,' he says.

I try to smile. But I think my sense of humour's gone.

And I thought I was being so clever: Onion Router, coded messages, book bloggers, Kiddie-Pads. How did they follow me? I'm sure ADAM didn't betray me. Why would he? He put everything into the campaign. *Maybe he's been caught. That's it. He was forced to tell.* Maybe he *did* come. And they forced him. *Did they shoot him?* I try to remember. *Was there anything lying slumped on the asphalt of the bridge?*

Maybe he's dead.

I tell myself to relax, he's alive. He's far too clever. He figured it out. He never came to the bridge. Cobain's just biased. He just hates ADAM. Maybe he's jealous? I wish he was jealous. ADAM will have tried to let me know. He'll be worrying about me. He must be holed up somewhere, worrying and worrying.

'Thanks,' I say. 'I mean, thanks for pulling me out of the river, for saving me.' I watch him.

'Again,' he adds.

'Yes,' I say. 'Again.'

'You really owe me now,' he says. His eyes narrow up.

I don't like that. I hate being guilt-tripped. I don't owe him anything.

'We need to get out,' I say. 'Can't we go already?'

'Brinkmanship,' says Cobain. 'There's no point in leaving the safety of this cover until exactly the right moment.'

'But look.' I point at the police launch. It's sweeping the river now from the South Bank right across. 'It's working this way.'

'So do we have a deal?' Cobain asks.

Incredible. Am I reading this right? The little hairs all down my back prickle. Is he suggesting that if I don't deal with him, he'll do what?

So I say: 'I can't decide anything until I make sure ADAM's OK. *However much you don't trust him,*' I add quietly.

Cobain laughs. 'You're sweet,' he says, 'but you don't get it. There is no ADAM.'

I look at him, puzzled. No ADAM?

'Where is he, then?' says Cobain.

In answer I pull out my mobile. 'I'll check,' I say. 'Of course there's an ADAM.'

'No,' says Cobain, so aggressively I jerk back. He stands up. 'Don't!' The boat tips, sways.

I'm not stupid. I wasn't really going to check. I was just doing it to wind Cobain up, see what he'd do. But as soon as I pull out my phone, I can see he's wired.

So I can't resist pretending, right in front of his face. Plus nobody tells me what to do.

I tighten my lips and give him a look.

But before I get any further, in one swift movement, faster than a cobra strike, Cobain swipes out at me and knocks the phone clear out of my hand. It spins up into the air. Makes an impressive arc. The lights of London twinkle off its screen.

The lights which are now back on.

And plunges down into the darkness of the Thames.

20

'Hope is Worse Than Despair.'
Anonymous

I don't scream or shout. I can't even think of an insult harsh enough.

'I'm sorry,' Cobain says, a strange, really-sorry note in his voice. 'I was just kidding you about having a deal with me. You shouldn't have tried to use that cell. You mustn't contact ADAM. I won't let you.'

'Won't let me?' I can't believe it. Since when has Cobain Reilly had a say over me? That's a joke.

'Get under the cloth,' he says, 'and hang on.' He loosens the mooring rope. The dinghy swirls into the current, casts a semi-circle, as if unsure which way to go. Unwillingly I tug at the sodden cloth.

'Let's get out of here.' Cobain pulls on the oars. I feel the dinghy suddenly shoot out under me and we're sculling downriver fast.

Cobain gives it everything. I can hear his ragged breathing. 'That was stupid, Tia,' he gasps. 'It really was.'

It was stupid to wind him up. But it doesn't let him off the hook. Without a word, I lie down on the bottom of the boat, and adjust the wet cloth until I'm sure even my feet are covered. I realise I'm trembling. My hands are trembling. My fingers won't work. And my phone's gone.

He knocked my mobile into the river. All my numbers. Gone. Jessica from my class, not just Jessica, *all* my friends, school, Grandmama, everyone. The only number I know by heart is Lacey's.

Mum's number. Gone.

I won't ever be able to call her again.

A breeze ruffles the cloth. It sticks against me, cold, heavy. Stench of wet cloth. I listen for the noise of the helicopter, wail of sirens. I lie very still, shivering.

I don't know how long I lie there. I'm very cold. The slap of river. The creak of oars. I cross my fingers. I hear Cobain. He's panting and puffing. I hear the boat groaning. The river running. The slap of paddles on water.

And I pray to God, *Please let us get away*.

Suddenly there's a pull and the cloth over me is yanked back. I flinch, expecting the worst.

'All clear,' Cobain hisses.

I sit up, squinting, and peer out over the water. We've come a long way downstream. The lights of

179

Westminster are way behind. Everywhere's dark. Only the moon, low and dim, lights a halo over St Paul's. We pull towards the South Bank. There's a bit of gravel, a few pebbles. I think we must be well down past the OXO Tower. I see the muscles in Cobain's arms straining as he turns the boat out of the current. His legs tense, braced against the dinghy. There's something reassuring about the strength it takes to steer us out of the current. If he were on my side, if we were really together, I'd feel almost safe. I let the thought go. He's not. Nothing's safe.

We swing in. There's a rush of water, a drag of shingle. I'm shivering even more. A breeze zips up off the river. It feels as if it blows straight into my bones, straight off the North Pole.

Cobain springs ashore. He grabs hold of the rope looped on the prow and hauls the dinghy in. 'Come on,' he says and holds out his hand.

I don't take it.

'Please yourself,' he says, 'but don't think we've lost them.' He points up at the wharf. CCTV cameras are trained on to the jetty. I pull my chin in and keep my face down. 'Big Brother is watching you,' he says.

I struggle to stand up. I can't see anything. Everywhere looks dark and treacherous. The boat rolls; the hull moves under my feet.

'C'mon,' he says impatiently, giving me his hand again.

'I can get out of a boat myself,' I say.

He shrugs and turns away. There's something disappointed in the angle of his shoulder. I step off the boat. The whole thing sways. I stagger and end up putting my foot into the shallows. I slop on to dry land and stand there on the stones, trying not to let him see my shivering.

'You can use mine,' he says.

I look at him. What? Use his what?

'My phone.' He holds out his mobile. 'I didn't mean to knock yours into the river. If you really want to check on ADAM, if you're so sure he's OK, use mine. It'll be a bit safer, anyway.'

I look at him, surprised. He really *is* sorry.

'OK,' I mumble. 'I won't sign in, or anything. I'll just check.' I don't say more. I know what I'm going to do. ADAM and I know how we message each other. I get online and, just like before, find the blogs. We've reached D in the alphabet. I use the code. I open up DarkBloggers, a site I used to love – when I had time to love.

I scroll down through the latest post, a review of a YA thriller. I think: *Who needs a book? My life will do just as well.*

Underneath is one post.

And I read:

181

*NO TIME TO ENCODE. URGENT. EVE – STAY AWAY
FROM THE BRIDGE. ADAM*

'Look.' I show Cobain with a certain amount of childish triumph. 'See!'

He doesn't look convinced and he doesn't answer.

But despite him, I feel reassured. At least ADAM is OK. And at least he tried to warn me. So I find the next code site and reply.

Glad you're OK. They nearly had me. I didn't get your warning in time. I guess there's no need to code this as you didn't. Plus they seem to have hacked everything, anyway. At least you know I'm not dead now. I'm just going to concentrate on trying to stay that way. Please make sure everyone who signed up for the HANDS OFF protests knows all their data is compromised. Like I said, any further protests will be just playing into the hands of the authorities and confirm the public's opinion that we all need snipping anyway, which is exactly what will happen if we get arrested. What a brilliant own goal that'd be. Ha ha. I don't have a plan for anything else other than #OpStopACTANoMoreChildrenInNeed, and staying alive until the bill's through – after which I'm hoping it'll be easier.

I haven't given up though.

I won't message again. There's probably no point in giving

you all my passwords any more, as long as everyone's warned.
Safer for us too. So I'm going off-grid for a while.

EVE

'Thanks,' I say to Cobain. 'Can I make a quick call too?'

He nods.

Quickly, I dial Lacey's number. She picks up.

I smile. Thank God, she's alive. 'It's me,' I say.

'Hi,' she says. 'Is it you? Really you?'

'Yep,' I say. I can hear she wants to ask a thousand questions, but I need to make this quick. 'Lace,' I say, 'just listen, do exactly as I say and then hang up. Exactly.'

'OK,' she says.

'I'm fine. I've been patched up, lots of stitches. The bullet tore a huge gash in my upper arm. I'm fine. But I need help. I want you to bring a change of clothes and anything I can disguise myself with and your bike and some money, as much as you can get. I'll pay you back later. I'm going to disappear for a while, so don't worry if after tonight you don't hear from me for a bit. See if you can get a contact number for my mum. She's working at the Shah Clinic, Ahmedabad. Bring everything and some food too, I'm starving. Go to the place we used to go – when we first hung out. Don't say anything. You know it. We used to go there on Sundays. That's all.

It's about ten forty-five now – so let's say midnight. Bring a sleeping bag too. I might need to sleep rough a bit. That's all. Don't tell anyone. I'll tell you everything else when I see you.'

'OK,' she says. 'Love you, Tia, so glad you're OK.'

I hang up. I'm annoyed she used my name.

'So where're we going now?' says Cobain.

I'm not sure if I should tell him. But I do anyway. 'Hyde Park.'

'At midnight?' he says. 'Are you sure about that?'

'I don't know,' I say. 'Nowhere's safe.'

'That's true,' he says.

'Thing is there's no CCTV there. So if I can get a change of appearance and some money, I can disappear for a bit.'

'But Hyde Park's huge,' he says.

'Don't worry,' I say. 'Lacey knows exactly where I mean. It's always been our special place.'

I slide Cobain's mobile off, and hand it back.

'Not a good idea,' he says.

'Pardon?' I say.

'Meeting up in Hyde Park. You don't know who set you up on the bridge. It's not a good idea to go to a place that's so lonely. Tia, get some sense. They must be tracking you somehow.'

'They were tracking my phone,' I say, 'but thanks to you they won't be doing that any more, will they?'

He leans in towards me, urgently. His hand closes over my wrist. I feel its warmth. He pulls me towards him, pauses, his face close to mine. My heart starts beating in a funny way. I can smell the tang of his skin. I can feel the warmth of his breath.

'And it's not your business,' I say. I twist my wrist free. 'And don't follow me this time.'

'And it's not your business where I go, either,' he says. 'I'll follow if I want.' And I can see he's angry.

'But you're stalking me,' I say.

'Pardon me,' he says. 'I thought I was saving you.'

'OK, saving me. Whatever.'

'Multiple times.'

'Well, you won't need to again,' I say.

'I'll leave you alone then. If you want to get yourself killed – go ahead. You're all yours.' And he throws back his head and rolls those eyes and turns around and walks off.

And I stand there not quite knowing what to do. Suddenly, strangely, wishing he'd said, 'OK, but let me come with you. I'll follow behind you. I'll be there – you know, just in case.'

A strange, sad little sinking feeling drains from my

chest into my feet. I handled that all wrong. I want to race after him, catch his arm, feel the warmth of his hand again, feel the breath of his lips on mine, go with him to Hyde Park.

But he doesn't even look back. He's just going to leave me here.

So I turn away. He won't give up, surely? Will he? Maybe I should have teamed up with him, promised to hack whatever he needed? He didn't get out on any plea bargain. He's the best friend I ever had.

I walk on. I don't look back. Although at every step I want to.

21

'Eve Was Framed.'
Anonymous

Greenwich to Hyde Park in an hour and a bit?

I start to compute. Best to take a bus. Avoid CCTV where possible. Try to get an older bus where the CCTV on board probably hasn't been updated. Don't go upstairs – they film upstairs from every angle. Don't go near the exit doors. Pull your collar up over your face. They say the distance between the pupils and the length of your nose are what identifies you. Keep your eyes down then. Stay near the driver.

Yep, that's best, but walk until you're nearly dry. Somebody will notice you're soaked and smelling like an old rag. Stay unnoticed. Stay invisible.

I start walking. My clothes stick against me, chafe my legs. I pull at them, try to get air between damp, clinging cloth and damp, shivery skin. I swing my arms. I stop swinging my arms: don't draw attention to yourself. This is taking too long. I should have said half past midnight.

Don't appear different. Check for CCTV. Stay on unwatched streets.

There're no crowds of people on the streets now, nobody to blend in with, just a few pedestrians hurrying by. What if the street's watched, though? Stick near the wall then. Cross into the shady bit where the lamplight hardly reaches. Walk fast, it'll keep you warmer. Plus at this rate you're gonna be late. I take the hoody off and tie it loosely around my waist, hoping it will dry quicker. I give in and look behind me.

Nothing.

The street is long and dark, except for the pools of street light spread metres apart. On either side there's nothing. Nothing except high walls of what could be warehouses. No windows. I strain my eyes, peer through the gloom. No Cobain. He really isn't following me this time. It's a good job I don't care. I don't care about green eyes or warm hands. It's a good job I don't need him to take care of me.

I get into Deptford. I'm a bit drier, but still shivering. I hang around at a bus stop, hiding my face, hugging myself and trying to unfreeze my fingers. At last a bus comes. Running late too. I get on. I don't have an Oyster card. I really hope Lacey'll wait for me. I just give the driver a sad look and hurry past. He nods. I sit down behind a tall seat and hunch low. Nobody else gets on.

He's definitely not following me then.

I rest my head against the cold chrome of the seat in front. I watch as the city blurs by. The bus is going to Victoria. I can jog it from there.

Hyde Park.

And I'm definitely late. I must be. Though I've no phone to check. I leave the roads and pavements behind, and cut out into the park. I try to hurry. The grass is short and flattens silently beneath my tread. Kensington and Knightsbridge are in total darkness. Each tree spreads an inky shadow. My heart pounds, as I dart from one pool of shade to the next. I half expect someone to be lurking there, lying in wait, but I find nothing, not even an urban fox. A night bird calls, a car in the distance, that's all. My heart's still racing. I stay out of sight. I slink quietly forward.

A slight noise startles me. I pause, freeze in the shadows. Was that a rat, a squirrel?

Nothing moves, just a drawing in of shadows.

Not Cobain then?

How could it be? He couldn't have followed. I don't have a pattern, there's no thick of the crowd to track. But

I remember his words, too. *'I'm not anyone. Not anyone can do what I do.'* And suddenly a wild hope runs through me.

I worry about myself sometimes. I don't know why I'm so cold when it comes to boys. I think it's because of my father. When you see how bad a relationship can get, it puts you off. Why was I so unfriendly to Cobain? All he ever did was help me. There was no need, whatever he'd done.

Suddenly I don't care if he robbed a thousand banks. And it wasn't as if he'd made a pass at me, either. And he would have come along. I just know he would, even if I wasn't up for his deal or anything. And he didn't mean to knock my phone into the river. And I have a sneaky suspicion that I'm mad at him because he didn't make a pass. Which is totally insane.

I think of his smile. He was always so totally on my side. I remember what he said. *'Tia, get some sense, they must be tracking you somehow.'* He was just trying to—

Suddenly my fear rockets to a new level. *'They must be tracking you somehow.'*

And they still must be!

I slide forward, switched to super alert. I hear something again. A rustle of leaves? But there's no wind? *Someone creeping behind me?* I stop. *Maybe I shouldn't stop.*

Maybe I should run. And then I definitely hear it, the crack of a twig beneath the weight of something. Something much larger than a squirrel.

My heart races. It pounds against my ribs.

'*Cobain?*' I hiss out, as loudly as I dare.

There's no answer.

It must be him.

'If it's you, go away,' I whisper. See what I mean? Why did I just say that? I'm scared, and if it is him, I don't want him to go away. Amazing. Totally amazing. I must be insane.

But there's no reply, anyway. So I move off, sliding swiftly again from pools of darkness into dappled spaces and then jogging out across flat, open fields of grass. Sepia-brown grass, blowing under the night sky. No one follows. I breathe deeply. Must've been Cobain. I don't know how he does it. I bet it was. I totally hope it was. I wonder if he's given up. Probably not. I'm strangely glad he's there. I start to relax a little. Strangely glad and strangely upset.

Far away the lights of Knightsbridge flicker on and off. For a moment a silhouette of houses are etched against the sky. Then Hyde Park is plunged back into a jungle of shadows. With a sudden sense of alarm I think: *Hyde Park is so big, so full of other dangers. Ordinary dangers, but still as deadly. Maybe I should have listened to Cobain.*

I hesitate beneath a tree. Should I go back? But I've already come so far. And back to what? And Lacey will be waiting. You can do it, I tell myself. One foot in front of the other. Stick to the shadows. You're almost there.

And then I start to worry. Will Lacey have been able to make it, get everything I need? I must be very near. I'm sure this was the place. Maybe just a little further?

Gently, I whisper, 'Lacey?'

I hear the crack of a twig again. I can't see anything.

'*Lacey?*'

No one answers.

I look around. I'm at the right place. There's the Serpentine – an ominous stretch of dark water – and there's the bench we used to sit on. I squint through the moonlight. Somebody's sitting on the bench. But it looks too large to be Lacey.

'EVE?' it says. It's not Lacey. It's a man's voice. 'It's OK, don't panic,' it says. 'It's me, ADAM.'

22

'If You Were Waiting For a Sign, This is it.'
Anonymous

'ADAM?' I say.

He stands up. He's tall and youngish, maybe in his twenties. I can't make out his face, it's hidden in the shadows.

'But I don't understand?' I say.

'Lacey messaged me,' he says. 'Told me she'd made contact with you. So I collected the stuff. I'm here to make the drop.' He holds out a rucksack with a sleeping bag attached.

'Oh,' I say. I'm slightly thrown. I know Lacey: she'd have wanted to come, even if she had messaged ADAM, even if she'd felt a bit scared about coming alone. She'd still have come.

'You've got something to give me?' he says.

'Yes,' I say. 'The passwords to the StormCloud for all the Darknet7 stuff. I was too scared to message you it

193

online, in case – well, you know, but now I'm not even sure it's of much use . . .' My voice trails off. I'm suddenly not sure of anything.

'That was smart,' he says.

But I didn't ask Lacey to call ADAM. I told her to listen and do exactly as I said. And to tell no one.

'And you mentioned you'd figured something out?' he goes on.

He steps forward. Behind him is a bank of bushes. As he moves, something glints inside them.

'Yes,' I say. I'm so curious to meet him, to see what he's like after all this time. I step in closer too. He's young and good looking too. Very fit! The glinting in the bushes is distracting. It catches my eye again. It looks really familiar. I step sideways, angle my head, trying to work it out.

'So what is it you know?' he says.

Yes, *very* fit. Nice voice too – calm, kind of rich, like real butter.

I smile up at him. 'I think the government may have masterminded some of the riots,' I say.

'Yes?' His tone quickens, like he's suddenly interested.

But it's weird, I'm late and he waited for me? I thought the drill was: exact time, exact place, dead drop, move on, if you're there or not. His rules.

'How did you know they'd set us up on the bridge?' I say. 'But I'm so glad you did, that you never came,' I add hastily. 'They had someone there, a sniper or someone and a helicopter. They nearly flipping got me!'

'Do you have any evidence that the government have masterminded anything?' enquires ADAM.

I know what's glinting in the bushes. It's a bicycle reflector. I can see it quite clearly now, round and red.

'It's weird, isn't it,' I say. 'We've messaged each other so often, and we've never met! We've worked so hard on all this – so it's totally awesome to finally meet you!' I dimple my cheeks with my special, special smile. 'I just wish they'd backed down and we could meet properly in daylight, in triumph. You know: *hasta la victoria siempre* style.'

He's very, very gorgeous, taller than Cobain, more regular features. His eyes aren't as nice, though.

Nobody has eyes like Cobain.

'I need to know what evidence you have,' says ADAM, 'then I can get it on to the campaign website.'

I think about it. How clandestine it's all suddenly become, how campaigning for what you believe in ought not to be like this.

And there's a bicycle stuffed in the bushes. Why is

there a bicycle stuffed in the bushes?

'Have you let everyone on Darknet7 know? That's the most important thing,' I say.

'Have you told anyone else about your suspicions?' says ADAM.

And why hasn't ADAM once asked me about the bridge? Or asked me about anything?

And suddenly, as if by some supernatural instinct, I'm scared. All the hairs on my neck stiffen.

And then I see it: a shadowy form, slumped beside the bike. What I thought was a log isn't. It's a boot sticking out. A girl's boot.

I go cold all over.

'Someone I know might have evidence,' I say.

And I look at ADAM and I know with a certainty that chills right through me that it's Lacey lying there in the bushes and that's her bike.

'Who knows?' he says. He leans forward towards me.

I stop my jaw from dropping slack. *Lacey's lying in the bushes*. Cobain was right.

He was so totally right!

Don't look shocked. Don't give yourself away. All along, it was ADAM. What's he done to Lacey?

'If you just tell me who knows and exactly what evidence they have, I'll be able to tell everyone – explain why carrying on with the protests might be playing into a government plot.'

I know I should say something now, tell him passwords – give him a name, any name, any password, make something up. I've got to keep him talking. *Don't let him know I've seen her.*

'EVE?'

My voice shakes. I clear my throat. 'Um,' I start. *Why is he still talking? Why hasn't he killed me already? THINK. THINK. What can you say? 'Yes, someone knows, and they have evidence.' That's it, he's pumping me. He wants to know what I know before he kills me.*

LIE. That's what I must do. Can I run?

'Yes,' I manage again, 'I hacked into . . .'

I can't run. There's nowhere to run to, only the park, huge and empty.

'You hacked what?' he says.

LIE. What was it Cobain said? 'I'd like you to hack into the websites of the Department of Justice, and get hold of some prison files.'

'Prison files,' I say. And I'm staring at the bushes. *Lacey?*

'Yes?' he says encouragingly.

'I don't know,' I blurt out.

'What did you discover in the prison files?' he says.

His voice suddenly loses its friendly tone.

What did I discover?

'Who else knows?' he says.

If I run into the lake – into the dark Serpentine? I could try and swim. If I dive underwater and try to get to the far bank – could I get away? I've got to try. There's nothing else I can do.

He takes a step closer.

I've got to move. I remember Mum saying, *'One of the first rules of self-defence is never let anyone get near enough to grab you.'* I can't remember why she said that. I back up.

'I think you'd better tell me everything you know,' he suddenly snaps.

'Yes,' I say. 'I mean, no. I don't know anything—'

But I don't finish. As I try to step even further back, he leaps, crashes into me. He grabs me with gloved hands. My heart stops. His hand goes over my mouth. I kick. There's no time to think. I bite. My teeth clamp down on leather. I try to hit out. No time to be afraid. But my shoulder . . .

And I'm down. I'm falling. He knocks me flat on to the grass. My head hits the earth with a thud. I hear my skull crack. Pain draws a silver line around everything.

I fight. I bite. I kick. I gag. I try to scream. I rip at him.

I kick and kick and kick. I'm not even afraid. My heart's pumping. I don't care. I don't care. I'm not going to die like this.

'Tell me what you know and who else knows it,' he hisses.

He smells. I can smell his breath. He pins me down. He's heavy, muscly. He's too heavy.

'Tell,' he snarls.

I jerk my head, trying to nod, like I'm gonna tell.

His hand loosens. His grip slips. I wrench my head round. I scream louder than I've ever screamed. My voice tears out of my throat, high pitched, terrified.

One hand grabs my throat. He cuts the sound off with a violent squeeze. I'm choking. *My God, I'm choking.*

I can't breathe. I try to kick. But my legs don't work. I try to push him off. *My shoulder.* I can't push him off. My head spins. It's so dark. I can't breathe. I can't fight.

Suddenly someone else is there. He grabs ADAM and wrenches him sideways. The weight shifts. I feel the grip on my throat ease. I punch at ADAM with my good arm, straight in the face. It's not much of a punch. I rake my fingernails across his eyes.

It's Cobain.

Cobain's here.

He's trying to get him off me.

Cobain lets go of ADAM for a second. ADAM tries to straighten up. Cobain bends down, heaves something from the ground. *It's a fricking paving slab.*

I choke. *My neck. My throat.* Cobain raises the paving slab. For a second he's silhouetted against the night sky like a god. The muscles in his arms bulge. The paving slab hovers, is poised. ADAM seems to straighten up, to meet it. Then Cobain brings the slab down on his head.

I hear the crack of concrete on bone. I hear a grunt of air escape from lips, smell it, thick and warm and animal. I feel the weight of him slump back over me. I'm jolted back to the ground.

I lie there, flattened.

Cobain rolls him off me. 'You OK?' he says huskily.

I rise shakily to my feet.

'Is he dead?' I whisper.

Cobain mutters something like: 'I fricking hope so.'

I sit up. I try to swallow. I raise my hand to my throat. It hurts. It starts to rain. The leaves patter with raindrops. 'Thanks,' I croak out. 'Thanks.'

Cobain doesn't answer. He squats down, searches through the man's pockets.

I want to say: *Why?* and *How did you follow me this time?* and *I know you did*, and *Why are you always following me around like my guardian angel?* and *I'm so glad you did* and *He killed Lacey*.

And *Is Lacey really dead?* and *I must get up and help her*. And *Of course she's dead. And I would be too by now, if not for you.*

Cobain straightens and holds up something to the light.

'What is it?' I wheeze, looking up at him, framed by the trees, a light blowing of rain coating his cheek.

'I'm not trying to rob him, if that's what you think.'

I wasn't thinking that. I wasn't thinking anything. I was overcome with a strange gratefulness; and tears are welling up inside, and they're hurting my throat.

'And the question you should be asking is: *Who* is ADAM?' he says.

'Who is ADAM?' I say. I don't get it.

'ADAM,' says Cobain. 'C'mon.'

I can't think. I don't know what he means. The trees begin to sway. The rain starts in earnest.

'Guess,' says Cobain. 'Here's his ID. Aay, Dee, Aay, Em. A.D.A.M.'

'I don't understand,' I whisper.

'Anti-Democratic Activist Monitoring.'

And I lie there and I still don't get it.

'A.D.A.M. wasn't anyone,' he says.

201

And the weight of what he's saying comes crashing down on me like that paving slab.

'A.D.A.M. is a government agency.'

23

'Nothing is True. Everything is Permitted.'
Anonymous

Cobain takes my hand. I don't resist.

'I won't say I told you so, but I fricking told you so.'

I nod. Even nodding is painful. 'He was going to kill me,' I croak. And then, after a pause during which rain pours down through the leaves, 'He killed Lacey. I think that's Lacey.' I raise a trembling hand and point at the bushes.

Cobain hurries and looks. I crawl after him. *Oh please God don't let it be Lacey.* My heart cuts as I register the slowness with which he straightens up from the body. I can't take it in. I crawl on.

Cobain tries to stop me. 'Don't,' he says.

But I must.

'*Lacey?*' I whisper as I reach the fallen shape. '*Lacey?*' I tug at her, hold her cold hand. See her little charm bracelet. See the golden charm I gave her. *For Ever*

Friends engraved on it.

See her swollen, blackened face.

Cobain squats beside me. 'C'mon,' he says, 'we need to get out of here.'

'But Lacey?'

He shakes his head. 'Nothing we can do.'

Nothing we can do? I can't speak. I can't feel anything. I can't seem to move.

Cobain helps me up.

'I don't understand,' I say. *Lacey dead? If I hadn't called her . . . ?* I can't move away. I can't leave her. And deep inside me, I'm trembling and trembling.

'Yeah, you do,' says Cobain. 'He killed Lacey and he was going to kill you. That was the deal. *"Bodies of two young girls found, robbed and strangled, in the middle of Hyde Park. Time of death approximately midnight. Search for their killer underway. Rioters suspected."* Big deal. Who cares? What the hell were they doing in the park anyway? You *do* know.' His voice is cold.

I twist my hands together. I try to call out, to whisper, '*Lacey.*' I feel my throat. It's so dry.

'With all the news focused on the riots, all the police time taken up, all the arrests they need to make, a double murder in the park will make the news for precisely twenty-four hours. And then it won't even be news. It's not even original.'

I stay quiet. I understand. He's right.

'Except he didn't know you're Tony Thomson's daughter.'

I take that in too. I'm not EVE any more, anyway. EVE is dead.

'And I told you so.'

All around me the night swirls. And he did. He did tell me so. But how was I to know? The rain is a steady drip through the foliage above.

'And it was my fault,' I say.

He puts an arm around me. 'No, you didn't kill Lacey. He did.'

'But if I'd never called her?'

'But you did, and that's all,' he says. 'Tia, this is the real world. It's time to grow up. ADAM is a government agency like MI6. They're just doing their job. Protecting the state, making sure the rich stay rich and the poor stay poor.'

I stand there. There never was an ADAM. I can't seem to get hold of that either. No ADAM. Vaguely I wonder if he's dead? What if Cobain's killed him? My mind flashes back to all those late nights, messaging out to ADAM. It did happen. We did organise rallies. There was someone. We did. There was a Darknet7. Lacey was all for it. She knew everything as well.

'Do you think they wanted Lacey dead too?' I say. 'Or was she just a way to get at me?'

'How much did she know about the way the campaign was set up?' asks Cobain.

'Everything,' I whisper.

'Then it's not your fault,' says Cobain. 'They intended to kill her anyway.'

'Poor Lacey,' I whisper.

'You both got too big. You were supposed to stop when they banned demonstrations. You both knew too much, and you were set up,' Cobain says.

I know he's right, but I still don't understand any of it. Why was I set up? And how? I really *don't* understand.

'It was a government operation,' repeats Cobain. 'Monitor the Anti-Snip Campaign. If it gets too big, discredit it. If that doesn't work, legislate against it. As a last resort, make sure it can't function again. Remove all key figures. And now they're rolling it up. They probably had a trace on Lacey's number too.' His voice breaks. 'I'm sorry, Ti,' he says, 'but all this was part of the plan.'

Nobody has ever called me Ti before. I like it. But I'm too confused to like anything.

The rain pours down. A radio crackles from the bushes.

'C'mon,' says Cobain. 'He's got some kind of walkie-talkie. Let's get going. The rest of them will be all over this place soon.'

'Oh,' I whisper, suddenly terrified.

'Move now,' orders Cobain.

I'm on my feet and moving. What a fool. Why didn't I ever question how 'helpful' ADAM was being? How he was always there, always wanted to be consulted? Knew everything, had all the answers?

If they catch us here now . . . I squeeze my eyes shut.

We're expendable.

I was expendable.

Just like that.

Did my father know? My father's in charge of this sort of thing. I know he boasts about it. Am I just a pawn in his repulsive game? My knees tremble. My father's game. Did he set A.D.A.M. up? I can hardly believe it. Just an acronym for some government surveillance office. He was in charge all along, wasn't he? Did he know EVE was his own daughter? No. I can't believe that. A.D.A.M. didn't know. So he couldn't have.

Could he?

Suddenly I don't know what to believe. Maybe he could have. Maybe I'm nothing to him. Like Mum, just another step in his climb to the top.

And he killed Lacey and was going to kill me. He knew who Lacey was. My mouth's dry. I can't think any more. Everything I thought was wrong.

'You OK?' Cobain lays a hand on my shoulder.

I nod. It hurts. I'm not OK. I feel like I've just been run over by a truck, like all the air inside me is squeezed out.

I try to answer. 'I don't know who to trust any more,' I whisper. Suddenly that's the problem. I don't know who to trust.

'Don't trust anyone,' says Cobain. 'Not even me.'

I let out a sound. It's not a noise I know or I've ever made before. It's not a cry or a whimper. It's just the sound of something crashing. And I'm walking and half jogging. And I don't know where I'm going.

Behind me I hear footsteps. I hear them, but they don't register.

'Hey,' calls Cobain. 'No need to run from me, though.'

I hear, and I don't hear.

'Ti!'

Don't trust anyone. Not even me.

Trust nothing. Trust nobody. Not even yourself.

And then suddenly Cobain is swinging me round and crushing his lips against mine and holding me tight. And he smells warm. And he's pressing his body against mine and his lips are moving; my lips are moving. My throat is hurting and my chest is burning. And I don't know what to trust. But deep inside me a strange fire is heating my chest and making blood pound in my legs. And I can't even trust that.

And my throat is hurting.

And my lips are burning.

And I'm kissing him back.

And after the kissing and the hurting and the burning stops, Cobain takes my hand and leads me forward, away from Hyde Park. And he kisses me again. And we carry on walking. And after that kiss, he kisses me again. And we're still walking. He keeps on kissing me. And I don't try to work it out. And together we walk and kiss.

And after everything stops, even the kisses, he holds me. There, by the very edge of the park, under the dark trees with the rain pattering over us. And I tremble in his arms.

And all he says is, 'You know what I want. Are you ready to help me yet?'

24

'Nothing to Lose Means a Whole World to Gain.'
Anonymous

I'm ready.

I'm going to team up with him.

I untrust him.

It's a new kind of trust. I trust him to be a yob, to think like one. I trust him to at least do that, like trusting a snake to bite or something. Or a star to shine.

And I untrust him with my life.

He's done a good job of saving it so far.

He laughs and stokes my cheek. 'The things you have to do to get a girl these days,' he says and laughs again.

'You wanted to get me?' I say.

'Yep,' he says, 'kind of. And I never give up till I get what I want.'

'Kind of?'

'You grew on me.'

I hesitate.

'I wanted you to help me,' he says. 'I'm pretty lost,' he adds as an afterthought, by way of an excuse.

'So that's why you wanted me?'

'Nope,' he says.

'Then why?' I want to hear it from his lips. I stare at them through the gloom.

He cups my face in his hand. He stares through the night into my eyes, and I can't really see his. They're not cat-green any more. They don't gleam.

'Ti, I said "don't trust even me" for a reason. But if it makes it any easier, I like you.' His voice breaks and he stops, looks up, shakes his head, seems to be fighting something.

'It's OK,' I say. 'I understand.'

I don't. But somehow here, with the park behind us, with Lacey dead, and everything I thought I knew shattered, understanding things isn't so important any more.

'Liking each other isn't enough nowadays,' he says, smiling.

And in that smile I do understand.

'It's dangerous.' The smile drops out of his voice. 'It might get us thinking we could escape and be OK.'

'We could,' I say, my voice cracking. I try to clear my throat. I can't even swallow. 'We could go away,' I croak.

211

'Go *where*?' He laughs. He runs a hand over my head, strokes my hair.

'Go anywhere. Go see my mum. Stay with her in Ahmedabad.'

'No, we can't go to your mum's,' he says. 'What would we do? How would we live? Eat her food? Crowd out her home? For how long? Get jobs – in a country where everybody needs one? Send postcards to our friends wishing them Happy Snip Day? I don't think so. We'd end up hating each other, hating ourselves. We can't escape.'

I close my eyes. There's no escape. No future. It's what I've always dreaded. But I won't believe it. There has to be a future. Even if it's only tonight.

'But we *could* go and see your dad,' says Cobain suddenly. A mischievous tone echoes in his throat. 'And fuck him up.'

My father? Suddenly it makes sense. *Grow strong, not up*. Yes. We could go and see my father. *And Fuck. Him. Up.*

And as if in answer, the lights over Knightsbridge come on. I see them stretching down towards Victoria, down towards Westminster. I smile. My heart suddenly lightens.

He won't get away with it.

'Just tell me how,' I say. 'And when.'

Cobain laughs. 'To bring down the system all you need to do is topple its pillars. Let's try – even if that's all we can ever do.'

'No,' I say, 'there's more to this, isn't there? When you first asked me to team up with you, you wanted me to hack into prison files?'

I remember how the friendly tone died in ADAM's voice when I mentioned prison files. 'There's something about prison files, isn't there?'

Cobain nods.

'What?' I say. 'Tell me.'

Cobain drops his hand from my face. 'I've been in prison, Tia,' he says. 'Inside, there's ways of surviving. If you haven't got anyone outside to send you money, you can get a job inside. Most of the jobs are pretty lousy. Or you can join up to certain education programmes – do in-cell courses and stuff.'

I wait as he pauses. I know more is coming.

'They had a programme inside called Citizen Awareness. If you signed up for it you got privileges – more association time, a few luxury items and extra TV channels, sport for example.'

'Yes?' I say.

'Citizen Awareness met every day and did stuff like

213

group work – learning about things like human rights, and how we weren't getting everything we deserved as citizens, how we should get angry about it. I thought it was weird at the time – like why would this government want to educate a load of prisoners about their rights, make them feel hard done by? But you don't really think about that when you're getting special treatment. The meetings were always really packed – inside, everybody needs extra privileges even if they've got folks on the outside helping them. The meetings got pretty rowdy, a lot of shouting and rhetoric, but that's inmates for you – they get worked up pretty easy. I got worked up. There's a lot to be angry about when you're in jail.'

I still wait.

'Outside the bank, in that crowd, I saw faces I knew. One face in particular.'

'Who?' I say.

'It was one of the screws. One of the guys who ran the Citizen Awareness. I did a lot of work for him. He got us pretty worked up about our rights and everything. So it was weird. Why was he there? Shouting out stuff in a mob? I mean, prisoners can get angry. Hell, I get pretty angry, but why would a screw get angry? The system works for them. Why would they want to bring it down? So I want to check the prison files. I want to find out how many Citizen Awareness groups were being run inside the prisons. I want to know if they're still running them. I want to know if they were grooming us for this.'

'Grooming?'

'Yep, if they set up all those Citizen Awareness programmes with the intention of stirring us all up, making us angry. Filling us up with stuff. And then letting us loose on the streets.'

I think about that. I think about how easy it would be. Radicalising prisoners. I think of the crowd on Saturday, how it only took a few to pull on a hoody, whip a bandana over a face. How, suddenly, as if by some signal, there were a load of hooded faces. How when you set a light to dry tinder it flares up.

How all you have to do to light a fire is dry out the wood.

'I thought I was fighting for a cause,' he says. 'I thought we all were, but now I'm certain we were used. And I want to find out why.'

'What did you do?' I ask. Suddenly I must know. 'Why did you go to prison?' I don't care any more if he's a yob or a hooligan or a bank robber. I just need to know.

'It's a long story,' he says, his eyes cast down.

'I really want to know,' I whisper.

'I didn't rob a bank.' He laughs.

215

I wait. The park behind us waits. The rain starts again.

'My people were travellers,' he says. 'That means you're off to a bad start. Your name's already in the system.'

'But surely . . .' I start.

He kisses me lightly on the forehead. 'Still so innocent.'

'OK,' I say. 'The system sucks and we're going to bring it down.'

He smiles. 'By definition travellers are liars and thieves and kidnap children,' he teases.

'But what did you do?'

'Had a lot of previous: resisting arrest, illegal squatting, unlawfully obstructing police and . . . shall I go on?'

I nod.

'All before I was eleven.'

'And after?'

'Ever seen the EAT THE RICH stuff?'

Who hasn't! Those amazing graffiti pictures with everyone who's anyone being eaten by the people. All the outrage! And so audacious! I remember every one of them. I loved *The Last Supper*, and totally adored the one of the Prime Minister being barbecued over a burning London skyline.

He waits while the penny drops.

'*You?*'

He flicks his eyebrows up,

'You drew those pictures?'

'I got six months.'

'Oh My God!'

'One day, when there's time, I'll tell you.'

'OMG!' I squeak again (relieved he hadn't robbed a bank! Totally glad he didn't need any plea bargaining! And completely Flipping Freaked Out in a Majorly Awesome Way that *he* drew those pictures!).

'I really will tell you,' he says. 'It wasn't for graffiti, though: I got the six months for something totally different.'

Cobain Reilly the graffiti artist!

'Can you wait, so I can tell you properly?'

I nod. I can wait. I need to wait! I can hardly get my head around it!

Plus I have an idea. 'Look.' I point in the direction of the lights. 'There's going to be an emergency session in parliament. They always light up these areas when they want their support. Tomorrow is the last hearing for the bill. My father'll be there. Let's go now, to his apartment, while he's out.'

Cobain hugs me.

And why not? What loyalty do I owe him any more? After all the hurt he's caused, the way he destroyed Mum;

would have killed me; has killed Lacey?

I don't owe him anything.

'He'll be in parliament,' I say. 'The place'll be empty. Let's go and dig out some prison files, clear your name and find out how to topple the system.'

'Now you're talking,' says Cobain and pulls my head back up towards him.

25

'Break and Enter a New World.'
Anonymous

My father's apartment is dark. No light shines out from the tenth-floor windows. I'm not surprised. He likes to control everything, even light switches. He goes round the apartment switching everything off, even the standby on the TV. '*Conserve and preserve,*' he says, as if everything is jam. But it's not really about that. He doesn't care about rolling blackouts. It's not even the fact that he has designs on the Ministry for Energy, after he has destroyed the Ministry of Youth and Opportunity. He just likes to control things. He likes to turn things off, shut things down, shut things up.

Like me and Mum.

I hesitate for a minute outside the glass door to the foyer.

'The porter'll be there,' I say.

Cobain shrugs.

'He'll recognise me.'

'Diversion then,' says Cobain. 'I'll divert him, then you slip in.'

I can't see how that's going to work.

'When you're in, I'll follow.'

'But how will you get past the porter?' I say.

He smiles sadly, as if I'm a five-year-old. 'I will,' he says. 'Don't worry.'

'OK,' I say. I'm learning fast. Seems like there's always another way of doing things, when you're around Cobain – ways I have no clue about.

'Just stay out of sight.'

I move off, go round the next corner and wait, wondering what Cobain is going to do.

Then suddenly I hear him banging frantically on the glass door of the foyer. At first nothing happens. But he doesn't give up.

On and on he hammers. *Bang. Bang. Bang.* I grit my teeth. It's somehow terrifying, somehow embarrassing. I chew my lip.

After four or five minutes the porter eventually opens the door. I don't stick my head round the corner to see it but I can just imagine the look on his face. 'Clear off,' he says, 'before I call security.' The same look is in his voice. My heart starts to pound.

'Please call security,' gasps Cobain.

I'm all attention. I wasn't expecting that. I don't know what I was expecting. Him to rush past? Crack a paving slab over the porter's head?

If I didn't know any better, I'd believe he'd just run a marathon. He's puffing and wheezing so hard, I can hear it from here. I get a terrible urge to stick my head out around the corner to see what's going on. Do I dare? Is he staggering? Doubling up? I can't resist. I duck my head round, just a little. I catch sight of Cobain sinking down on the pavement, as if he's going to pass out.

A man steps out from the doorway. It's the old porter, the one with a large muscular neck and a small chin. He obviously hasn't got a clue what to do. I smile. This scenario wasn't in my father's drill book.

Tentatively, he stoops over Cobain.

'I'm OK,' wheezes Cobain. 'But some kids need help – just down the street. Some yobs set on us, we got beat up. Can you help?'

The man steps out a little further from the door and pulls out his walkie-talkie.

'Are you sure, pal?' The porter looks doubtful.

Cobain nods. 'Go on, please,' he says. 'As soon as I catch my breath, I'll follow you. Can you call up a few more guys? Have you been first-aid trained?'

The man nods. 'Have the yobs gone now?'

'I think so,' says Cobain. 'Please hurry.' His voice has a tone of command so seriously similar to my father's, I flinch a little.

The man hears the change in his tone too. He nods, but he's still unsure. He speaks into his walkie-talkie anyway.

'Yes,' says Cobain. 'Please call the police, and an ambulance – and again, please hurry.'

'OK,' says the man, pulling out a mobile now and stabbing numbers into it. 'You OK?'

'They need you more.' Cobain points down the street, looking like he's fit to bust.

I can see the porter's worried. He shuts the entrance door. I hold my breath. The locks click to. Will it work? He hurries off, down the street.

I can't believe it.

I step out. By the time I reach Cobain, he's already on his feet, leaning against the door frame.

'Quick,' he says. 'Key in the door code. Creep through the foyer. Stay low. Standard CCTV setting won't catch anything below one metre. And hurry. We haven't got long.'

On the tenth floor the lift creaks to a stop. The door opens.

'Watch the CCTV,' says Cobain. '*Always watch the CCTV*. When it swings away – *go*.'

I watch the CCTV. I'm learning.

'I'll follow on the next swing.'

We take it one at a time. The camera swings slightly to the right to cover the landing. I'm out and into my father's apartment, while the camera angles itself back at the fire exit, next to the stairwell. I leave the front door slightly ajar for Cobain, and then I draw all the curtains before I put the side lights on.

Then I hit the fridge. I grab the fruit juice and swig it down straight from the carton. I break off a lump of cheese.

'Nice place,' says Cobain. I whirl round. I'm not sure how he does that, just appears so silently. I look around Dad's sleek, masculine apartment and compare it with Pat's house. Yes, it's a nice place.

'Cheese?' I hold out the rest of the lump.

He takes it.

Then he waits and looks at me. I nod. I know what he means; this is my place so I get to decide what happens next.

'OK,' I say, 'I'm going to hack into my father's computer.' Although hack isn't the right word really. I know all his passwords, I've known them ever since

I figured out how to survive him. Know his comings, know his goings. Know where he keeps his money. Know how to access it. Know how to cover my tracks. I know all his passwords.

'You can do what you like. There's food,' I say.

'I'll take a wash, if it's OK with you?' he says. 'Need to get all that park business off me.'

I notice the dark blood-splatter crusted across his top, sprayed across his face, and I nod.

Yes, wash off ADAM and all his DNA. I'd like to do that as well: shower, shampoo, face scrub, nail scrub. Scrub him off. I don't look in the mirror. I don't want to see the bruises.

'OK,' I say. 'We've got fifteen minutes, maybe more?'

'We won't make it more,' says Cobain.

'Bathroom's that way,' I say, 'and . . .'

'Don't worry, I'll cover my tracks. No one'll know I was ever there,' says Cobain.

I smile. I untrust him to do that. I'd like to give him the best towels, cologne and scented bath oils. But I know that'd betray us, so I just nod instead. Nodding hurts. 'I'm just going to scan through his stuff and pick up anything pillar-toppling.' I grin. It gives me a nice feeling.

I swig the juice again. I top up the carton with a bit of water. I completely remove the rest of the cheese and shove it in my pocket. Better to let my father think the supermarket delivery forgot it, or question his own memory, than find a half-eaten wedge covered with my DNA.

Know his comings, know his goings, know how to cover your tracks.

I head straight for his study, sink down on to his desk chair. It smells of him. A cloying, soapy, new smell. I raise my hand to my mouth and pinch my nose but the smell remains.

Getting into his laptop is easy. So is accessing his files. The hardest bit is knowing what I'm looking for.

I try files labelled *Five-Year Planning Around Energy Consumption* but they're full of calculations and statistics and reports.

I try a file search with *Stop Children in Need*, and I get up so many hits I don't know where to start. But it interests me, so I begin trawling through. When the state starts toppling, the first pillar to go has to be the whole Children in Need thing.

I copy files to my account in the StormCloud, but one comes up with a twenty-minute copy schedule, so I click escape. And I'm floundering about, running my cursor up and down the long lines of files, running out of time.

I notice one called *Mass Impression Management*. It's a

weird title. I'm curious. I glance at the clock: ten minutes left. I decide to open all files with names that hit a nerve. Perhaps I'll strike lucky.

I open up *Mass Impression Management*.

And there it is.

Bingo!

I've struck lucky.

Exactly what I've been looking for.

Struck *unlucky* more like it.

Exactly what I've been dreading.

26

'Find Out What You Want. Destroy Everything in Your Way.'
Anonymous

The title of the first file is:

OVERPOPULATION AMONGST THE LOWER
DEMOGRAPHIC IS A THREAT TO NATIONAL
SECURITY AT-A-GLANCE BREAKDOWN OF
KEY FIGURES

I run my eye over the 'key figures'.

The figures are boring and I skim through them,
noticing how my father is building a case against the
working classes and using jargon to sanitise his intent,
calling them 'demographic' as if they are not real people.

Population growth

Overall	+33%
Amongst the middle demographic	−2%
Amongst the unemployed	+32%

Taxation

Middle & Upper demographic	76%
Lower demographic	24%

State-paid-for consumption
Health

Middle & Upper demographic	14%
Lower demographic	86%

Schooling & associated child services
Dental/transport/free school meals

Middle & Upper demographic	44%
Lower demographic	56%

Prison places

Middle & Upper demographic	28%
Lower demographic	72%

Unemployment benefit

Middle & Upper demographic	17%
Lower demographic	83%

Social Services including over-80s' provision

Middle & Upper demographic	13%
Lower demographic	87%

Housing provision & benefits

Middle & Upper demographic	31%
Lower demographic	69%

Anti-social behaviour & policing

Middle & Upper demographic	27%
Lower demographic	73%

I shake my head. So typical. The concluding bullets say it all:

CONCLUSION:
- This state of affairs must stop.
- Poverty is real, but need not be.
- It is our job to secure the future of the country.
- We must conserve wealth amongst the middle and upper demographic.

SUGGESTED TARGET MEASURES:

1. Lowering population figures amongst the least productive demographic of society by 32%.
2. Growth in the unemployed categories of person must be reduced to (zero) 0%.

My hand trembles above the touch pad.

Initial emergency measures must be considered to reverse this trend.

ALTHOUGH POPULATION GROWTH REMAINS STABLE, OVERPOPULATION AMONGST THE LOWER DEMOGRAPHIC IS A THREAT TO NATIONAL SECURITY. Their numbers must be contained.

This is it. This is his campaign. This is the pillar I need to topple. Quickly, I read on:

AT-A-GLANCE OVERVIEW OF DEFENCE STRATEGY
Strategic Campaign: No More Children in Need

And here is the summary, condensed in a nutshell.

Objectives:
- The sympathies of the middle demographic must be established.
- The message that poverty is real but unnecessary to be disseminated.
- Convince the nation overpopulation is the problem.
- Demonise the unemployed.

Delivery Options
- Televised speeches as part of a nationwide TV campaign.
- *Images focusing on damage done to innocent children*:
- *Suitable images*:
- Picture of starving babies
- Young, abused, house-bound mothers
- Violent fathers
- Extreme emaciation
- Disturbing physical abuse
- Foetal alcohol syndrome with simulated in-uterus abuse
- Haggard, prematurely aged parents
- No-fun lifestyle (compare happy holidays snaps/lively birthday-party images of childless couples) etc.

Slogans for distribution
- Would you want to put your children through this?
- Don't you think it's time we ended child abuse?
- Enough is enough.
- We must fight this together – one civilised nation, one solution.
- Voluntary Sector statistics published widely.

Positive Media Campaigns
- 'Hi, I've chosen not to have children.'
- 'Parenthood is a decision I've chosen not to make.'
- 'Stay young. Don't be a mum.'
- 'I'm so glad I'm not a dad.'

Negative Media Campaigns
- Overcrowding kills.
- Who wants to breed like rabbits?
- Are your kids the problem? Are you to blame?

Incentives Rationale
- We have a responsibility to our planet not to destroy it.
- Overpopulation is the biggest threat we face today.
- Should we let the un-conscienced few determine the future of the world?
- The un-conscienced few – those who will never make the right choices – those who don't care about society – the planet – those who will never care about their children either. *They do not deserve the right to be a parent*.
- Payoffs/extra benefits for childless couples.
- Free university fees for sterilisation.

The No More Children in Need Programme

- Start in prisons within six months: All convicted prisoners will be sterilised.

- Public debate on this at formal, government-controlled consultation conferences. Feedback taken via comment sections on government websites.

- Big posters with single slogans, single images.
- NO MORE CHILDREN IN NEED. Image of emaciated, bruised, staring-eyed children with hands held up pleading.
- Launch full-scale Snip programme within the five-year framework.
- Snip suitability reassessment schedule at four-year periods.

Still in shock, I register a link at the bottom of the document. My mouth suddenly dry, I click on it.

Propaganda Calendar for Garden of Eden

Phase 1
- Power outages (point – we can no longer afford to power our country)
- Establish on-going recession

Phase 2
- Squeeze the lower demographic
- Target them with curfews
- Additional 'poverty taxes'
- Freeze salary increments for lower-paid workers
- Introduce austerity measures

Phase 3
- Fund project *Garden of Eden* through A.D.A.M.
- Monitor public unrest
- Monitor underground social media networks
- Provoke or create rioting to discredit 'anti' campaigns
- Radicalise inmates in prisons to discredit any bona fide protesters
- Start race riots to divide cohesion of 'anti' groups
- Increase policing budgets (make the middle demographic pay for it)

- Harass them with stop-and-search campaigns
- Increase parking and road offences
- Up insurances to 'cover' unemployed liability
- Create food shortages
- Introduce rolling blackouts
- Create fuel shortages
- Extend pensionable ages
- Develop special anti-riot teams using army specialists
- Announce a state of emergency/ curfews/outlaw public gatherings
- Permanently remove key agitators and campaigners – use shoot-on-sight powers
- Use necessary force
- Arrest and convict all illegal protesters
- Roll up *Garden of Eden*

Phase 4 (Long-term Goal)
- **Enforced sterilisation of all unemployed demographic.**
- **Eradication of 'undesirable groups' in society.**

231

The cursor is shaking. My hand is trembling on the touch pad. I found it. I don't know what to think.

So blatant. I can't quite believe it. I glance up at the clock. I save the whole file quickly to the StormCloud. Time's running out.

We must conserve wealth amongst the middle and upper demographic.

It's just like its file title – *Mass Impression Management*. All a way of manipulating impressions. All those kids – all of them, set to be snipped.

The end of a class.

I can't believe it. It's a kind of genocide.

- *Create food shortages.*
- *Introduce rolling blackouts.*
- *Create rioting.*

'Although population figures remain stable . . .'

There is no overpopulation. It's all lies.

'*Enforced sterilisation of all unemployed demographic.*'

I sink back down on to the desk chair, my legs weak.

'*Permanently remove key agitators and campaigners – use shoot-on-sight powers.*'

This is much worse than I imagined.

'*Monitor underground social media networks.*' That's me. I was 'monitored' – Darknet7 was monitored right from the start!

'Long-term Goal: Eradication of "undesirable groups" in society.'

I push my knuckles into my eye sockets. I rub hard. I hear Cobain in the hall, closing a door. I hear the door behind me open. I drop my hands to my lap.

'My God,' I say, 'you've got to look at this.'

I can't add anything else. I just can't believe it.

There's a soft snake hiss, as if someone is letting out their breath in a long, taut sigh. The silence suddenly becomes heavy. There's a cloying, soapy smell. I half raise myself up, point at the stuff I've found. 'Cobain,' I say, 'we've got another Iraq on our hands. There were no weapons of mass destruction. There is no overpopulation. They'll *never* believe what I've found.'

'No, they won't,' says a voice.

But it's not Cobain's.

I whirl round in my chair, a cold shock travelling down my spine.

'No. They won't even get a chance to consider it,' says my father, and his voice is soft and reassuring and completely deadly.

27

'Change You Don't Have to Believe in.'
Anonymous

My father closes the door of the room. He crosses to the ox-blood-red leather Chesterfield. He gently hitches his suit trousers over the knees. He hates creasing them. He sits down. He leans back and crosses his legs elegantly.

'So, Tia, you have decided to come home.'

He's smiling. It's a bad sign. I look at him. I can't believe it. *I can't believe it.* I look wildly around – at the door. *Cobain?*

'And you've decided to take an interest in government issues,' he continues, so mildly that the blood in my veins freezes.

I try to clear my throat. My voice is stuck. I drag my sweater up to cover the bruising on my neck. My mouth is dry. I can't speak.

'Come, come,' he says affably. 'You're not a child any more; you shouldn't look so surprised.'

My eyes bulge.

'We all have to come to terms with the fact that the tooth fairy does not exist and Santa Claus is a construct to improve consumer spending.'

I remember that Christmas at Grandmama's when Mum was still with me. I was only four years old. I remember creeping down late – it was the middle of the night for me – I wanted to leave a cookie out for Santa, by Grandmama's huge fireplace.

I remember seeing my father, the way he crossed over to me, picked me up, his hands pinching my tiny shoulders.

I remember him saying, 'Go back to bed, Tia. You're not a baby any more. You need to face the fact that Father Christmas does not exist. I will have a word with your mother about it. Go back to bed. There are no reindeers. There are no elves. There is no reward for being good.

'Your mother should really have told you all this. I'll let her know how disappointed I am.'

Oh, I remember.

'How could you?' I say. It's all I can say. I gesture feebly at his computer. '*How could you do all that to everyone?*'

'Now, let's be very clear, darling. Do all *what* to whom?'

'How could you?' I repeat.

'Do you mean: how will our purpose be achieved? Or do you mean why?' he adds very pleasantly.

'You know what I mean,' I stutter.

'You're very dishevelled,' he comments, 'and you've got some nasty bruising.'

I try to drag my top still closer around my neck.

'And I believe you've been at a rally. Is that it? Were you too scared to come home because you got a little carried away on behalf of other people?'

I can't answer. I just stare at him, his slim, black-suited self, so composed, so utterly in charge. *Suddenly I realise he likes this*. He's enjoying it. He's not pleased to see me. He likes my distress. He likes having the advantage. *I must try not to show him how disturbed I am*.

'*You ordered the army to shoot a baby*,' I try to shriek. My voice comes out like a whine, and I gasp for breath.

'And, darling, what is all this about you being the new Jesus and attacking our banks? You know perfectly well if you need money you only have to ask.'

He knows about the attack on the bank. He's seen the video clip. His daughter, out on the streets with a crowd of thugs. I try to read whether he's angry, what he's thinking, but his face is as inscrutable as a mask.

'I wasn't anything to do with it,' I squeak. My voice is so high pitched it hardly comes out at all.

'Tia, Tia,' he warns with a sweet smile. 'You're getting hysterical. You're going to have a conniption. You know how I feel about conniptions. I had to put up with it from your mother; I'm not putting up with it from you.'

'*You killed a baby*,' I whisper.

'Do you *really* believe that?' he purrs, taking his phone from his pocket with that same sweet smile. '"Killed" is a frightfully strong word, my dear, for a very disagreeable business.' He turns his phone off. 'For everyone involved – I might add.'

'You did, you did.' I'm shrieking. I'm whining. I'm hyperventilating. 'You killed that girl, Daisy. You killed Lacey. I wasn't the one who set that mob on the policeman, it was you. You did! It was all under your orders!'

'Your hysterical reaction tells me you aren't thinking properly,' he continues mildly. 'When you calm down, I'll explain everything to you. I don't have to, but I can see you've got hold of the wrong end of the stick.'

I close up my mouth. Stay in control, I tell myself. Pull yourself together. You're not the same person he used to bully.

'You're such a silly girl,' he says. 'The government is

there to protect you. You really don't understand anything. We're big and strong and you're small and weak – it's only natural you should be frightened of us. But *we're not* the enemy. No one is trying to kill anyone. The real enemy is nature.'

Nature?

I look at him, confused.

'That's right. The real enemy is hunger and starvation and not enough to share out to everyone.'

'You mean, not enough to share out to anyone who . . .' I can't finish my sentence.

'There you are!' He throws his hands in the air. And he's still speaking in that bland, even tone, that same soft, never-changing pitch and that deadly smile shining from his eyes. 'You don't understand. Have a little faith, Tia, and study nature if you want to learn how the world works.'

I grit my teeth.

'Only the strong survive, my dear. Charles Darwin was quite right about that. Underneath all that pretty fur the grizzly is a vicious beast. And he'll rip your throat out if you forget it. But you like to cuddle up to teddy bears, don't you, dear? You forget that only the strong survive – and why shouldn't you? You've always been protected by the strong; you've never had to face

238

reality. Tia, Tia, believe me, you are such a child.'

He's started.

'Have a little faith in what I say.'

I sink my head.

'If you're not the predator you must by default be prey.'

Another of his lines.

'The poor, you see, are always with us – even Christ, I believe, commented upon that fact.'

He really has started. Anything I might have said, would have liked to say, is lost now.

'And our job at the moment is to make sure we are always with the poor.' He smirks a little at his own cleverness. 'Because if their numbers overrun us, who will provide for them – let alone provide for us? We've got to do something, you see – for their sakes. We can't have a world where everyone is out of work, now, can we? We can't have a world where nobody is clever enough to run society; you really *do* have to agree?' He speaks straight at me in the voice of one who knows the facts and asks the questions merely as a matter of routine.

And I watch as a little glob of spittle collects in the corner of his mouth.

'The poor consume far too much of our available

resources and produce far too little to justify it. More mouths to feed, more brains to educate, more bodies to treat, more faeces to dispose of. I know. I know. It's unsavoury, but it's not good enough, Tia, really. Somebody has to stay strong, stand up, be brave and say: *No*. Someone has to be firm and lead this country.'

He stands up at this and waves his long forefinger towards some distant point out of the window.

'And I know,' he continues, 'that it must all be dreadfully unpleasant for you – quite intolerable for someone your age, so preoccupied with having fun. I wouldn't have such a state of affairs happen to *anybody* – let alone you, my dear – but we live in a changing world and someone has to do the Devil's work.'

He smiles that calm smile and then suddenly spins round. He points his finger directly at me. His voice changes.

'And you really must let me do my job, Tia, and stop having panic attacks every time something disagreeable happens. You must stop this self-centred hysteria – and stop trying to out-think me. You never will, you know.'

He crosses over to the desk, closes the laptop.

'And definitely stop prying through top-secret affairs that you don't understand.' And with that he firmly pushes the top of the laptop to with a click.

And his hand descends over my wrist.

And if I'd thought of going, had any idea that I might leave the apartment – ever again . . .

It dies.

28

'I'd Rather Risk Prison Than Live it.'
Anonymous

I don't know if it's years of being overruled, or some inbuilt terror hard-wired into me, but at his touch I collapse. I can't oppose him. I'm too used to surrendering. My mind bends against it. *A scream a day keeps submission away.* I try to scream, warn Cobain, but no sound escapes. I don't want to submit, but like a lamb to slaughter, I'm led off, out through the study, down the hall, up the flight of stairs, to the spare guest room where I stay when he's in London. *Dear Father, who art the Devil, cursed be thy name.*

But as we pass the bathroom opposite my bedroom, I tremble. Where's Cobain? I hope to God he heard my father come in, has left, hidden himself – anything? But I hear the slight squeak of the shower door and all the blood drains to my knees. *I must warn him.* If my father finds him . . .

Fear forces me to speak.

'How come you're home so early?' I squeak. My voice is loud. Too loud? Not loud enough? *Please hear me, Cobain. Please understand. I couldn't help it. I didn't hear him come in. Don't turn on a tap. Don't give yourself away.*

'Why, my security guard called me the minute he saw you and your friend enter the building.'

I look up in alarm. I thought we'd got in OK.

Cobain. He knows Cobain's here too.

'He was concerned, of course. He knew how anxious I was to find you.'

Where's Cobain? Has he hurt him already? There's no sound coming from the bathroom now.

My father lets go of my wrist and opens the bedroom door beside us. 'You need to rest, Tia, and I need to make a press statement to let the nation know you've come home safely.'

I don't move. I'm not going to be locked up in my room like a naughty child.

'Now, young man, come out of the bathroom,' snaps my father.

For a nanosecond I freeze. I take it in. Cobain's alive. My father knows, is in total control. I listen for some indication that Cobain has heard, will comply, won't comply, understands, and I'm poised like a wave at full height before it crests and breaks.

243

And then my father pulls a gun from his pocket.

A gun?

I didn't know he had a gun! If I'd known he had a gun, I'd have looked for it, checked, done something.

'Cobain!' I shriek. 'He's got a gun.'

My father smiles. 'There's nothing unusual in owning a firearm, my dear,' he says. 'In the States they've been doing it for ages.'

There's silence from the bathroom.

'A few years ago, we got a very difficult amendment through the House,' he comments, almost to no one in particular. But I listen. My father doesn't speak to hear his own voice. He flicks the gun up and points it directly at the bathroom door. 'Do get dressed,' he calls, 'and do come out quietly with your hands up.'

I can't get over the fact he's got a gun. Is this what it's come to?

'But now, thankfully, in England and Wales,' he continues, as if he hasn't just threatened anyone, 'in the case of burglars, anyone can use "reasonable" force to protect themselves or others, or to prevent crime – especially against known felons. Householders are protected from prosecution as long as they act "honestly and instinctively", in the heat of the moment. "Fine judgements" over the level of force used are not expected;

the Crown Prosecution Service knows this. The law is there to defend hard-working, law-abiding, peaceful citizens.'

Fabulous. I knew listening to him would pay off. He's made his point very succinctly, with all his usual aplomb. Cobain must come out, with his hands raised, and do everything my father says, or he will be shot down in cold, legal blood.

How typical. Typical of his need to control. Typical of the way he twists everything to his advantage.

Typical of the man who devised the Snip Bill.

I look at the space between me and the gun. My eyes dart forward and back, measuring our chances. If I kick out, will I be able to knock it from his hand? If I leap forward, will he shoot me?

I don't believe he'll shoot me. So I lunge forward fast.

But my father's faster.

Without adjusting his grip on the gun for one second, he lashes out and pins me against the wall. 'Really, my dear,' he says mildly, 'you should be a lot more careful around guns.'

Effortlessly he propels me through my bedroom door. His grip hurts my shoulder, twists open my old wound. I try to speak, try not to double up in pain, try to splutter something out, but all I can manage is: 'No.'

My father pushes me further into the room. He doesn't lower the gun. 'Oh yes, I think you will,' he says.

'No,' I say again. 'You can shoot me. How about that? How will that fit in with your acting "honestly and instinctively" in the heat of the bloody moment?' And I fling myself back at him, back through the bedroom door.

'OK, I'm coming out,' shouts Cobain.

'I won't shoot *you*, my dear,' says my father, 'but you will go quietly into the bedroom and you will stay there like a good little girl. And I really don't appreciate you swearing at me.'

'Go on!' I say. 'Go on, act instinctively.'

'If you don't do exactly as I say, right now, I'll shoot your young man.'

Of course. Of course he will. Why did I ever imagine for a moment that I could outplay him?

'I hadn't intended to,' says my father very silkily, 'but if you don't do *exactly* as I say, you'll be forcing my hand.'

Point made. I step again through the open door to my bedroom, noticing that 'do exactly as I say' has become his new favourite catch phrase.

'That's a good girl,' says my father. 'Your young friend and I are going to have a little chat, and he's going to tell me everything that's happened, everything he knows.

Then, once I've had a chance to think and made a few arrangements, I'll decide what to do next.'

Of course he will.

My father closes the door on me and says, 'I'll brew you a nice soothing pot of Earl Grey tea soon, my dear, if everything goes to plan. Don't worry about your friend at all, I'll have him taken very good care of.' And he locks the door.

A chill runs down my spine. *'Have a little chat.'* Goosebumps shiver up my arms. *'Made a few arrangements.'* My skin crawls. *'I'll have him taken very good care of.'*

I hear my father step away. I jump to the door. I try the handle. I pull on it. I scream, 'Please, don't lock me in!' But he doesn't answer. I know him, he won't answer again, not until he's ready, not if I scream the whole flipping place down, even if it means silence for a week.

And I hear the bathroom door unlock and open.

I hear my father say, 'That's a clever boy. Hands up high. Don't speak even a word, or it will be the worse for you. Straight ahead, down the stairs, that's it.' And footsteps.

My heart is banging on my ribcage. This wasn't supposed to happen. What will my father do to Cobain? He'll disappear. *He'll just disappear.* I'll never know. *Nobody'll ever know.* I suddenly see Cobain's eyes, his smile. He'll vanish, like he'd never lived at all. All record of him. Gone.

I sit on the edge of the bed. I'm shaking so badly, I can't stop my legs from knocking together.

I fix my eyes on the door handle. Any minute my father can walk in again. No, he won't walk in again. He just wants me to sit here expecting him to, expecting that pot of tea, planning how I'll beg and plead. He won't walk in again. But I still start planning how I'll beg and plead anyway. *Was that the front door?* I'm sure it was. Has he left? Has he taken Cobain away?

Stop it, I tell myself. *Think*. Your father will not go out now. He's just playing you. Probably opening and closing the front door to mislead you. That's the kind of thing he likes to do. And there's no point in you planning any speeches, arguments, promises. Even if he does come back in – which he won't – they'll be of no use. He'll savour this now. He'll sit up all night working out a diabolical plan. He'll let his devils out. He'll enjoy it. This is what he loves: total control over someone. Cobain's still in the apartment. He won't call in any specialist unit until daybreak, until he's figured out how to break Cobain.

Use the time sensibly. Use the time to wash, to change, to prepare, to figure out how to get out. If you don't,

Cobain *will* disappear. And you can't let that happen. Figure it out, Tia.

I walk through into the en-suite. I wash my face. I'm too restless to stay there. I want to clean my teeth. I force myself to clean my teeth. I need to shower ADAM off me, but somehow taking off my clothes will make me too vulnerable. I cross back to the bed. I sit down again. I stare at the door handle.

I try to think.

If the door won't open, what will? If I can get into the rest of the apartment, where will he keep Cobain?

Come on, Tia. You're a boarder. You've done this before. Every boarder at every boarding school knows how to get out without being caught. Think.

I cross to the window. I look out over London. The sky is all moon-washed stripes. The streets everywhere are dark. There're no lights, not even in the Square Mile. I shake my head. I can't believe it. A handful of inner-circle officials can subject the nation to all this misery – scare us half to death, starve us, trick us.

Think. Think. Think.

I check outside my window. It's a good forty-metre drop. These split-level apartments go up more than twelve storeys. I know there's no escape from here. Or as good as. Our building doesn't have a fire escape on this side. The fire escape runs down by the lift shaft.

But there's always an escape. Isn't there? Doors? Windows? Chimneys? Dumb waiters? Cheap plasterboard? Loose hinges? Connecting doors?

Arise, ye wretched of the dormitories. You have nothing to lose but your chains.

Chains? Ropes? Rope ladders? Diversions? Drainpipes? Trees? Rooftops? Balconies?

Bedsheets.

Sometimes the olden ways are the golden ways. Bedsheets, knotted together with bath towels and anything that'll reach down to the kitchen window below me.

I'll do it. I'm not going to end up like Mum, broken. I'll find Cobain.

I brought him here. I told him we had time.

I'll save him. And we'll escape together.

Since all this started he's been finding me and saving me.

It's my turn now.

29

'A Limit is Only Something We Haven't Destroyed Yet.'
Anonymous

In the dead of night, I strip the bed. I tie the bottom sheet to the duvet cover. I get the bath sheet and tie that on too. I think the knots are good. I test them by looping the whole thing to the iron frame of the bed and yanking on them as hard as I can. The bed squeals across the floor.

I turn on the TV to drown the noise. Not that you can hear much through the solid walls and floors of this building. I know – I've been listening for the last two hours for that cry of pain, for any sign Cobain's still in the flat.

And he is. I know.

About half an hour ago I heard a thick noise. A series of thumps.

With the TV on, I drag the chest of drawers across the back of the door and jam it under the handle. I don't want that pot of tea being brought in just as I'm making it out of the window, do I?

The TV drones out.

'Since the shooting of Daisy Collins, known to most as Eve, mother of the future, thousands march across Britain towards Parliament Square, under the banner: We March for Eve . . .'

I check the handle can't move.

'Daisy Collins has become a symbolic martyr . . . Many more thousands have joined the campaign since her death. The protesters hope to arrive at parliament in time to oppose the no more children in need Bill, due for its final hearing tomorrow . . .'

'We're going to march all night if that's the only way,' says a spokesperson from the student union of Reading University. *'And we will not be stopped by unlawful bans on gatherings or spurious curfews introduced without proper legislation . . .'*

Gently I shunt the bed across the room. I jam it frame first up against the window. I unlatch the casement.

There, in the half light outside my window, dark against the night, is the skyline of London. Away to the east, it's strangely rosy. I stick my head out. Fire engines wail out, not so very far off. I can smell burning too. Six metres below me is the kitchen window. Below that is the next apartment in the block. Then a forty-metre drop.

The kitchen window's got two louvre blades at the top, which are always open. They'll be my way back in, once I'm out of this room. I wonder how I'll reach in through those narrow louvres with only one arm to unlatch the main casement, how I'll hold on to the rope with the other. How my shoulder will take it.

But I will.

Won't I?

Though once I've left this room, there'll be no way back if I don't. I'll be left dangling like a piece of washing over a precipice of thin air. Or I'll fall.

Oddly, with the window open, I can hear noises in the downstairs of the apartment better. Someone is talking. A door closes. There's a muffled shout. An ominous silence.

I have to.

A chill shivers through me. *If I don't, they'll kill him.*

But I could fall straight down on to the concrete below. I stick my head out again and look down. Dark street. Concrete pavement. I look at the sheets all tied together, ready to go. And suddenly I think, *I can't do it.*

But I can't sit here either, waiting for my father to do his worst. Remember Cheltenham, I tell myself. You walked a ridge pole and shinned down five floors on an old Victorian drainpipe. And that was just to go to a quarry party on Leckhampton Hill. You can do this.

And suddenly I know I *am* going to do it. And instantly, before I can reconsider, I measure out six metres of sheeting. I'll tie the rest around my waist. I'll have two free hands then. I can dangle. I get an even better idea. I'll use my spare school backpack.

I get it down from on top of the wardrobe, empty it out. Pens, text books, bits of paper fall to the floor. I rig up a rough harness. I need to test it. How can I test it?

I could test it on my teddy? At least it won't strangle him! But there's no point. I'm just wasting time. Grizzly bears will rip your throat out. Who needs grizzlies. If the harness fails, I'll fall thirty metres on to solid concrete.

Before I've got time to change my mind, before I think how stupid it is to even consider testing a life-saving harness on a teddy, I slip it on. I secure the sheet around the bed frame. It's gonna have to do. I check I can click free from the backpack, if I need to, and I push the window wide.

My heart hammers. My throat sticks. I'm hanging on to the sheeting so tight I daren't even brush my hair out of my eyes. And I haven't even got out of the window yet.

Beads of sweat break out on my forehead. Best to ease myself out backwards, like going down a ladder.

You can do this.

Don't look down.

254

I climb up on to the bed. The mattress bounces unsteadily beneath me. I test the sheet-rope again, yank at the knots. Will it bear my weight, or in one yielding shriek tear and drop me to the pavement? It feels good. You can do this, Tia. You can do this.

And I want to do it. That's all I can think. I want to. I won't let my father win. I will save Cobain. And I will leak that MIM file. I'll expose the whole thing. I'll stop the bill.

A shiver runs down my spine, and I suddenly feel very close to that girl and that baby, to Daisy and to Lacey. Their ghosts seem to draw near, their deaths seem to demand something from me.

'Here goes nothing, Lace,' I whisper. 'Save me a place on that old freedom train if I don't make it.'

So with a last pull at the knotted loop around the bedstead and a tightening of the knots around my waist I start.

I crouch on the windowsill and, holding on to the bed, lower my legs out. They dangle uselessly. Knots tighten in my stomach. Everything's knotted.

I just hope to God they hold.

30

'You Are Only Ever as Strong as Your Weakest Link.'
Anonymous

Now that I'm half hanging out of the window I wonder how I'm going to do this? If I'd dropped the rope down first I could've tried climbing down it, but now I've got it tied around my waist, I can't.

I wish I'd watched rock-climbing programmes, or circus acts or something, because I don't know what to do. My hands slip, slick with sweat. Beads of perspiration trickle down the side of my face.

Don't look down.

I play out what I can of the sheet. I grasp hold of the last bits, just where it's tied to the bed frame.

I lower myself out.

The wrench on my arms is instantaneous. I can't hold on. My bad shoulder's on fire. I wind my legs around the rope, which hangs down below me and then loops back up to my 'harness'. I dig one heel into the top of my other foot with the 'rope' in between, like we do in gymnastics. The pull on sinew and bone eases a little, but it's not a strong sisal rope like the ones we climb at school. It stretches and slips. And I slip with it.

And I slip completely out of the window.

And I haven't got the strength to pull myself back in.

What the hell have I done?

I swing a little to the right. *Save Cobain*. I sway back. *Stop the bill*. I let go with my bad arm, and ease it down the sheet a bit. I wish I'd tied knots in the sheets. It would've made it much easier. I loosen the hold with my good arm and let my bad shoulder take the weight. The pain's too much. I slip. I can't do it. My arm goes weak. I slide. A rush of air, damp pavement. Rain on concrete.

And I slide.

My knees scrape the brickwork. *I'm sliding*.

I try to hang on. The 'rope' slips again and I can't get any grip on it. For a moment I dangle. I twist. Then I *really* slide. I thrash my feet against the wall, trying to create enough friction to slow me down, and I cling to the slipping sheets for dear life. And then suddenly the sheet-rope is ripped from one hand.

The backpack harness brings me up short with a terrible jerk. My shoulder. *My bad shoulder*. I spin a full

257

circle, in the kind of agony I've never felt before.

And come to an abrupt stop.

Dead level with the kitchen window.

The fall knocks the air out of me. The backpack gives a little. The snap-strap around my waist digs in, and I can't seem to get my breath. I'm swallowing air. I'm hyperventilating. *My shoulder.* I look down.

A giddy, nauseous rush flushes through me. My mind swims. I'm going to black out.

And I'm scared. I'm so scared I can hardly move my fingers. My heart pounds. I'm going to fall. All my intestines seem to melt. The sheet will rip. The backpack will tear. I'm going to fall.

But I don't fall. I just sway and twist outside the kitchen window.

I can't hear anything any more, except a voice somewhere. Maybe the TV. Oh God, I hope Cobain's still in the flat. He must be. He will be. Right now my father'll be planning something more for him. Some new horror. My father will like doing that. Little by little he'll set about breaking him. He won't hurry. He'll savour every minute.

You've still got time, Tia.

I reach out for the window. My fingers lock on an open louvre. I scrabble with my feet. There's enough window frame to lend a toehold. I take the strain off the backpack. I cling to the window.

I'm going to have to reach in with my bad hand.

A light goes on in the hall beyond the kitchen window.

Someone's coming.

I freeze, clinging to the window. A shadow passes across the corridor from the sitting room to the study. *Please don't let him come into the kitchen.*

Without even registering the pain, I reach through the open louvre and release the catch on the window frame. Maybe I've still got time to get in. Hide. Stay out of sight?

The bloody thing opens outwards!

The light in the hall is still on. I can't do this. No time. My father could come at any minute. I'm going to have to manoeuvre to the side, stay out of sight.

Which side?

I toe-inch my way to the left side of the window and freeze.

Someone's coming into the hall. They're speaking on the telephone. It's my father. He's checking an HDPad. He's holding it in one hand and pressing a mobile against his ear with the other. He walks towards the kitchen.

My heart stops. All the blood in my chest forms into

one thick clot that rises up to my throat and sticks there. Something at my temple pounds. I feel dizzy. This is it. He'll find me.

Oh God, don't let him find me.

He's coming into the kitchen.

31

'Direct Action Gets the Goods. Particularly When it Involves Stealing.'
Anonymous

I turn to stone. I close my eyes. I can't face him. I can't bear it.

But there is no sudden shout, no rush to the window. No cry of anger. Very slowly, expecting the worst, I open my eyes.

My father is standing in the middle of the kitchen.

My father is standing in the middle of the kitchen.

A bolt of electricity shoots through me. I close my eyes again, then re-open them.

He's still there.

I stare at him. But he doesn't stare back.

The light from the night outside is so dim, I can't even tell whether he's facing me or not. His head is silhouetted by the blue glow from his HDPad and he's listening.

'No,' he says. 'No, Prime Minister, no direct action.'

I can hear him so clearly. I hold my breath. *I daren't even breathe.*

'I'll organise press coverage for tomorrow. Yes, she's here, and under lock and key.'

He doesn't know I'm out.

There's a pause. He seems to be nodding and typing something into the HDPad.

'I shall release a new photo of her and say she's been here since the afternoon. The bank job was a hoax. Yes.'

A crazy hope starts to fire up under my ribs.

He hasn't noticed me. I may still be able to outwit him. Get Cobain out of his power and . . .

He jams the phone against his ear with his shoulder. His hands are full. That's why he hasn't turned the light on. And he's talking to the Prime Minister.

I hold my breath.

'Let me assure you, I have everything under control, even that terrorist Reilly. I'm arranging for his extradition as we speak.'

Extradition?

'We'll find out what he knows, if he's linked to any bigger picture.' He nods. 'You can rest assured . . . not a whisper of extraordinary rendition . . .'

He listens. 'Clearly . . .'

He puts the HDPad down. 'To Eastern Europe, or the Middle East . . .'

With his spare hand he opens the fridge door. A flood of light shines on the counter. I freeze.

'I can think of about five black sites where they'll be able to extract the kind of complete . . .'

Extraordinary rendition? Black sites?

A loaf of French bread is still lying, half eaten, on the side, cheese, olives, hummus, pickles, a newspaper, keys, briefcase with breadcrumbs on it.

'. . . Irregular, but the Chief Justice must be made to sign . . . extrajudicial transfer.'

I shrink against the glass. My father reaches into the fridge and takes out a half-empty bottle of wine.

'As for my daughter, I shall announce she's unwell. I've arranged for a visit from a psychiatrist and the Commissioner of Police. Leave her to me. We'll start with a Section Four,' he says smoothly.

A Section 4?

He puts down the wine, picks up the baguette and tears a hunk off with his teeth.

'Oh, she'll tell me everything. I'll make sure she stays out of circulation.' He chews and waits. He swallows, picks his teeth. 'Until the bill's through . . . until we've settled things.'

His voice is calm. He picks up an olive, pops it in his mouth. He lifts the bottle of wine again, eases the cork out with his thumb, lifts it to his nose, smells its bouquet.

'Yes, I quite understand.'

He moves towards the kitchen door.

He hasn't seen me.

He doesn't flick on the light. With the bottle under his arm, balancing the HDPad, phone pressed between his ear and shoulder, he delivers a deft kick with his right foot to the fridge door and he knees it shut.

He's leaving.

I watch his form retreating down the hall. I hear the door of his study being kicked. It clicks to, bounces shut and clicks open again. It does that. I've noticed. It comes open all by itself just as if it knows. I press my forehead against the cold glass. I get my breath back. The knot of blood and tissue clamped tight in my throat dissolves. I dare to move.

I nudge open the window and, hauling myself in with my good hand, I slide my legs through first, as quietly as I can. The light in the hall is still on. The kitchen door is still open. For a moment I am half in the room and half suspended outside over the damp pavements.

Extraordinary rendition.

He's going to fly Cobain to a state where he can be tortured.

264

My heart's hurting. My fingers are hurting. I must have been gripping the window frame so tightly, all the blood in my hand is gone. My fingers are numb. Numb and white.

My legs are through. I feel for the kitchen counter with my feet, lower myself on to my bum. I ease my body in after, twisting my head down. On the counter I balance. *I did it.* I take a few deep breaths. I unclick the backpack. *I just climbed out of my room and I'm here.* I shove the backpack outside the window and lock the window shut again. No cold draught to give me away.

I glide to the floor. I look at the loaf and wish I had time to take a bite myself. That's when I see the keys.

His keys. *His car keys.* And a mad, wild idea jumps from the counter right into my brain.

And I pick them up. And pocket them.

Very carefully I tiptoe out of the kitchen. Where will he have locked Cobain? There's only one place: the front closet. It's a coat closet and it locks on the outside with a bolt. I pray Cobain's in there. He must be in the coat closet. The only other place is my father's bedroom. That has a key like mine. But my father wouldn't want him in there.

Not with all his things. Not if he intends to sleep tonight.

Very quietly, I creep down the corridor. To the left is my father's study. The door's very slightly open. My father is still talking on the phone. I crouch beside the hall table and listen.

'Tomorrow afternoon – another emergency session . . . clamp down,' he's saying. 'Get the bill passed first . . .'

I pause. I can see him dimly reflected in the door of a glass-fronted bookshelf.

'Special licence to treat future protesters as criminals? 'I see.'

He clicks off the mobile. He hesitates, then he picks up the wine bottle. He looks around. I can see he's looking for a glass. There's no glass.

He'll go back to the kitchen to fetch a glass.

Oh crap.

Like a ghost I slip past his door and vanish. I slide two steps into the visitors' toilet. I straighten up and freeze. I hear my father stride out of his study, put his mobile down on the hall table, pick up something and walk off towards the kitchen.

Through the gap by the toilet door hinges, I see straight down the corridor. I see him put on the kitchen light. I see him open the cupboard for a wine glass.

And then he sees the flipping backpack.

It twists and slaps against the window.

A cry of something between rage and surprise escapes him. He spins on his heel. I take a deep breath. My heart hammers. He charges down the corridor. I close my eyes. Straight past me, straight past the open toilet door. *Thank God.* Straight up the stairs towards my room.

I step out of the toilet. For a moment, I hesitate, scan the hall. His phone starts ringing. It's there on the little table beside me. Instinctively I reach for it. Instinctively I press reject.

His phone.

Like pieces of a puzzle, an idea falls into place. Mum's number. His phone.

I pick up his phone.

I need a phone that can't be traced.

And then I turn. I race for the front door.

For the coat closet.

And for freedom.

32

'War Can Be Fun When You're Fighting For You.'
Anonymous

My father's so sure of himself, isn't he? He's so sure that I must have dropped from the room and gone, or I'm still in it. If he'd taken a minute to think, instead of being so sure of himself, he'd have realised nobody had left the flat, that the harness and sheet stopped at the kitchen window, and unless I dropped the remaining thirty metres – I had another plan.

But he doesn't think females can plan.

I race to the closet, snap back the bolt. Above me, I can hear my father start hammering on my bedroom door.

'*Cobain?*' I whisper. There's a dark shadow hunched in one corner. He's here. *Thank God*, he's here.

'*Get up*,' I hiss. '*We gotta go.*'

Cobain doesn't need telling twice. He's on his feet.

'*Be quick, be very quiet,*' I say.

He nods. He glides past me out the door. But before he goes a step further, he turns, shuts the coat closet – and slides the bolt back. Clever Cobain. Then he pauses, looks at me. He's somehow thinner and older, as if something has aged him terribly. And then I see the bruising.

I extend one arm, reach out, take his hand. I slip it into mine. It's warm. I feel my throat lock. I can't swallow. His hand's so warm.

'Ti?' he says. His voice is husky. He looks at me and whispers, 'Thanks,' through split lips.

Upstairs, I hear my father still hammering on my door, kicking it, I think. Quietly I cross the hall. I lead Cobain past the dining room. Softly, together, we close the vestibule door behind us. I squat down and slip back the bottom bolt on the front door. Cobain tiptoes up and slides back the top one.

I can see he's in pain, but together we ease the door open, and almost as if we're one being, we flow out, pressed against each other, his arm round me, my arm round him, his warm hand resting on my shoulder. Out into the lift-shaft lobby. Out towards the stairwell.

'Remove your shoes,' he whispers. I remove them.

'Old burglars' trick on staircases.' He smiles and I notice one eye is puffed up and nearly closed.

It works. We close the fire-door gently behind us and not a stair rattles; there's no click of plastic sole or hard heel to give us away. We run, light-footed, down the stairs, escaping, twisting like gymnasts round the corners, never letting go of each other.

We race as best we can towards the basement.

On the lower-ground floor, car park level, we pull our shoes back on and barge out into the underground car park. We hurry together, hand in hand, out into the rows of parked cars, down the aisles.

'Wait,' I say. I chuck Cobain my dad's car keys.

He catches them.

'Can't drive,' I say.

'Where's the car?'

'Not sure.'

Cobain limps to the nearest bay of cars and clicks the door-unlock on the key. A flash of light comes from somewhere. He turns, clicks the key again. I look, trying to pinpoint the flashing headlights. 'Over there,' I whisper. 'I think.'

'Let's go,' he says.

By my father's BMW, we embrace. I'm careful not to hug him too tight. Even his cat-green eyes are dark. He doesn't speak. His head is bending over me. His lips are searching for mine. He finds what he needs. I find what I need. We press together very gently. Just for a second, I feel his hard, slim body against mine and it feels strangely like I've come home. A mad sense of well-being washes over me.

He draws away. He takes a short breath. He lowers his face and rubs the tip of my nose with his forehead.

'You OK?' I say. I know he's not.

'I'll live,' he says.

'I'm so sorry,' I say.

'Hey, smart kid,' he says. 'You rescued me.'

'Yeah,' I whisper back.

And I did.

And I have a crazy feeling. Like the sun just broke through the clouds, and it's the first day of the holidays, and I just opened a crisp packet and won a tenner. And I did rescue him. But I don't tell him from what, although I think he knows.

'C'mon,' I hiss. I drag open the car door.

'You saved me,' he repeats, as if it's a first for him too.

I'd like to say, 'Again,' but he's still three ahead. So I just smile and try to figure out how long it will take my father to work out what's happened.

Not long enough.

My blood starts to pound in my neck. He'll miss the phone very quickly. I pull it out of my pocket. Maybe

I shouldn't have taken it? He'll know I was inside the house. When will he miss the car keys?

Please don't let him miss them till daylight.

I slide into the passenger seat. Cobain sparks the engine. Please let us get away before he realises. The purr of expensive machinery breaks the silence. Thank God for tinted windows, thank God for bulletproof car doors.

The car slides into reverse. Cobain backs it out of the parking bay, takes the exit ramp.

As we curve up and out of the garage, I search for the auto-barrier release. It's right there in the little cash-well by the gear stick. I take it out, point it at the exit barrier, press. The steel barrier arm to the street rises up noiselessly. I bite my lip, hold my breath, half expecting there to be an armed squad of police waiting outside, staking us out, but there isn't. Nobody's there, just the dark night and the empty street and the smell of burning.

'Where to?' says Cobain.

I don't know. Away. Anywhere. A place I can think. 'Let's get clear of the city,' I say.

'North, south, east, west?'

'Hit the nearest highway,' I say. I remember Mum's beach hut in Hastings. Just a clapboard shed, but it's got a roof and a shower room. 'Head south,' I say. 'Get over the river.'

By the time we make the corner, we hear them, police cars. Sirens, long and shrill. They fall and rise, ululating in the grey dawn. I try to work it out. Us? Or fires burning somewhere else?

'OK,' mutters Cobain, 'time to see what this babe's made of.' He swings the car out on to the main street and hits the gas.

I pull my belt over me and buckle up. 'Stick to the speed limit,' I hiss.

He nods. 'Until they find us,' he says grimly.

Until they find us.

Which they will.

I sigh. Hiding out in a beach hut isn't going to work, is it? We can't just drive off as if nothing's happened. We can't just sit and hold hands and watch the sun set over the sea. Live on nothing but fresh air. Although I wish we could.

How long will it take them to find us?

No time at all.

So while Cobain navigates the streets, I open up my father's phone. I still have a mission to finish. My heart's hammering away, but I'm calm. Strangely calm. I've suddenly got a wild idea. Maybe it's the madness of the moment; maybe it's the feeling of freedom, of having saved Cobain, of outwitting my father. Of no hiding place left. I don't know.

When you've got nothing, you've got nothing to lose.

'I'm going to message Darknet7,' I say.

And everything to gain.

Cobain shoots me a look. He laughs. 'From your dad's phone?'

'Yeah,' I say.

He laughs again. 'Nice one.'

'They'll read it, I know, but so what?' I say.

'Yeah, so what?' he says.

'I've gotta let everyone know what I've found.' I tell him about the *Mass Impression Management* File.

He grips the wheel, shakes his head, swerves to avoid a badly parked car. There's a pause.

At last he speaks. 'Are you saying there's no overpopulation?' He presses the fingertips of one hand on his forehead, as if the idea won't go in.

'Yep,' I say.

'And they're snipping prisoners, and lying to the nation?'

'Yep.'

'Christ,' he says. He goes very pale. I can see his knuckles, white on the steering wheel, his cheeks drained.

274

'I'm gonna message it out,' I say.

'Yeah, do it,' he says.

So I get up the Darknet7 login page. 'They'll start to locate us, as soon as I go online,' I say. I don't know how long it'll take. 'A.D.A.M. is still out there.'

'Yeah, they'll locate us,' says Cobain. 'But they'll have to catch us too.' His jaw is set. 'And we won't make it easy for them.'

I smile, Cobain smiles. I love that. So undefeated. Like we can outrun the world.

I bite my lip. Feel a sudden rush of tears. Swallow them back. *Just do it*, I tell myself. They were going to locate you anyway.

So I open up Darknet7. I log in. I load the MIM file on to the ADMIN page. I publish it, and I send a message out to all the campaigners. 'This is TIA THOMSON. EVE is dead, but I've got some information you're gonna love.'

And then I wait. How long will it take? I listen for police sirens. Nothing new. They're not looking for us. I cross my fingers. Not yet.

I check the website to see if the whole file loaded up OK. Make sure it wasn't encoded in some way.

And I can't find it.

The Mass Impression Management file just isn't there.

I go back into ADMIN.

It's gone.

I go to download it from the StormCloud again. And then I realise it's useless. I could do it a thousand times.

It's never going to upload.

'What's up?' Cobain glances over at me.

'I can't do it,' I say. 'Someone from A.D.A.M. must have set up a keyword search that automatically deletes anything containing sensitive material from being uploaded to the Darknets.'

Fabulous. It's not gonna work. Maybe there's even an alert or a hash tag or a symbol loaded on to the MIM file to trigger that on other sites too. Wonderful.

'Try it again,' says Cobain.

'I just did.'

We're screwed. No matter how many times I upload it, the file will delete itself.

I rack my brains. What can I do? Apart from running through some kind of decontam or pro-spam software, I need to upload it to some place from which it can never be deleted. Where it isn't even stored! And I need to do it quickly!

Shit. Shit. Shit.

A.D.A.M. knows I have the data now! Even as I'm thinking this, they'll be trying to hack my account in the StormCloud. I've really screwed myself over this time.

'Keep going,' says Cobain. 'Remember "*For ever until victory*".'

What I need is a network of computers fast enough to un-stress the formatting and then upload everything simultaneously to a myriad of sites – computers which can onion-route the document through a global setup, pre-loaded with all kinds of bugs and malware, so the whole file can then trojan-horse its way through the entire world.

Before A.D.A.M. gets to it.

The idea makes me smile, anyway.

'Isn't there anything we can do?' asks Cobain.

'Not with just a mobile,' I sigh.

And that's when we hear the police car turning into the street behind us.

'That was quick,' he says.

And I'm surprised at my own naivety. *Of course they wouldn't be wailing their sirens when they're stalking us, would they?*

Not just one police car, a whole bevy of them.

'What'll we do?' I shriek.

'Panic,' says Cobain.

33

'The Police Say We'd Miss Them, But We Have Pretty Good Aim.'
Anonymous

Behind us a flare of light bursts out. Headlights dazzle the wing mirrors. Cobain flicks the driver's mirror up.

'Hang on,' he says.

I press my lips together, draw in a deep breath. Cobain jams the car down into a lower gear and hits the gas. We surge forward like a jet taking off. We zip past closed shops, grey in the early morning. I get a vertigo rush and am thrust backwards against the seat.

'Woo,' says Cobain, 'this babe can move.'

I glance over at him. His jaw is set, his hands are tight on the wheel, I think he's enjoying it. I can almost see the way he lifts the car over the speed bumps and guides it round the corners, down the empty streets, as if he's flying one of his model aeroplanes.

I glance behind. We've lost the police cars. They're way behind. It's very strange. It's like being in a movie, except we're not.

And I know that if I'm going to make any difference to kids being snipped, I don't have a lot of time left in which to do it.

And I want to make a difference. I want all the tragedy of the last three days to count for something. Can that baby and his mother; that girl, Daisy, who took my rucksack; that policeman by the bank; Lacey; can they all have died for nothing?

With a tingling down my spine, I feel them very near: the girl, the guard, Daisy, Lacey. And the sad little ghost of that baby. He seems to wail in my ear. He seems to weep for all the playgrounds he will never play in, all the cuddles he will never have, for the future he was robbed of. And beside him in the shadows crowd countless other unborn children, all crying too, all weeping for their stolen futures. I shiver. They're so *very* near, almost as if they're in the car, here with us.

And I look over at Cobain. And I try and read his expression, try to see if there's any happy ending written there. But I know there's not. This isn't a film. This is the dawn of the day on which the No More Children in Need Bill will be passed.

And that's what'll happen unless somebody does something to stop it.

So I have a choice. I can hold on to the dash in front of me and chew my lip off, and be haunted for ever by all those ghosts, or I can do something. And I know which one I'm going to choose. So I tell my heart to stop making such a fuss, and I tell my brain to come up with whatever it is I must do.

And it does.

A truly mad idea.

I have my father's phone. So I'll just pretend I'm him.

But first, while Cobain is hitting the gas, I sign in to my @tiathomson account. I write a new message. One that gets me smiling even as I type it.

This is TIA T. LEADER OF THE PACK, AVENGING CHRIST CHILD ON ALL BANKS. *Got some info here you're gonna love – straight from the Lion's Den.* And then I give it to them.

THE GOVERNMENT HAVE DROPPED THE SNIP BILL.

And then I press: *Share.*

It's so mad even I can't believe what I'm doing. Then I open up my father's address book. I scroll down until I see PRESS COVERAGE.

- Media NewsCaster
- CCC Corporation
- Universal Com News

- TV Now

I cup my hand over the phone to distance the sound of the police sirens. I wedge myself securely in my seat with my knee on the dashboard, so that every time Cobain swerves round a corner, I'm not thrown sideways. And as we race past pavements and rubbish pods and traffic lights blinking, I dial up the first number under PRESS COVERAGE.

It's still very early, maybe nearly 5 a.m. A bored voice drawls out: 'Hello Media Caster, please listen carefully; you have a choice of connects. Press one for news items. Press two for existing contacts. Press three—' I don't wait for the rest of the list. I hit one. I get another choice of options. I get through to someone. They can obviously see whose phone I'm calling on, because they're suddenly apologising and connecting me up to somebody very important who says, 'Tony, how can I help?'

'This is Dr Thomson's PA,' I say, cupping my hand more tightly against the wailing sirens.

'Yes?' The voice is just as helpful.

'Dr Thomson would like you to run an announcement in your first release this morning.'

'Of course.'

'Shall I go ahead?'

'Please.'

'OK. This is it: *The government, in light of huge public outcry, will not be sitting on the No More Children in Need Bill today.* That's it. Got it?'

Cobain shoots me a look. He mouths out: 'YEAH!'

'You mean the bill's been dropped?' says the man on the other end of the line, a sudden eagerness in his voice.

'Off the record: yes,' I say, 'but you are not to quote that. Dr Thomson will be making a public address on the matter at 8 a.m. today, outside the Houses of Parliament, and he will give press interviews immediately afterwards. Can you organise your people to be there?'

I catch Cobain's eye. He rolls them in a funny way, and I nearly get the giggles.

'Please run the announcement in this morning's news,' I continue.

'Can you assure me that we'll get first deal on this?' he says. 'Exclusive interviews?'

'First deal?' I repeat, not quite sure what 'first deal' is.

'Can you hold back on this story, so that our media companies get first run, first scoop at it?'

'I'll get back to you on that,' I say.

'Can I speak to Dr Thomson?'

'He's resting,' I say. 'He has a big day ahead.'

One of the police cars behind lets out a hideous howling.

'And there's enough disturbance going on as it is,' I add.

'Yes, of course.'

'How much cover can you give this – the whole country, plus national and local TV?' I add, as if I'm reconsidering giving him exclusive coverage.

'Yes,' he says. 'We can have it out there in under an hour on the channels, and in print for a later delivery run. As we speak I'm assembling a team.'

'OK,' I say. 'Good. I think Dr Thomson would be fine with that. You better get going.'

'Thanks,' he says. 'Let Dr Thomson know we're grateful.'

I hang up and throw my head back on the head rest and snort out a huge laugh.

'Nice one,' says Cobain. And he reaches out and squeezes my knee.

I smile back at him. 'Well, you did say we should Fuck Him Up,' I rejoin.

Before he can answer, a police wagon appears, as if by magic, just in front of us. The engine grates as Cobain slams the car into second. Brakes squeal. He takes a sudden sharp corner.

'Can you send out a message for me too?' says Cobain, as soon as he's slung the car past a petrol station, and cut through an estate.

'Yep,' I reply. 'What d'you wanna say?'

He laughs. Behind us sirens wail.

'*Prisoners unite, you have nothing to lose but your freedom.*'

I start typing.

'Not really,' he says.

I obediently stop keying it in. 'I want you to message out: COBAIN HEARTS TI,' he says, 'in caps. To the universe.' He smoothly changes down into third gear, takes another corner, jumps a kerb and we hit a dual carriageway.

I really smile. '*Do you?*' I whisper.

'Maybe,' he says. Then his poor swollen mouth twists up. 'Maybe not.'

A warmth spreads across my chest, and it's like the sun broke through and that's so flipping clichéd. But I don't even flipping care if he doesn't mean it. I just love him for saying it, right now when everything's so screwed.

I bend down over the phone. I'm gonna send it out anyway.

A message pings up on Darknet7. I can't see the source, but it reads: *OPERATION STOP ACTION: NO MORE CHILDREN IN NEED. WE MARCH FOR EVE. ALL*

SUPPORTERS SHOULD HEAD FOR PARLIAMENT SQUARE.

'I tried,' I say. 'But I don't think the morning news is going to be in time to stop anything.'

I check the other action nets. All are alive and pinging and scores of messages are saying: *PARLIAMENT SQUARE NOW*.

I rub the window free of condensation and peer out. People are on the move. Cobain turns off the main highway into a narrow alley. Behind us the police cars are still sirening out.

'If everyone jams into Parliament Square, what the hell's going to happen?' I say. Desperately I message *STOP. THE BILL HAS BEEN DROPPED. IT'LL BE IN THE MORNING NEWS.*

I send it. But it's no good. It's drowned. They're too many messages. I try again, but it's all so much bigger than me now. I let the phone drop slack in my lap. The messages run on like a torrent. Picturegrams of marchers from every district in the UK drown the networks. The nation has chosen what it wants to do. I look at Cobain. He glances over at me. I shake my head.

'It's too late to stop it,' I say. 'There's going to be a bloodbath.'

He just nods. 'You're such a minister's daughter,' he says.

I raise my head at that.

'You think you should have it all under control, don't you?'

I shrug.

'It was always so much bigger than you,' he says. 'Bigger than anyone, even than your dad.'

And I think about it. And he's right. The people don't want the bill. That's all. They were always going to oppose it. They were always going to march against it. I didn't do anything, except harness that opposition for a very short while.

'So what now?' I say.

'We've got a few minutes before the police get here,' he says. 'But it's enough.'

'Enough?' I say.

'For me to stop the car and for you to bail.'

'Bail?' I say.

'Likelihood is the police will gun us down as soon as it's cleared with your dad.'

I nod. It's possible.

'And one of us still has to let the world know.'

'I guess,' I say.

'Or this thing won't stop.'

He's right. That network of fast computers needs setting up. That *Mass Impression Management* file needs salvaging and sending straight out, even if I have to remotely hack back into my father's computer to retrieve it.

'So at that corner, I stop. And you jump.'

'And then?' I say.

'And then nothing,' he says. 'That's all.'

34

'May We Meet One Day in the Burning Streets, and Warm Our Hands on the Old World.'
Anonymous

'I want to explain something,' he says. 'Before you go.'

'OK.'

'About me – us –'

A strange look settles over his face. 'I thought I'd have time to tell you, you know – one day, you and me, lying somewhere far away, sharing stuff, with all the time in the world.'

We reach the corner. He slams on the brakes.

'I'd have made you laugh. Not just at my life as a traveller's kid and being moved on all the time – or the things I got up to in care homes and foster families – though some of that was mental . . .'

He reaches across me, shoves my door open.

'And EAT THE RICH was the maddest thing of all.' He laughs as if we're already under swaying palms, lying snuggled up somewhere in a lazy hammock, on a fairytale beach, by blue, blue seas.

His hand falls on to my lap.

'And I'd stroke your skin and tell you about being caught for something entirely different.'

I gulp, swallow the feeling in my throat that threatens to choke me. The door scrapes across the kerb.

'EAT THE RICH?' I say, trying to put off the final moment. 'Why eat the rich?'

He smiles. 'Jean-Jacques Rousseau. *"When the people shall have nothing more to eat, they will eat the rich."*'

I want to cry. I want to kiss him. My heart swells up. I grip the seat.

'I created something for the media. And the media created me. "The Epitome."' He sighs. 'I lived up to it. That graffiti! The Bigger, the crazier, the more daring the locations, the more insulting the images, the better! I loved it.' He laughs again, as if those were the good, bad old days.

His hand is lying on mine.

'I gave Vandalism and the Criminal Damage Act a run for its money, I can tell you. And I learnt all about surveillance. Did you know the Environmental Health Office has as sophisticated surveillance technology as the Department of Defence? Totally nuts.'

The police sirens wail nearer.

'I wanted to be as big as Banksy.'

'You were,' I say. 'Bigger than Banksy.'

'They never could pin it on me.'

I turn my hand over and curl my fingers into his.

'Vandalism carries a ten-year sentence. And that's just for the spray paint.'

His hand is warm.

'Did you know graffiti falls under the Incitement to Terrorism Act.'

I shake my head

'They were totally pissed at me.'

'But it was just graffiti.'

He looks at me. 'No. Wrong. It was not "just" graffiti. I'm as guilty as hell, Tia. I intended to bring the system down.'

He keeps hold of my hand, clutches the wheel with the other. 'I felt I was owed something. I was angry, cheated. When I knew I couldn't have what everyone else had.' His nails dig in. 'Nobody was gonna have it.'

I look at him. A bead of sweat is rolling down the side of his face.

'Sometimes that's what it all boils down to. All that stuff you felt you were owed, that home, that feeling of safety, of being loved, that childhood that you didn't get. It was yours and you were supposed to get it.' He twists his lip. He doesn't let go of my hand, but takes the other one off the wheel, grabs the gear shift, rams the car back into first and revs the engine.

'But last night, in that cupboard, I realised it isn't all about me. I know, don't say anything. And I still want a fairer world.'

I look at him. I force a smile.

Dimly I hear the car radio announce: *'Crowds are already gathering in Parliament Square.'*

He looks steadily at me and smiles. And we're smiling. And it's funny, because here we are in a stolen car, with nothing but a stolen phone on us, and half of the country's police force on our tracks, and a bloodbath about to start, and we're going to have to leave each other, and we're holding hands and we're smiling.

The radio drones on . . . *'Two factions seem to be uniting – those who march for EVE, Mother of the Future, and those that hail the Messiah, Tia Thomson, Daughter of the Devil, with her "Shank a Bank" message . . .'*

He squeezes my hand.

'So you bail. I'll pick up the police again and keep them on my tail. I'll lead them as far away as I can. And you know what you've got to do.'

He's right. That's all there is left. If he can draw the police off and I can get the MIM file out, all this will end.

'But,' I say.

'It's not hard,' he says. 'You simply swing your lovely legs through the door and step out. It's just another goodbye.'

But this time it isn't. He won't be coming back. He won't be following me any more. There'll be no more rescuing.

'Reports are coming in that Dr Thomson will shortly announce the Snip Bill is to be dropped. TV cameras are already being set up outside the Houses of Parliament . . .'

'Hey, you're smart,' he says. 'You'll be OK.'

'But they may catch you,' I say.

'They were always going to catch me,' he says.

'But we'd be together,' I whisper.

'It's better this way,' he says. 'Go and finish it, and just don't forget I saved your butt a couple of times.' He sees my face. 'Hey, I've always wanted to drive a car like this up the motorway.' He flicks up an eyebrow at me. 'Fast.'

'Just don't let them catch you,' I whisper.

He grips the wheel. I swing my legs through the door.

All of a sudden he reaches out, kisses me. I gasp, unprepared for the flood of panic.

'It wasn't ever going to happen anyway,' he says. 'You

and me and the future.'

There's something in his eyes.

'I'm sorry, Ti,' he says.

This is goodbye. The final goodbye.

'I'll message you,' I say. 'I will, on Darknet7, on the book blogs. I will.'

'Whichever way today plays out,' he says, 'it's too late for us. Get out now and just forget about me. It'll be much safer that way.'

I look at him.

'OK, I'll convince you,' he says. 'Prisoner 5074. Bill Fifty-six, Section Eight. All right?'

I shake my head. I don't get it.

'Under Act of Parliament 304, twenty-second of September.'

I still don't.

'I was given one year for Attempted Burglary and Criminal Damage. I served six months. They failed to ever pin EAT THE RICH on me, but I was caught on CCTV during the very early riots, smashing a window with a hammer. They let me have it then. It was all they could get me for, but they seriously wanted to get me. They manipulated the image.'

'You were looting?'

'No. The shop was on fire. There were some kids

trapped inside. *They* were looting. I just smashed the window to let them out.'

'But . . .' I say.

'There you go again, being all naive,' he says. 'Those kids weren't ever going to testify on my behalf, were they?'

I pull a face. It sucks. It all flipping sucks.

'Please listen,' he says. 'When you go down for something you didn't do, it hurts. I was easy prey. I already wanted to bring the system down. But there's been another reason why I've been so angry.'

'What?'

'I want you to remember that I fought them,' he says, 'but they were stronger. They held me down.'

I search his face for a clue. Any clue.

There's a screeching of tyres.

'Ti,' he says, 'I'm telling you all this, because I'm trying to make this easier for both of us. You and me. It wouldn't have worked out, OK? Not after everything you've fought for. Get it?'

'No.' I step out of the car. 'I don't.'

He revs the engine.

'I'm on your side,' I say stubbornly. 'I don't care if you've been in prison. I'm proud that you sprayed EAT THE RICH everywhere. I don't even care that you were turned and became a real yob.'

'Ti,' he says in a voice that breaks my heart, 'you deserve a future. A nice, straight guy. A better family than the one you've got.

'And I can't give you that. I'm a wanted terrorist, with a long police record, and I've already had the snip.'

35

'Attack Fails Sometimes, But Submission Fails Always.'
Anonymous

I duck out of view. I stumble along the street. The air's cold, nearly spring, still winter. It must be about 6 a.m. *Cobain's had the snip*. The first shafts of early dawn are tinting the sky rosy pink. Like blood seeping through a bandage; grey, sterile gauze.

I feel so tired. I can't seem to get my mind around anything. *Cobain. Cobain.* My stomach clenches up in pain as if the knife has sliced me open, made its clean incision into my groin. I have to stop, to double up, to lean my head against the cold brickwork of a building, press my lips tight and try to push back a sudden flood of saliva.

Prisoner 5074.

And as if in a dream I catch the face of a child. A glowing, bright-eyed girl with a soft, round face, with dark hair, with green eyes. There might have been shouts of laughter, a tumbling of tickles, stories at bedtime, traditions at Christmas.

Nausea rises up again. I brace myself against the wall. I raise my head and look up into the dawn. Red streaks bleed out across the sky. I must stop this.

All of it.

A voice in my head says: *Only you can.*

Oh, Cobain.

I won't let it happen again.

The voice continues: *Only you know how to survive your father.*

The sky over Cheapside is still glowing with the fires of last night. *You can't do anything to stop the protest now. It's grown beyond you. It will take too long. Now you must do what you set out to. Where can you find a computer?*

Desperately I try to think. *Nowhere. Not at this time.*

What else can you do? I open up my father's phone. I could call him. I could find the words to make him stop.

If he calls the Prime Minister, orders the army to back off?

Cancels the Snip Bill?

He could do that.

They're already on the move. I can even hear them, through the early dawn, chanting '*Parliament Square. Parliament Square.*'

Find a way. Make your father back down.

Stop the Bill. Stop the bloodbath. Make all the sacrifices count.

I lean my head against the brickwork and groan.

But groaning won't fix it. The voice in my head snorts: *I hope you didn't leave Cobain so you could groan.* I straighten up. I race to the end of the alley. There they are, placards held high, banners, the tramp of feet, the repeated refrain: '*Parliament Square. Parliament Square.*'

I leave the alley and make my way towards them.

'What's going to happen?' I ask when I join the steady stream of marchers. 'It's so early.'

'The early bird catches the worm,' says one.

'The worm has turned,' says another.

And all the time the drum of feet. The echoing cry: '*Parliament Square. Parliament Square.*'

'We'll burn the Houses of Parliament if we have to.'

'But,' I say, 'they'll open fire. They'll call the army.'

'Let them,' says a third and I can see a light in their eyes that has spread from the burning buildings and caught fire to something in every one of them.

'Who cares,' says one man suddenly, fiercely. 'They got my daughter.'

His daughter. I don't know what to say. They got his

daughter. I walk along with them. More people join us. They start to chant again.

'They've cancelled the buses,' says someone randomly.

'Like that'll stop us,' says another.

Nothing will stop them. Nothing. Not a warning from Darknet7, not water cannons, not sharpshooters, not the army. Nothing except a backdown from the government.

And then I know what I must do.

I must give up trying to find a computer. I must leave Cobain to his fate. I must get to Westminster. I must lure my father there. I must confront him. I must find his weakest spot, expose it and, with his underbelly wide open, deliver him to the crowd.

Then they will stop.

And the thought of doing that puts the fear of God into me. I shiver, but even as I shiver, I pull out the mobile. I press the phone number of the flat. It rings. It's picked up. I listen to the silence before I hear his voice.

'Who's this?'

I open my mouth. I croak. My brain stops.

How best to trap him? If I show him my hand?

'It's me,' I say. I hear his sigh of relief. I hear his thoughts. *Ah, so it's Tia. Good. I know how to control her. I yet may save the day.*

I'm surprised at the calmness with which I speak. 'We need to talk,' I say.

'I think we've already had our conversation,' says my father. Menace laces his voice. Just the right amount. I know each inflection, each phrase, each nuance. *Intimidate Tia.* Not enough to terrify, too much to ignore. 'And I think you'd better stop being silly and come home.'

'No,' I say. I don't know where I get the strength to disagree with him. My heart is beating so hard I've forgotten to breathe.

'No,' I repeat. 'I won't come home. But I will meet you.'

Again, that unheard sigh of relief. His confidence returns. He clears his throat. I hate that sound. It means he will shout or whisper. I think I prefer the shouting. It's so much less frightening.

'*You will not curb the Devil in me,*' he whispers.

Before he has a chance, before I lose my nerve, I say: 'You will meet me and I will call you to say where and when – otherwise I will expose to the world exactly who I am.'

'And who do you think you are, Tia?' he whispers.

'I'm your daughter,' I say, 'and I'll tell them why I ran away. I'll tell them why I led a mob against a bank. I'll tell them everything I read on your computer. I'll post the whole thing on the Internet. You won't survive it. You've deceived the entire nation. You've destroyed people's lives. You want to know who I am?'

He does not reply.

'I'm your nemesis.'

There's a silence. He draws in a long, deep breath. He clears his throat.

'I'll tell you where,' I say and press the end-call button.

36

'One Solution: Revolution.'
Anonymous

He knows now the danger he's in: public disgrace, resignation, investigation, ruin. He'll come to wherever I say. He'll do whatever I tell him.

For a moment my brain turns to jelly. *Live deliberately. Lose hope. Take freedom. Society is like a stew. If you don't stir it up, a layer of scum floats to the top. He'll never come. He'll outsmart me.*

'*No more games. No more defeat the Snip Bill. Get back at Daddy. Play at saving the world like Mummy. This time we play for real.' Don't think about Cobain. Just grow up. It isn't all about you. You've made your choice. Focus on your father. Get him to come. And you must stop him. Stop the carnage.*

But where?

Somewhere that counts. I fall into step with the march. Our last stand. I know exactly where. Parliament Square. I'll speak to him there, in front of everyone. But how to manage it? He won't agree to speak in public.

How can I play this more cleverly than him?

Give him a loophole? Promise to keep quiet? Allow him to publicly 'find' you? Denounce you? Redeem you? Claim he needs to spend more time with you? Resign for family reasons? Make him think he's cleverer than you.

I don't think he'll resign. But it might work. At least it might get him to the square. Play it by ear, then. Find a way to confront him. Disgrace him.

I pull out the phone. I slide it open. I call. He picks up. His voice purrs. I don't wait to see what hook he's baited for me, I say: 'I'll meet you outside Westminster, right outside the Houses of Parliament, behind the police cordon, on the podium you set up for later. We can keep this private, if you do *exactly as I say*.'

He draws in his breath. He is not used to being bullied by anyone. Before he can confuse me, I say, 'Make sure you have your work mobile on you.'

And I slide the phone shut.

I get to Parliament Square.

There's a sound like a wave crashing on shingle. A shout goes up. I crane my neck forward, trying to see what's going on. More new security measures? Booing echoes from behind me. Somehow I must get up to the front of the square outside the Houses. I must get as near to the police cordon as I can.

People start jeering. I elbow my way forward. There's another bout of hooting. This time it's a bit louder. Maybe my father's up there already. He won't show himself, though. I push forward, and I step out faster.

What will I say to him? *Please stop all this? Please drop the Snip Bill. Can't you see people hate it? Can't you see they won't take it?*

Up ahead the sea of people boils over: mums, dads, little kids, students, pensioners. And there, too, are the black balaclavas stretched across faces.

'HANDS OFF OUR BODIES!' shouts someone.

I wince. I remember Lacey. I let the thought of her rest just for a moment. I touch my shoulder. The wound still aches. 'Won't forget you, Lace,' I whisper. Then I push it all out of my head.

A chant reverberates back down the street. 'HANDS OFF OUR BODIES.' *It's like déjà vu.* Overhead the air starts vibrating. Underfoot the pavement shudders. I push everything out.

Kill the fear in your head. Kill the hope in your head. Kill the memories in your head.

The tramping from the protesters almost drowns out that dragging sound again, but not quite. I don't waste time guessing. I know what it is. I duck through a gap between a couple in front of me. I glance behind me. More than twenty thousand people. I peer ahead. More. Thousands and thousands more. I'm halfway across the square, hemmed in on all sides. We won't stand a chance. The police will cover every exit.

Just get to the cordon. I shove myself between people, pushing towards the barricades, and the crash barriers, and the scaffolding. Just another few metres.

Here at the front, I'm surrounded by a familiar mob: big, square, male shoulders; stubbly chins; angry fists; sweaty armpits. I press up against them, squeezing my way forward.

It won't be OK. My father will stop at nothing. The government won't back down. They'd have to resign. The road shakes again. The juddering underfoot is unmistakable. Even the crowd hears it.

Kill the fear in your head. Don't give up now. We are the Barbarians at the gate. We are wolves in your fold. We are the ghosts of our children.

I wouldn't put anything past my father. I bite my lip. I pull out the phone.

I message him: *I'm here. I'm coming to the front, make sure you tell the police to let me through.*

I am his nemesis.

I am the one he overlooked.

305

I am his Achilles heel.

This is it. I suck in air. My knees are weak. *Oh, Cobain. Hang on in there for me.*

I will never let you defeat me, Father.

I'm almost there. Push through. Excuse me, please. Elbow your way. Excuse me, please. Excuse me.

There's a roll of noise from very near. Suddenly I can see the cordon. A loudspeaker hails us.

'STOP THE PROTEST. GO HOME. WE WILL USE FORCE.'

The water cannon roll into view. They line up along the front of the Houses of Parliament. A cloud rolls across the sky. In slow motion the cannon on each tank swings round and points directly at us. A battalion of soldiers jog in, back up behind the police front.

I'm here.

Huge buildings tower on either side. Big Ben. Gothic spires. They swim in and out. *Keep going, Tia.* The protesters at the front are yelling. The police line sways. People surge forward. Like cattle we crush together. Someone screams, 'Stop the bill! We are the people!'

We are an image from the future.

We are the first drops of a flood.

We are the lightning on the horizon.

We are the sound of the coming storm.

We are the wolves at your door.

Riot helmets, face visors, body armour, neck protectors, knee pads, gas masks, bullet-proof vests. The riot police link arms, stare straight ahead like zombies.

Excuse me. Please. Excuse me. Let me through. Let me pass.

A helicopter overhead suddenly illuminates the crowd, spotlights over us, pauses, searches. Its blades flicker.

The time has come. The helicopter is looking for me. I twist my mouth into a sad little smile. I shade my face and look up, tracking the whirring wings. It circles back.

Kill the fear in your head.

Kill the hope in your head.

Kill the future in your head.

I edge right up to the police line.

The helicopter hovers. *It knows I'm here.* Its spot searches, seeks out girls, settles on faces, one by one. It's looking for me.

I try to compose my face, wipe off any trace of fear. I continue edging forward. The helicopter hovers, runs a face-recog scan. They know who I am. *Tia Thomson, daughter of Dr Thomson, Minister of State.* He's playing some game. He's cleverer than me. I don't duck my head. I hold it high. The spot settles on me. The blades whirr. The spot locks on.

307

Me.

'YOU.' The loudspeaker hails me directly. The crowd around me shifts.

'DON'T MOVE.'

The demonstrators continue pressing. I can't help it, I tip forward.

'Stop pushing!' I say.

I sway, try not to move. The cold March morning condenses around me. Out the corner of my eye I catch glinting on a rooftop. *Of course they've got sharpshooters*.

Suddenly everyone's focusing on me.

I won't step back. That's for sure. Behind me the crowd wants to see, they're really shoving. I thrust out with my arms. I push forward. I elbow-poke my way up to the front. I don't care.

The helicopter hovers closer. The spot steadies on my face.

I pull out the phone. I call his work mobile. He answers.

'OK,' I yell. 'I wanted to settle this with you discreetly, but if you want it this way . . . I've got copies of all your files, all your five-year preparations of this bill. With one flick of a finger on my touch screen, I can let every person in the world know all about the way you've conned them.'

It's a lie. I can't.

I hold my breath.

He clears his throat. His voice purrs. 'I think you'd better come up for our little chat then.'

I look up, let my hand and phone fall from my ear. On the stage the police cordon parts. A man steps from behind their shields. And there he is. Cool as the morning. Right in front of me.

There already.

One step ahead.

37

'Seize the Means of Destruction.'
Anonymous

The police take up position.

'*Praise the Lord!*' shouts my father.

The crowd fall silent. Such a strange choice of expression.

My father extends an arm to me, helps me on to the stage. 'Thank you,' he says to the crowd, 'for delivering back to me my daughter.'

They don't know whether to boo. They boo anyway.

My heart bangs. My stomach feels like I've swallowed razor blades. How is he going to play this? His long-lost kidnapped daughter returns? His deranged Christ-child avenger is defeated? I don't think the crowd will care. They don't care. The booing doesn't stop. Neither does the chanting. 'DOWN WITH THE BILL.' Quite right. They're here to defeat a bill, not to watch a family reunion.

But they expect something. What do they expect? That I can somehow fix everything? Will they feel betrayed, if I can't? Do they think that right at the end I've tried to switch sides? Will they lynch me, pull me limb from limb?

'TIA!' shouts the mob. 'SHANK A BANK TIA!'

I salute them. I give them the victory V. One wrong brick, one wrong move. We won't survive. I won't survive.

My father reaches out, as if to put his arms around me. I stand up straight as he dips nearer. I say, 'I'll tell them.'

'No you won't,' he says.

'I'll tell everyone,' I repeat. The unspoken word: 'unless' hovers in the air.

'Think of your mother; spare her that,' he says.

How dare he try to play me with my mother.

'Drop the bill,' I hiss. 'Let these people know. Let them go home. It stops now. No more riots.'

'Oh, yes, it stops now,' he says.

That was too easy. He's planning something.

'There won't be a riot,' he says. 'If anyone dares to raise an arm, take off a T-shirt . . .' He nods at the rooftops. All are manned with sharpshooters. He nods at the wings of the square, mounted police who have blocked us in.

'You forget them,' I say in a shrill squeak. I can't help it. I gesture at the hooded men at the front, the balaclava'd

311

faces, the backpacks being opened, the hammers being brought out. 'You created them,' I say, 'and they don't care.'

He hugs me a little tighter. 'Nobody can rescue the lower classes, my dear. They can only be taught a valuable lesson.'

'I'll send your files. They'll go viral,' I say. 'It'll be the end of everything . . .'

'I don't think so,' he whispers back. 'As we speak, Internet coverage has been suspended, mobile phone networks are going down.'

'They won't be for ever.'

'They won't need to be,' he says. He glances up. I look up too. It's nearly eight o'clock. Big Ben is silent. It rises like a monolith. Only a pale sun is shining, way off, down behind the river, illuminating the skyline in a ghostly show of silver grey, like an age-old etching. I stare at it as if I'm going back in time.

'Just long enough to take care of business.'

And that's when I see the red laser spot.

Hovering over my chest.

38

'There's No Government Like No Government.'
Anonymous

I duck, twist. The red spot finds me. I stop. I look out into the crowd. My heart is banging.

I hear their voices again, far away.

'TIA! SHANK A BANK!'

I can't think, can't threaten. You can't outwit a red dot. Can you?

My father holds me very steady. I wince, try to stand straight, as I feel the weight of his hands press on my bad shoulder.

'I'm so sorry, Tia,' he whispers. 'Really sorry. If you stand very still you might be spared. I gave orders not to kill you, if you're sensible. So when you're inclined, raise your hands up and surrender. They won't shoot you then.'

I don't believe him. He'll kill me, when he's ready.

He's lived up to even the lowest opinion I ever had of him.

'But I'm your daughter,' I say. And it's ironic that here he is, deciding the fate of so many unborn children, of so many fathers, and yet he is the one who should never have been allowed to be one.

'That's what your mother says,' he rejoins. 'But you haven't behaved in a very filial way, now, have you?' His voice as ever; mild, reproachful.

And I can't believe it. I didn't think he could sink any lower. Even now at the very end, he insults her. Am I not his daughter then? I pray to God I'm not his daughter.

The spot settles on me. The crowd near the front sees it. Somebody screams. My heart explodes in my throat. I'm trapped. *Kill the fear in your head.* My breath just stops. *Oh, Cobain, where are you now? What would you tell me to do? Should I just raise my hands then and wait to be shot?*

I don't know what to do. I can't think any more.

And I remember Cobain saying, *'You're such a minister's daughter. You think you should have it all under control, don't you? It was always so much bigger than you.*

'Bigger than anyone, even your dad.'

And I think about it. And he's right. The people

314

don't want the bill. That's all.

Attack fails sometimes, submission fails always.

And now I know just how to attack.

'OK,' I say. 'I'll submit.'

My father's press on my shoulders eases. I raise my head. He removes his hands. Very slowly I raise my arms in a motion of surrender. And I look him in the eyes. And for once I'm not afraid. 'Please, Dad,' I say, 'you can back down. You can announce it's all over. Everything's set up, the media believe that's what you've come here to do. There'll be no disgrace. Please? I beg you?'

He doesn't even bother to smile. So, even more slowly still, giving him as long as I can, I twist and face the mob. I nod at the red spot, still hovering over my chest. So now they know.

An angry roar goes up.

Then, still very slowly, I spread my raised arms to mimic the Crucifixion.

The roar becomes thunder.

My heart sticks to my ribs. My tongue feels heavy. 'I'M TIA THOMSON,' I shout, 'AND I'M ON YOUR SIDE.' I don't say it to anyone in particular. I'm not telling them what they should do. I just say it. Like all information has got to be welcome.

315

The red spot hovers. And my blood is pounding so hard I feel faint. And I'm praying they can't shoot me down in cold blood, not right in front of forty thousand people, not in front of a nation of TV cameras.

My father laughs. He seems to think that me raising my arms means he's won. And suddenly I feel really sorry for him, because he doesn't see what he's created. Not just me: a daughter who'll defy him to the last, not just Mum, a doctor who'd rather work in the slums of India than be within ten metres of him, not just a nation who hate him – but a mob of thugs who have armed themselves against him and are baying for his blood.

And if I could, I'd raise up a hand to stop-signal them back, or press my palms together to pray to them to forgive him, but I can't because I have to keep them raised, because that's *exactly* what he's instructed me to do.

And I know it's too late anyway. Because even as I watch, the mob is surging through the police line, trampling batons and visors and bullet-proof vests underfoot, lashing out at soldiers, swarming over barriers and barricades and upturning water cannons and, like a dam breaking its bank, the crowd overruns every obstacle.

Nothing stands in its way.

Only the TV cameras are left, like islands in the flood.

And suddenly I'm surrounded by the mob and dragged off the podium and pressed up against them: big, square, male shoulders; stubbly chins; angry fists; sweaty armpits; and they're protecting me and they're passing me back through the crowd and they're yelling, 'DEATH TO THE OPPRESSOR!'

And they turn on my father. They drag him down.

He calls out to me, 'Tia!' And in that one word I hear his defeat. But it's no use. It's come too late. I can't save him now.

And I want to say, *'Father, this is the Britain you created. This is your handiwork. I hope you enjoy it. I tried to get you to stop. I begged you. Why wouldn't you listen?'* But I can't. I can't say anything.

And the police don't know what to do. They're under siege from every side, and some of them look like they're waiting for instructions, and some of them try to keep order, and some try to get the water cannons upright.

And no shots ring out.

And nobody's in charge.

And hands pass my father into the belly of the mob. And he goes down. And there's arms with hammers being raised, and boots being brought down. Pounding that thumps into something yielding.

And a grunt of satisfaction ripples through the crowd.

And I hide my face, while the mass push forward.

And stamp down.

At last someone screams.

Riot police surge towards me. Wield batons. Shove. Push. Crack down on arms and skulls. They charge into the crowd, thrusting us aside. I'm pressed tight. A helicopter whirrs low. A voice hails, 'DISPERSE.'

The mob stumbles aside. I stagger, nearly fall. People squeeze back.

'GO HOME.'

Officers reach the place. The yellow of their high-visibility vests strangely bright. One bends over. A head blocks my view. I can't see anything. Officers are signalling a helicopter. Whirring blades. Gust of air. High-speed wind. Dust in my eyes. A stretcher. So quick. Helicopter lifting something red.

'He's dead,' shouts someone. 'Tony Thomson's dead.'

'We've won.'

The mob thins, pulls away, leaves behind the stained pavement.

A tremor goes through the crowd.

And it's over.

There's a roar behind me.

Cheering and cheering and cheering starts.

'*Hasta la victoria siempre!*

Not the End

'Hasta la victoria siempre!'

'For ever until victory!'

Che Guevara, June 14, 1928 – October 9, 1967; Marxist revolutionary and guerrilla leader

'Revolution is a series of moments worth living.'

Anonymous

It's a bright April morning. I walk down to Westminster Bridge. It's been fifteen days since Dr Thomson died in the final demonstration against the Snip Bill. The Prime Minister has made an announcement. Two announcements, actually. The first one simply says: *Dr Thomson lost his life trying to hold back an angry mob during a rally against the deeply unpopular No More Children in Need Bill, which he spearheaded. The police are carrying out investigations and anyone with further knowledge should come forward.*

Nobody has.

There've been a lot of interviews and questioning. The investigation is ongoing. It appears no arrests have been made.

The second announcement is more simple: *The No More Children in Need Bill will go to a binding referendum in the autumn. Meanwhile a special commission has been set up to re-examine the figures on overpopulation.*

323

The rioting has stopped. For now.

Mum's number was on my father's phone. I called her. She's flown home with Dr Shah. They didn't want to stay at the London flat. I didn't either, so we're all crowded up in a flat in Vauxhall with Dr Shah's brother and his family. It's fun. I love curry, and I'm learning how to do this weird dance with lots of finger movements and neck stuff. It's a laugh, though I'm crap at it. I blame that on my bad shoulder. Well, that's my excuse, and I'm sticking to it! (Although Dr Shah actually did some microsurgery on my scapula, and it's masses better.)

In fact Dr Shah is awesome. He's got a superfast computer, and he lets me use it. He says it's a Delhi Devil and he'll get a cousin to send me one.

I spent one evening on it hacking into HMP files. I found all the records of Cobain Reilly and I erased them. I traced every digital footprint connected to each alleged misdemeanour he'd ever made, right back through police interviews, court hearings, witness statements, CCTV evidence, even to the childhood orders made to place him in care. They never quite caught him for all the EAT THE RICH stuff. Clever Cobain. But they knew it was him. At one point I had to stop. Just seeing his face again made me go all shaky.

But I told myself off. Being all emo over him wouldn't

324

get the job done. And I'd promised him, so I pulled myself together and traced the solicitors' papers, probation department reports and the documents relating to the charges made in Wandsworth Police Station.

The criminal damage and attempted burglary case was *definitely* a put-up job. You could tell that just from the notes.

Anyway I made history of the whole lot of it, including his fingerprints, eyeball ID and DNA. I even got into the archives of Media NewsCaster and corrupted a certain image of a hoodlum with cat-green eyes.

He hadn't lied to me. The CCTV footage of him breaking the shop front was so amateurishly manipulated that any appeal court in the land would've seen straight through it. If his appeals had been heard. Every one of them had been turned down. The footage had subsequently been used in so many media campaigns, I had to set advanced searches and tracker bots out on it to find all of them. You know they even had video images of his green eyes in Outer Mongolia!

While I was at it, I gave Cobain a whole new history and Internet profile. I even hacked into Imperial College and gave him a place on a course entitled Applied Aerodynamics and the Mechanics of Flight, just in case he ever wanted to study the technology on how to develop those unmanned air things. I had to fabricate a few GCSEs, of course, and some advanced qualifications to fix it, but I didn't think the College of Hard Knocks would mind.

Since then I've put an alert on any mention of him, at any time or place, across the whole country, from the day he disappeared until now – with zero results. I extended that to an international search. Nothing's been flagged up. It's as if he's disappeared off the entire face of the globe.

Apart from that, I've been to two funerals and cried a lot.

Spring has come. Today is a lovely day. The sun's sparkling off the river. The shops are opening up again. The smell of burning's gone. All the trees have suddenly come into blossom. The pavement is coated in tiny petals, white and pink, like confetti.

Every day I post a message out. The message simply says *Westminster Bridge twelve noon*. No codes. Every day I walk down here. Today I'm going to stand exactly in the centre of the bridge and wait five minutes. No point in staying longer. He won't come. But I'll lean over and throw a little bunch of dandelions I've picked into the river.

I suppose they caught him. I can't bear to think of anything beyond that.

Up ahead the bridge gleams in the sunshine. Three double-decker buses are ploughing over it, and it's thick with people.

I told Mum about Cobain. I told her everything. She held me in her arms and pressed me close. I cried.

'Find him,' she said. And then she went into the kitchen to talk to Dr Shah and Dr Shah's brother.

I sat there red-eyed, biting my lip, trying to be glad that I was with her again, trying to be happy for her sake.

She came back later and sat by me. 'Dr Shah says we'll open a surgery here. He's spoken to his brother and asked if we can join his practice for a while. It'll be tight – three doctors in one small clinic for an extended period – but we'll make it work.'

'Make what work?' I ask.

'Dr Shah thinks we can pioneer the same kind of reconstructive surgery we've been doing in India. He thinks we can reverse the snip operation. He's going to offer to start the work *pro bono* for all those who've suffered at the hands of Tony.'

I smile through my tears. My mum is such a good person. Dr Shah is such a good man. I should be so happy.

* * *

It's nearly midday. I thread my way across the bridge. The sun is very bright. It's glancing off the iron fretwork and blinding me. I head for the point in the very middle, clutching my posy. With a sinking heart I see someone else has got there first. A boy. I hover – perhaps he'll move off. I can't leave until I've completed my little ceremony. I blame Grandmama – all that training in tradition.

I edge closer. There's something about the angle of those shoulders, a certain tilt and slimness. I hope he'll go soon. He's bending his head over the balustrades, looking down into the water. There's something familiar in that shock of black hair too. *Something achingly familiar in the angle of that back*.

My heart stops.

A bolt of electricity jolts through me. I can't quite get my breath. *I can't quite believe*.

I start to run. I'm flying round people. *I can't believe*. I can't think. *Just run*. I'm sucking in air. My heart's flying. The sun's in my eyes. I can't see. I stumble on a loose paving slab. I drop the flowers. They scatter on the pavement. I stretch out my arms. I go flying forward. *I'm going to fall*.

He turns. He holds out his arms.

I fall.

He catches.

'Oh,' I say.

I look up into his eyes. His green eyes.

I grin back, hopelessly lost for words. I reach into my memory, and all I can come up with is: 'But I thought you were caught; I thought you said it was goodbye.' I don't know why I'm babbling that out.

I can't believe it.

He sweeps me into his arms. 'I told you not to trust anyone. Not even me,' he says.

'You're really here,' I squeak out.

'You know me,' he says, 'the bad penny. I never give up, till I get what I want.'

'You're squeezing me,' I say.

'Got to. You nearly took a tumble there,' he says.

'And you saved me,' is all I can manage.

'Again,' he says.

And he doesn't loosen his grip one bit.

Acknowledgments

Anonymous for their slogans

Minty Barnor

Sakky Barnor

Beverley Birch

Joy Coombes

Ruth Eastham

Naomi Greenwood

Sophie Hicks

Jane Howard

Caroline Johnson

Claire Cartey

Nigel Baines

Jane Burnard

'I believe the children are our future. Arm them well,
and help them fight for their rights.'
Thank you, everyone.

Read on for an extract from SIEGE also by Sarah Mussi ...

9.22 a.m.
Friday, 18 September

The windows start rattling. They're small, thick things, made of cheap blast-proof plastic, suitable for our kind of school. They mask another sound, something like popcorn popping. I tilt my head, trying to make it out.

It's coming from the gym, from morning assembly. Must be some surprise show for Own Clothes Day. Something like a cheer goes up; people start screaming, chairs scraping, fireworks firing. They're having fun. I stare at the ceiling. If it hadn't been for stupid Connor I'd be in there enjoying myself.

I fix my gaze on the ceiling tiles. The rattling stops. I can still hear humming. That means Lock Down is still on. I stay tense. Miss Carter's going to pick on someone now. Rub it in. *See what you miss when you're late for school.* The rattling starts again. A sharper, crisper, popping noise. Another bout of screaming. Louder, or am I listening harder?

Then there's a crash, like a door slamming, the patter

of feet, like someone's sprinting. That don't sound right even to me.

Two benches away my mate Kady looks up.

I chew my lip. Miss Carter is still looking to pick on someone. She already sent Tariq to the Head's office. Could be anyone next. Although if she's sent him, she mightn't want to send another; might look like she can't cope. But sprinting in the corridors. Someone's gonna get it for sure.

Another crackling sound and definitely running. I cross my fingers under the bench. Miss Carter don't care if you ain't done nothing. She'll pick on you just the same. Please don't let it be me.

Miss Carter screws up her face, spins on her heel and marches towards the door. She snorts as she moves. She's going for the source. Good. I flex my ankles, breathe out slowly, uncross my fingers.

Before she makes it to the door some kids bust in. Two of them. No polite knock. No note. No uncertain hovering.

I half rise, alarmed. Now we're *all* going to get it. My head starts banging. That's so unfair. They're so stupid. They walk right up to Miss Carter. They crazy? She opens her mouth in a snarl. She ain't seen such rudeness since Psycho Sam.

There's something about the way they do it. With no fear. Even Psycho Sam picked his battles. Suddenly I'm on automatic. I ain't seen kids act like this before. Something's up. I start backing up towards the tech den door. I'm out my seat. Am I crazy too?

I can't help it. Something ain't right.

I crouch, ready for anything.

One of the kids pulls out something. He's smiling. My mouth drops slack. Looks like a gun. Can't be. It's realistic though. He's gone loop. Must have. He's *so* going to be on the Volunteers' Programme next week. It happens, you know. It's not just a rumour. The End of Your Education. You Are Now Officially Slave Labour. He shoves the gun at Miss Carter. Must be one of those copy weapons they sell everywhere.

It's not.

And then there's this noise and this hole appears in Miss Carter's forehead. A small, red, round hole. It's got delicate edges that unfold like rose petals. She's grunting like some kind of tribal pig. Then I see the blood and her eyes and her mouth starting to sag open, and it's all gone mad. And the kid is wheeling round with an impossible grin on his face, waving the gun at us. And somebody is screaming. They're all screaming. Except me.

For one mad second I think they've come to liberate

us. Do Away With Teachers. Do Away With Detentions. But I'm wrong. The boys' eyes tell me. I can't make out who they are. I'm so shocked I can't make out anything. They're out of school uniform; could be anyone. Don't stare at them, Leah. Don't make a sound. I'm too shocked to make a sound. School uniform makes you a school kid. Those two ain't school kids no more. They've bust loose. They don't care about students versus teachers. They've fricking bust loose. They don't care about nothing. They're just doing destruction. One of them is kicking over the teacher's stool. Aliesha's screaming, Kady's screaming, all the kids in detention are screaming.

I see Anton moving for the door to the tech den. I back up further. I forget about Kady and Aliesha and the screaming others. I'm going to follow Anton. Kady's a drama queen and Aliesha's a loser, but Anton's smart. I like him. He likes me. And what good will it do staying with Kady and Aliesha?

The first killer seems unsure whether to fire at me. Instead, he raises his gun. He points it at Aliesha. He swings it towards Kady. They're both screaming. He likes the screaming. He says, 'Eeny meeny miney mo. We are the Eternal Knights.' And then he shoots Aliesha. She falls. He carries on shooting.

I'm almost at the door to the tech den. Almost through

it. Anton is nearly there too. I look at Anton. I'm thinking: *Get out. Hide. Get out. Hide. Get out. Hide.*

Suddenly Anton is right beside me. 'Run,' he hisses.

I leap from the lab, burst through the tech door, don't bother with no one else; I'm into that tech den like a bullet. I pull at chairs and bins and leap the benches. Vials and shit crash to the floor. I tear through it, swerve shelves, rip through air like it's got a sell-by date.

Footsteps crash behind me. Them? Kady? Did she get out? Not her. Must be Anton. Clever Anton. He's in Year Ten, different, not really Challenge School material. It better fricking well be Anton.

I can hear ragged breath right at my back. Someone's bellowing. And getting closer. Up ahead is Lab Two. When I reach it, I see it's empty. Ten metres empty. I weave in between the lab benches, ducking, leaping, twisting. How good a shot can those kids be? The floor's covered with smooth plastic tiling. Treacherous. If I slip, I'll crash. A booming, popping, shrieking tears past me. Christ, they're shooting at me!

Holy shit! My only chance is to get across the lab. I topple a pile of books, kick over the apps systems. My lungs can't make it. I got one chance. On the other side of Lab Two is the Level A corridor, but down some stairs, round a corner, past office doors and toilets, the

Level B corridor leads to the Humanities wing and the side entrance.

One chance.

Get to the exit. Challenge Schools are built on the transparency system. It's going to be impossible. They call it the Nowhere To Hide build. But that's them. We call it the Know Where To Hide. But do I? And even if I know somewhere, they will too.

Just run.

Just pray.

Just make it to the side entrance.

Is Aliesha dead? If not, she needs help. She always needs help.

Is Kady dead?

Go back?

Out. Of. The. Question.

This is it then.

There's a deafening roar behind me. They're into Lab Two, only ten, fifteen metres behind me.

I run.

Just before the steps to Level B, I sprint, stopping at the turn of Level A; I take the stairs. I'm in the air. I scream, my arms outstretched in front of me. I hit the ground still running and tumble forward. Keep running.

I turn towards the toilets.

9.30 a.m.
Friday, 18 September

People sometimes ask you what you'd do in an emergency, like there's time to plan. You can't plan. You don't think. You just do something. It's like there's this thing in you that kicks in and you're on automatic. Action that comes straight from the brain and the character and experience.

I turn to the toilets.

I whirl. I see the kids reflected in the Level B windows of The Crossing. Think of a mall or a prison. Levels in tiers of glass from a central, open-to-the-roof highway: The Crossing. Level A (floor one), Level B (ground floor), Level C (lower floor), four wings L, M, N, O – shaped like an H.

There's a pounding behind me. Very Close.

I shrink into the toilet alcove.

It's Anton.

'Humanities!' I hiss at Anton.

There's a sudden scream cut short from somewhere.

Anton and I race out into the Humanities corridor. There's the exit at the end of it. Run for the exit. Someone else is running for the exit. They pull at the door. They can't get out. Then I realise it's Total Lock Down.

Total. Fricking. Lock. Down.

Not your poxy lie-on-the-floor-till-the-bells-go Lock Down, neither. I'm talking the full Secure and Seal System devised since the last lot of riots when kids thought it'd be fun to nick all the computers and burn down the schools. I'm talking: metal door grilles, steel window blinds, smoke-sensitive water sprinklers, perimeter-fencing electrocution, high-voltage fields on every side of the building. Lock Down that the police can initiate from the safety of their little Lock Downed stations.

The kid at the exit is screaming and screaming. He's tugging on the fire bar, but it's not opening the doors. He don't know you've got to have the fire alarms going to open the doors during Total Lock Down. The fire alarms'll only go if they sense massive carbon dioxide or something on the *inside*. Carbon Dioxide Activators are another new system the government's designed to Keep Kids Safe. Aka: Stop kids escaping. Stop kids setting off the fire alarms for fun. Like that's fun even.

I think he's a kid called Theo, in Year Eight. He's always out of class, roaming. His screaming draws the killers. I hear them dropping down the staircase I just jumped from. They're squealing in glee and racing out of the stairwell behind us. Hide. Forget exits. Forget Theo. Desperate, I search around. Lockers. Thank God for fricking lockers. I duck into a space behind the lockers. My heart's pounding fit to bust. Anton's too. He ducks in with me. Anton smells of fresh laundry. The two boys race past. I watch. Holding my breath. Heart exploding. They reach Theo. One of them says, 'Any last words for Mummy?'

Theo is crying, begging, screeching. One of them says, 'We are the Eternal Knights.'

I don't wait to hear it. I nudge Anton and we make a run the other way. While I'm running, I hear shooting. I imagine the blood splatter on the exit door that didn't open.

Theo, the little kid who liked to be free.

The corridors are empty now. Everyone's in assembly, aren't they? That's where it started. Didn't it? We must have been the only ones to escape. Except the new Year Sevens. They have their own assembly in the library. Did the killers go there first, before the Detention Lab? There's no way out. And the library runs the entire length of The Crossing on Level B. No way past it. Get to the library then. If they're all dead in there? Lie down too;

play dead. If they're not? They can't kill everyone. They'll run out of bullets. Hide at the back. I'll never make it. Everywhere's on Lock Down. Even the toilets. I stop. I swerve. I nearly bash into Anton. I head back down the Humanities corridor to the library.

Hide with the Year Sevens.

Dead or alive.